UNDRESSING
SHADOWS

Postwar Germany
The Story of Two Women

A Novel by
Ursula Tillmann

URSULA TILLMANN

ISBN-13:978 148 1238601

For Lotte
and Waltraud

Tired of waking
I long for the night.
Undressing shadows
Folding their gowns.
U. T.

PROLOGUE

With tiny steps she tip-toes along the edge of that dark hem, retracing fading stitches of a gown worn out over time. Careful, not to stumble on that garment her shadows have woven those past fifty years. Unable to shed the past, unwilling to forget she moves along. Still waiting after all this time.

She realizes, history is a matter of opinion depending on geography. The chronicles of victors remain meticulously stored in archives for generations to come. Don't you dare question what is written. Oh yes, she knows. Don't doubt, for they know better. Although they were not there. So what about the suffering of women and children who mind landscapes when men battle on foreign soil? Anywhere.

Most of their stories stay hidden. Untold and unwanted within the big picture of world events. A nuisance. And, in particular, deemed mathematically unimportant.

Victors and losers, friends and enemies. Where to draw borders, permanent lines? At the end it's all the same. For all involved. Despite written documentations, one way or the other. The past doesn't care. It just is, as all stories.

What began by pure chance later unfolded by necessity, because in those days choice was a luxury few owned. I did not witness the beginnings, because it happened before my time. But I saw enough later, as a child. And the talk, the terrible gossip and degradation of displaced people. A nation divided among its own people and wounded so deeply, leaving scars for generations to come.

The end of the Second World War is only the beginning of unspeakable brutality for many civilians. In particular in Germany, the loser of the conflict. Fourteen million Germans flee from the Red Army in East Prussia, Pomerania, Silesia and other German territories beyond the rivers of Oder and Neisse in the middle of the winter. A war lost and with it the soil of their forefathers.

Expelled by the Russians, who are now master of one fourth of German territory in the east. The Soviets want those lands vacated. Promptly and without delay for a Polish population, which is being chased further west out of their own country to enlarge the Soviet territory. Joseph Stalin is enacting the resolution of the Allied Forces from the 1945 Potsdam Conference to shift Germany's borders westwards with the expulsion of all Germans from areas in the east.

Stalin has permission by decree. And although the excess of brutality is not part of the Allied order, it is not prevented during actualization. There is no pardon when it comes to kin liability of Germanic peoples. That's the idea, the thought and the deed which follows. For the victors, every German is guilty. Even if they were only bystanders.

And Stalin is clever; five months before the Allies give the official go-ahead of expulsion in the east, his soldiers get to work. The same happens in Czechoslovakia where 2.5 million Sudetenland-Germans are banished. Not orderly, but in savage ways which include rape and execution at random. Many captured Germans, not only soldiers but civilians as well, are shipped to Siberian labor camps to rebuild his communist empire.

Germans know what it means when people fearfully whisper: "The Russians are coming". They run for their lives.

In haste they leave all possessions behind to trek on foot toward the west. Outlawed, chased like cattle by the Red Army. Ahead of the gunfire but often within. Many too old and weak to escape unimaginable cruel revenge.

Fourteen million civilians are on the move. Displaced and deported, dishonored and starving while low-flying planes spill their firepower with machine-guns on anything that moves below. To kill. Mostly women, children and old men.

Two million expelled Germans die on the long walk to the west. And the living? At a loss of their land, homes and loved ones. Dead souls marching.

Blunted, desperate. Demoralized and dammed. Stripped of self respect over and over when they arrive after the war in West Germany in the rubble of Hamburg, Cologne and Düsseldorf where nobody wants them.

"There are three curses: Wild boars, potato beetles and displaced Germans," many in the West say of their fellow *Reichsdeutsche* (German Nationals) upon arrival.

The west cusses the overwhelming number of expelled Germans from the eastern Hinterland. Those people are considered an additional burden in a landscape already crushed, flattened and on its knees.

In the west fifty percent of all houses are destroyed while food is rationed. Hunger is a constant companion after this lost war. And two million German soldiers are still missing.

Perhaps unbearable grief can be shared, but how do you feed an additional twelve million people from the east? Survival is a lonely task few are willing to share. But then again, desperation creates more than bystanders. Didn't the famous German composer Richard Wagner say, when man has it good he is bad. And when man has it bad, he is good?

Those words of an artist will put a nation to the test.

But where to begin? And who takes the lead? The women, of course. How could they not? Millions of men have died in the war, several millions are still missing, most of them in prisoner of war camps.

Men who survived are haunted by guilt. Many are mental wrecks after years in the trenches. And later at home, rejected by their own children. It's up to the women as after every war. Not by choice but out of necessity a new self-confidence leads to female domination in postwar Germany. The burden of a country in rubble, hunger, demoralized men and neglected children weighs heavy on their shoulders. Meager food supplies, surrounded by nothingness force women to rise to the task.

Inventive, they join forces. And prevail. Despite human nature. Like in America, where women across the country cook, can and pickle food to be shipped to the starving people in Germany right after the war. Women demonstrate for months in front of the White House when politicians delay shipments of humanitarian aid for nearly a year. They picket and shout their demands until freighters finally sail from New York to Bremerhaven to ease the hunger of the former enemy. An event which marks a return to humanity.

The question of easing hardship is no longer tied to culpability.

What can be more forgiving than sharing bread with your former enemy?

LOTTE WON'T TALK about times which bear those horrible memories of displacement, fear, looting, death and hunger. Not today. She won't even complain about the rejection and treatment by her fellow West Germans upon arrival in the Rhineland. They have said it all. Let it be done and rest.

"How do you undress shadows?" she once asked me. "How do you fold their gowns before going to bed? I can't figure it out."

And I don't have an answer either. So when I visit her for the third time that week in her small cottage, which she is sharing with her son Albert and daughter-in-law at the outskirts of Düsseldorf, I simply hold Lotte's hands. So boney, pale and cold. Hands, which did the work of a man but also comforted and caressed like a woman.

"You came today, what joy," Lotte says while leaning back on the couch, hugging a pillow like she used to hold me when I was a child.

"Isn't it Monday? Shouldn't you be in school?" she asks.

"We have the day off," I reply quickly. And I will not make the mistake again of reminding her of the present, more than three years after the fall of the Berlin Wall and reunification of Germany.

Officially I am here in my former homeland on assignment for American newspapers. I have three months to file newsworthy stories. Foremost however, I am looking for mine. I am on a quest to solve the riddle of a family secret. And Lotte is my gatekeeper to the past. The last and only one who is still around to speak about those years. All others of her generation in my family are gone.

Only Lotte is left to break the silence. She knows, I am certain. But will she tell?

"Don't ever skip school. Do you hear me! Never. It's education, ah yes, education, not the land you own. There is no eternal entitlement to land. Never. Even if you own the soil under your feet. Haven't we seen that over and over, especially in East Prussia and Pomerania. My father never understood that education and not simply the possession of acres is indestructible. How could he? He was a farmer. The land under his plow was like the flesh to his bones. And my husband was just the same. Earth and blood. *Ach ja,"* she sighs.

Lotte closes her eyes for a brief moment, searching for memories. Pictures of a landscape, her homeland Pomerania once part of Germany, surface. She visualizes her family's estate with hundreds of acres of healthy crops beyond the stonewalls of the farmhouse. Fields with potatoes and golden grain, edged by poplars along the horizon cross her mind; lands owned by her ancestors for generations. And Lotte as a young girl, glowing with expectations.

She smiles and I detect a sparkle in her eyes when she goes back there in time, before the war, remembering abundance and the lightness of days. She won't go any further forward in time to that winter of 1945 when they lost everything; when they ran ahead of the gunfire and were chased off their land. They were among millions of civilians fleeing from the hatred of the Russians, an angry nation who wanted revenge.

Lotte's pictures of the past stay simple. It's Pomerania before those dark days and then the postwar camps in the Rhineland. There are no landscapes, places or persons for the times in between. Just attempts of survival spiked with shadows which linger day and night. But she won't go there. Not today, not for some time. I have to guide her carefully one year at a time if I want to learn the truth which sealed the lips of my own forefathers.

"Tell me again how you met them after the war," I ask her in order to fast forward those years of horror before she came to the West. "But not just bits and pieces. I want to hear the whole story."

Softly she strokes my cheeks. "Of course, Christina. You need to know. But where should I start? My generation learnt too late that we lived in a hypnotic state of deception. Hypnosis by free will at first but manipulated by leaders who knew where to push buttons. Like in trance we marched along. Cruel events happened during that war, that's true. But does that justify the massacre against German civilians by Russian troops at the end of the war?"

"If you talked about displacement and numbers, politicians were quick to point the finger at German concentration camps, at war-crimes of our own nation. We had to shut up and sulk in our own sorrows. No, we could not expect empathy. How our people suffered is only an addendum in history books. Losing a war should not minimize what we endured. But even today the guilt-factor suppresses open discussions.

"You see, before you were born in the fifties, this was a country in ashes where everybody just tried to survive. Hungry, exhausted and shamed, stripped of dignity and self-respect after Germany surrendered to the Allied Forces."

"We were the walking dead, like ghosts we searched for new directions but most of all food. Yes, there were moments we envied those who weren't among us any longer. And before that many in our country were brain-washed. They were told stories over and over until the lie became the truth."

"We didn't know any better, we were in denial of reality." She glances at her hands. Pale and skinny. They look just the same as fifty years ago when she arrived in the Rhineland. But it was hunger then, not age that marked her body.

That was after the war in the summer of 1945, when Germany surrendered to the victors USA, Great Britain, France and Soviet Union. Those nations took supreme authority and divided Germany into four sections.

One area, the Rhineland which initially was under the control of the British became a dual-zone by '48 when the Americans joined their administration. At that time millions of expelled Germans had already arrived in the west. The Allies were overwhelmed by their numbers. The logistic of building temporary camps was an enormous task. Feeding those new Germans became a nightmare. Until the fifties temporary shelters turned into permanent slum housing.

What about those West Germans? Didn't they care about their own countrymen from the east?

How do you stay compassionate and willing to share on an empty stomach? How do you split nothingness? That is the question.

1

Her eyes are glued to the east but her view is lost. She doesn't know if she is coming or going. Lotte Marlow is sitting on her small shabby brown leather suitcase in front of a wooden shack. Her black jacket and ankle-long skirt look dusty, as if dawn is still upon her worn-out clothes. Her sunken eyes are dull, her beauty faded. She looks aged beyond her thirty years. Emaciated. The madness of nearly two years in refugee camps at the end of the war in her own country, trekking from east to west, then north to south have left their marks. She is unwanted and often despised.

The agony of landscapes wandered after her displacement has rewritten the lines in her face, leaving traces of dust from rubble of fallen cities from east to west. The war has repainted the land gray and grim. Visible not only in towns but also in faces of expelled women who are now in allied camps.

Women everywhere. They embody the survivors of a man's game.

Females who lost their husbands, women with orphans and women who are still scared of uniforms. And the power of men who wear them, even if they maintain now that these are the liberator's uniforms worn by Brits, Frenchmen and Americans.

But soldiers rape women, don't they?

Who to trust? Where to go? No one can tell. The wounds of the long trek are not bleeding any longer. Time has bandaged visible scars. And what's hidden inside is nobody's business.

It is May '47. The shanty town with thousands of displaced persons at the edge of Düsseldorf in the Rhineland at least has small huts with wooden walls to lean on, to rest and pause in privacy. The ghastly stinging smell is gone, an odor from camps overcrowded by hundreds of people in small barracks sharing suffocating space and privacy.

The stale smell of humans which even stray dogs avoid, that stink has vanished. But so have thousands of people, too weak, tired and malnourished. Left behind during the trek to be buried by kind strangers in shallow graves along roadways.

Last winter was the worst. Chronic hunger became their daily companion. Most days they did with barely 400 calories per person; the equivalent of three slices of dry bread without butter. The death rate of German civilians rose to four times the prewar level. Among children that death rate climbed ten times. During the first twelve months after the war ended nearly half of all babies were stillborn. For many death came from illnesses aggravated by acute malnutrition.

Lotte still feels drained, numb and tired of life. A reflection of the camp's monotony. This is not life, it's waking death. Right after starvation, suicide is the most common cause of demise these days.

Better walk away when detecting such madness in the camp. Who knows who is next? So she avoids talking to others to keep her own thoughts in line. She only functions by gliding slowly through daily routines consisting of meaningless tasks to shorten the hours.

Waiting. Day after day. But for what?

For whom, she knows. Lotte has family and no permission to resign. But the shadows are everywhere, dressed in fine clothes, dancing and mocking her every thought. Her attempts to scream are stuck in her throat. So she keeps silent. Most of the time. Not for own benefit but her family's sake.

Her husband Otto and son Albert have gone to the canteen of the refugee camp in the British zone to eat and then again beg for work. As every day. Any job, anywhere in this land. Lotte stays behind. Her hunger cannot be stilled by potatoes and cabbage. Granted, the British soldiers are kind and try their best to feed millions of displaced. But most German refugees from the east are restless. After regaining some form of physical strength they now want to leave the camps.

Close the gate and open a new window. Go. Run. Somewhere. Anywhere. To work, feel purpose once more. In agony many refugees however only fantasize about their imminent return to Pomerania and East Prussia. They want to go home to plow their homeland in the east.

Such illusions, haven't they heard? Don't they know how the wheels of politics are changing the landscape? Of course not. Not here, not in their world of nonexistence.

Restless, useless. It's all around her. Like a virus those feelings have infested themselves and spread through every camp across the country. Twelve million displaced people from the east with too much time to think about nothingness, with dim hopes of a future and even darker memories of their past. And Lotte is only one of them. What's to become of her son Albert? The boy is eight now and has never been to school.

For moments Lotte indulges in the luxury of dreaming about Pomerania, her homeland some seven hundred miles to the east. She can see the red brick schoolhouse, the laughter of her siblings on their way back to their estate in a Landau carriage, pulled by two black *Trakehner* horses driven skillfully by farmhand Johannes. Her memories stand in sharp contrast to the ruins of downtown Düsseldorf.

Lone burned out high rise structures appear like skeletons against the gray skyline. People stumble over stones and debris with no particular place to go. Lotte allows herself one more glance at her carefree past in Pomerania before she suspends her memories.

Stop it. This is madness, Lotte tells herself. If she won't take the lead by standing back and putting her husband and son first, the suffering will have been in vain. Doesn't she still have her loved ones? Every eighth male in the country has died in this war. Two million are still prisoners of war in Russia. She feels engulfed in self-pity as most of her countrymen; lamenting the hardship of postwar times. Whose fault is this anyway? Abruptly she pushed her thoughts aside. Desperation and hunger leave no energy for soul-searching or feelings of guilt. Not here, not now.

Lotte stands up and straightens her skirt, which has grown far too big for her skinny body. She reaches for her worn-out suitcase, her last familiar possession.

"So you are all packed then, always ahead of yourself," she suddenly hears the voice of her husband Otto. A few steps behind him she spots her son Albert with a tall slender man who is wearing polished black riding boots, beige pants and a checkered gentleman jacket.

The visitor looks out of place and time in this camp of rotting souls. When he steps forward to address the family, he does not offer a handshake, an otherwise common courtesy of respect in this land. The stranger just stands there, scrutinizing the family like regulars for selection of a battalion. Such arrogance and superiority. Hasn't he heard, the war is over.

"Good heavens, this place gets worse every time I come here. The smell is unbelievable, how can anyone live like that? I guess, that's why I am here. By order of the local committee my family has to take in more of you people," the man says. "Refugees, I mean. Or displaced, if so preferred. Heaven knows why? There are already seven extra mouths from the east to feed on our farm," the stranger says.

Damn the government's new enacted billeting, he thinks. The Allied Control Council in Berlin is meanwhile confiscating living space with increasing speed to get a handle on the problem. Not only for bombed out Germans in western cities but also for refugees from the east in overcrowded camps. That's why they are placing the war-homeless into undamaged houses across the nation. By order, not choice. Ideally the occupancy of 2.4 persons per room is the norm.

The norm? Normality? There is nothing normal during postwar times, the stranger thinks. Even at the beginning of the war he never experienced such unpredictability. It was better then for him and his family on the estate. They lived well during those first years of war, until the Nazis also drafted farmers and forced them to march with the *Wehrmacht* (German army) toward Russia to expand *Lebensraum*.

For a brief moment the stranger's agonizing memories seem to mellow his harsh attitude in this camp. He takes another look at those displaced Germans with a flicker of empathy now lighting up his eyes. Poor souls. It's not their fault, he thinks. But it isn't mine either.

"What can I say? I am here on government order," he continues.

"You'll even get paid for working the fields. You know, plowing, seeding? Do you know what I mean? Have you ever worked on a farm?" he asks while looking at Otto who just stands there and seems slightly agitated by the stranger's demeanor.

The Pomeranian farmer feels intimidated. But not Lotte. She is beyond insult while leaning forward to catch every syllable of the man's words.

Work, Lotte thinks. Purpose. Open space. Farming. Perhaps fresh apples and cherries. She pinches her husband gently in the back to encourage his response. But Otto just stares at the man until he finally mumbles.

"Farmhand? Yes, I suppose I can do that. Plow fields, plant potatoes".

Can he really? the stranger thinks. That man appears emaciated, worn out. Just another mouth to feed without a good day's work to show for. He now hesitates as if rethinking his choice. There are stronger workers in this camp. Aren't there? When Lotte looks at his face, she senses his deliberation. And she acts quickly.

"My husband is a very hard worker, he knows everything about farming. You won't regret taking him," she pleads. "He is relentless, you'll see. He needs this job. My Otto is the hardest worker you'll ever meet."

Women, the stranger thinks. They all say the same; always defending their man. He is not convinced. Should he take that boney worker back to the farm? Halfhearted he points at Otto.

"Alright then. We'll give it a try. Get your stuff and come along. We have a long way back to the farm," he says. Otto looks dumb-folded. He did not expect an offer of employment on the spot.

When you hope and wait for such a long time, the decisive moment always comes too soon. He is confused.

"Right away? Now? What about my wife and son?" Otto asks. The man seems in a hurry, he wants to get home.

Tragedy is about location, Otto thinks. What if that man had lost his farm during the war and I was him? Would I react in the same manner? Perhaps or quite certain? It's geography which make us unequal, Otto decides for himself.

Disparity decided by history within one country. How bizarre is that?.

"Now listen, you want that job or not?" the stranger says. "There are thousands in this camp and millions of you all over Germany who are looking for work. I don't have time for arguments. Take it or leave it." With those words the stranger turns around to walk away.

"No. Wait, please stay," Lotte calls. "How about it, *Mein Herr* (Sir)? You'll get three for the price of one. I can milk cows, help in the house and garden. My son can do farm chores as well. We'll work just for our keep. Take my husband, please, but let us come along too. You won't regret it. I promise."

From squire to servant. Second class citizens. That's how it's going to be. She can see it clearly now but will not complain. What's the alternative? Exactly, nothingness, she thinks. Swallowing her pride, she watches Otto tearing up. Pleading is not a new experience for Lotte. Her words have strength but also sincerity. They come from a place where you go, when you have nowhere else to arrive any longer.

"A fine feisty woman you have there," the man responds while grinning at Otto. "She'll get along just fine with my wife. Alright then, let's try it. But your wife and son will only be on probation."

The Marlows nod and keep silent. Probation is a leap forward, Lotte thinks. It is a release from camp. A step toward regaining hope. An escape into open spaces to familiarity like Pomerania. She feels her blood pumping beneath her skin, streaming back life underneath her pale cheeks. Slowly she returns to her senses, overcome with joy as if going home to the east. Within ten minutes the Marlows are ready to leave the camp.

The trip by horse and wagon takes longer than an hour. They ride from the city through two villages onto a gravel-road into the country without noticing any visible damage from the war. No bombed out houses, no rubble or that horrific sewage smell so familiar from the camps. A different world, a place awakening memories and hopes of better days to come.

Lotte hugs Albert who points eagerly at cows and horses in pastures along the way. They ride in silence without knowing the man's name or the place they are going.

Following blindly without trusting. Just moving forward.

"Up there, this is it," they hear the man finally announce. The large estate with five separate buildings and a main mansion appears beyond a private roadway, bordered by tall oak trees.

"Ten Eicken", they read engraved in white letters on an oval brown wood sign above the entrance. After riding another five minutes up the hill, they stop outside the stables on the east side of the mansion. The man jumps first off the carriage, eager to be done with his task of bringing more refugees to his ancestor's place.

"Here, unhitch the horses and then report to the main house," the man says to Otto. And without another word he leaves the Marlows standing there alone in the yard.

Pomeranian farmers on foreign pastures in the Rhineland.

Arrived. But forlorn.

Driftwood of a lost war.

East meets west. One German nation by history but two different worlds by fate.

2

Our daily bread. But for how many more days? Hopefully there will be enough flour on Ten Eicken to make it through the week. Shortages everywhere. Another bulk of grain has to be delivered to town officials to feed the hungry in the city. In addition five hundred pounds of potatoes as well as three pigs, fourteen chicken and eight dozen eggs will also be picked up from the farm in two days to fulfill the quota of the district's obligatory food collection. That is the law these days. What about apples, peaches and pears? They come later. After harvesting the fields.

With strong fists Hilda Eicken squeezes the sticky bread dough in the wood trough on a stool. That was a maid's job before the war but dire times make servants out of mistresses.

She bends down like a boxer over his capitulating opponent.

Punching the soft dough with her knuckles. Adding more white flour here and there to make it firm. She will form it later when the yeast gives rise to cut chunks for making loaves.

Hilda feels the strain of effort in her spine, tiring her body and aching her muscles. But twenty large loaves need to be baked today. So many people to feed and care for. They are hungry. All the time.

Postwar years of immense scarcity lick plates clean at every meal, there is not a crumb left. No waste ever.

Hilda doesn't mind hard work. But she could use some help in the house as well instead of employing more and more field workers on the farm. Wiping the sweat off her forehead she pauses for a moment to straighten her back, when she spots outside the bake-house three strangers. They look pale, thin, forlorn and displaced.

From the east, she thinks. They carry their geography like a brand with their meager appearance; malnourished and tattered clothes.

Hilda scrapes the dough off her hands and folds her apron. She is wearing a light blue cotton dress, her blond hair is braided. When walking outside toward the group, she holds out her hand to greet them.

"Welcome to Ten Eicken," she says in a friendly tone. "And you are?"

Otto takes off his black cap and steps forward. "The Marlows, new farmhand with family."

Lotte and Albert respectfully remain a few steps back in anticipation. They learnt their lesson on the road during their displacement. Too often premature trust chased them off farms further east, when they knocked on doors already half-starved and asked for bread.

But with millions trekking westward, alms became a rarity. Kindness an exception. The release of aggressive mongrels became the rule. Stumbling forward with hunger day after day, not only distance but also resentment found growth. Life in camps later restored some of that lost trust in general but not faith in particular. So at that moment, in the yard of Ten Eicken, the family simply stands there and waits to see what comes next.

"Marlows? East Prussia?" Hilda asks now.

"Pomerania," Lotte says while stepping forward to greet the woman who seems friendly enough. Hilda takes her hand and puts the other gently on Lotte's left shoulder.

"Pomerania, oh yes. Beautiful land, rich farm country, honest and hard-working people," she says while looking at Lotte for a long time as if trying to read her thoughts. She can see what needs not to be mentioned, she can feel the obvious. And she is humbled by the sight of these displaced people.

How did they survive? She can only imagine. With encouragement, she guides them through the main entrance toward the kitchen.

"Come on in, this is your home now too, " Hilda says. She speaks quickly now, like a tour guide who wants to avoid question which find answers before asked. "You'll see in no time you'll love it here. Ten Eicken has been in the family for over three hundred years. Yes, it's quite large, lots of work with seven hundred acres in this valley. There are also two lakes with trout and thirty acres of pine and oak forest. Our nearest neighbors are way beyond those hills," she points to the west.

"Come along with me to the kitchen, you must be hungry and thirsty. There isn't much but more than in the camps. We'll also find you some clothes and perhaps a pair of shoes for the boy. You've met my husband Ernst, he picked you up in Düsseldorf. He'll talk to you later."

What a change, kindness at last. A retrieval of normality, of feeling human again, Lotte thinks. And such beauty after all those months surrounded by filth. Lotte feels mesmerized by the moment, as if stepping back in time or forwarding her existence. It's not the lavish estate, she decides. But Hilda, that wonderful creature in front of her, radiating warmth and comfort. She is moving Lotte to tears, helping already to mend what lies within. With her dusty sleeves, she quickly wipes her eyes to regain posture. There is something in particular she needs to address right away.

"Your husband mentioned this may only be probation for me and my son," Lotte says while eating a thick slice of bread with sugar beet syrup. There is no butter. "Probation, he said," Lotte repeats, as if that word contains the threat of returning to camp soon. But she wants a clean start. Better to settle matters up front before too much trust disappoints later. The lady of the house will surely understand that?

18

"Probation. What nonsense. Don't you worry now," Hilda says. "I promise, you'll stay together as a family."

That husband of hers, what did he tell them? Still snot-nosed despite a lost war, notwithstanding injury and loss of relatives. Such arrogance, a family disease Hilda cannot cure. But she knows the power of her persuasiveness. It always works. And it will keep the Marlows together, right here on Ten Eicken. As a family under one roof. Yes, Hilda knows what's best. Hasn't she carried the burden of running this place by herself for the past few years. After the men went to war? And what about later, when Ernst returned home wounded from the frontline? Unable to take care of himself, let alone lead the business on the estate.

No it won't be a problem to keep all three Marlows on the farm. Hilda is certain. While finishing their meal in the kitchen, they hear footsteps echoing on the wooden hallway floor.

"Come here, don't be shy. Wilhelm, say *Guten Tag* (good day)," Hilda catches the running child and hugs him while lifting him toward her shoulders. "I'm too old for that," the boy objects, "I'll be six this summer." The boy is neatly dressed with shiny black shoes, short Lederhosen and a dark green shirt. His blond hair is cut short. Wilhelm looks at Albert with curiosity, noticing the poor outfit of the boy. His worn out dusty shoes, dirty spots on his black knickerbockers and mended beige shirt. He utters a quick greeting while freeing himself from his mother's arms.

"Wilhelm, this is Albert, he is only two years older than you,." Hilda says. "You'll have a new playmate." It is Hilda, who is now ready to tear up. She needs to talk, say something. Explain to that stranger in front of her. A woman will understand her pain caused by the war.

"He is all I have left. My little boy Wilhelm," Hilda says to Lotte. "His father Walter Eicken was killed near Stalingrad in Russia. He was the older brother of Ernst. You may as well know before others gossip. Yes, I later married his brother. When my first husband Walter went to the Russian front, he knew I was pregnant. But he died before Wilhelm was born, he never saw the child. But he knew. That counts, doesn't it?"

Hilda keeps talking. Why, she cannot explain. But she feels a kinship with this stranger. A recognition and familiarity of sorts which animates to share. The similarity is obvious to Hilda. She too was treated like an outsider when she first came to Ten Eicken.

In a sense, we are two of a kind, she thinks while looking at Lotte.

"Two years after the Red Cross informed me of my husband's death, Ernst asked me to marry him. I think he was in love with me all along. So I finally said yes," Hilda continues. "Those times were hard, I was twenty-one and alone with an orphan in this huge house ..." She suddenly stops talking. She doesn't want to think about it any longer. The pain is constantly there, especially when she looks at her son Wilhelm. He is the living image of her dead husband. She must not think about it. At least not so often, she reminds herself.

The women walk in silence through the long hallway of the main building followed by Otto and the two boys. Hilda opens a few doors to shows them the layout of the mansion.

Such a huge house, but the rooms are furnished Spartan. Only a few paintings decorate those white spacious walls. Carpets and curtains are missing. The Marlows keep silent but Hilda senses their curiosity.

"Looted," Hilda states matter of fact. "Taken by the mob from the city and also by soldiers. Desperate times lack consideration. Those looters weren't just hungry, they were after valuables, so they took the antiques and our silver cutlery too. Items which probably ended up on the black market. When the British soldiers marched in we had to move to the village and stay with friends. Later even the Americans requisitioned Ten Eicken and used it as their headquarter for several months. Darn war." Again Hilda abruptly stops talking. What is she complaining about? Ten Eicken was only plundered and now some items are missing. The Marlow Family lost their farm and land. Their only possessions are the clothes they wear.

The group has reached the end of the hallway on the ground floor. Hilda points to the wide wooden stairway.

"That's off limits. Not just for you but all of us."

"Who lives up there?" Albert asks.

"The rest of the family," Hilda says with disinterest in her voice. And that is the end of the conversation.

They step outside, walk past the blacksmith building and foreman's cottage. To the left is the barn and mill. Ten Eicken is a huge estate but in dire need of maintenance, repairs and painting. Whatever money is earned on the farm has not been used for upkeep for quite a few years. That neglect is visible. The war won't do as an excuse. The mill, a half-timbered house typical in the Rhineland, has a coat of white fading paint. The black horizontal and vertical wood trim needs work as well. They climb the stairs to the first floor above the mill.

"We set up only one room as we didn't know there would be three of you," Hilda says. "But there is an adjoining door to another large room. You'll have lots of space. Yes room we have in abundance but that's it. We suffer shortages as everybody else these days. Why don't you get settled and then we'll carry on. Meanwhile, I have to get back to my baking. There are lots of mouths to feed on Ten Eicken."

"I'll come with you right away to help," Lotte offers. And while both women walk back to the main house, Otto smiles. He grins inwardly for the first time after two years with relief. This is way beyond probation for his family. The warmth and kindness feels permanent.

Glancing out of the window he loses his view for a flash beyond the valley. But the moment passes, and as if now fully awake Otto abruptly stops his comfortable line of thoughts. He cannot allow permanence, his family will surely go back to their farm in Pomerania right after the politicians have sorted out this mess. Isn't that the plan? To return to his homeland and claim his birthright? Looking at his son Albert, Otto promises to never shelve that thought.

He is not alone with those hopes of returning home to the east one day. But time will write its own history. Like millions of displaced persons, the farmer from Pomerania will sit on a packed suitcase in vain until the day he dies.

3

The fields are plowed and seeded. Farmhands on Ten Eicken work the horses long hours. Every day. There is no time to idle. In the country the weather sets the pace for sowing and reaping. Tomorrow it may rain, the hay in the pastures is dry and has to be brought in by nightfall to be stored under the roof in the barn. The feed for the cattle is valuable, not one leaf of grass must be wasted. If the cows don't eat, there won't be milk or butter for people. That's how farmers think. And that's how they act in comparison to people who were born in the city.

Ernst Eicken is running across the pasture. He sees Otto and waves at him several times, advising him to stop loading hay on the cart.

"We need these two horses, Hektor and Pfanni. Unhitch them right away and bring them to the stable. My mother and sister want to go in the *Landauer* to the city. Hurry," Ernst pleads.

"But what about the hay? We need those horses to bring in the hay. It looks like rain overnight, the hay will rot in the fields," Otto says. He is a farmer with heart and soul. And he cares. Dark clouds in the west of the valley confirm his concern. Can't Ernst see that too?

"What can I say, they want to go to Düsseldorf so get those horses ready for the trip," Ernst says with resignation in his voice. He knows it is wrong to interrupt the work in the fields but his mother demands, she does not request. Father and son learnt that lesson over the years. She conditioned them well to her needs.

Otto shakes his head in disbelief while clouds move closer toward the valley. This is not the first time a private affair has taken priority over the work on the farm. It's a repetition of events on Ten Eicken. And Otto knows what lies ahead. He'll have to drive Agnes the "Queen" and her "Princess" daughter Gisela, as he secretly calls them, to the once glamorous Düsseldorf shopping area of the *Königsallee*. To stroll and parade as if the war never happened and postwar times are none of their concern. A mockery to other women who sort in rags every day through rubble.

Hard times? Where? Not for mother and daughter. Not here on this estate. Agnes and Gisela are one of a kind, inseparable they demand as one entity. Convinced live owes them. And who dares to differ? Nobody within their family. The queen and her princess are the carriers of a family disease. An incurable arrogance and assumption of entitlement.

"They do this on purpose, I swear," Otto says later to Lotte.

"As it gets busier in the fields their urgency of using the horses for pleasure trips increases. They'll ruin this farm in time, that's how it always ends. I've seen it before, this wild ride goes straight toward the abyss. They are chasing the horses to that bottomless pit. City women. No one raised in the country would act this way," he curses.

"Stop talking, it's none of our business," Lotte halts his flow of words. "We are working for Ernst. You are talking about his mother and his sister. Those excursions are not the fault of your boss. Isn't it true that he works just as hard in the fields as the farmhands? Granted, he has some of the same allures as his mother but he is not lazy. So stop mingling in other people's affairs and mind your own business." Lotte is angry now but Otto keeps lamenting.

"Why doesn't the old man stop the extravagance of these women?" he says. But Otto doesn't wait for an answer. He knows by now as everybody else on the farm what's really going on. Although the old man Gunter Eicken is the owner of this estate, he is defiantly not in charge. That's obvious. His wife Agnes spends the money as quickly as it is earned. With rising inflation money isn't worth much any longer anyways, so today the women bring old fur coats along to trade for evening gowns on the black market in the city.

Why can't they get more cash? Because the credit line at the bank is overdrawn as well. But what can Gunter do? Agnes was raised in the city, she has no understanding of the land, the hardship of farming and meager income during postwar years. She doesn't want to know. So her life of dissipation is financed by selling substance of the estate. One parcel of land at a time.

It shames the old farmer when selling off his forefathers fields to satisfy the needs of his wife while at the same time betraying his offspring of their rightful inheritance. But for Agnes he'll do anything.

What a delicate creature, what a wonderful woman, Gunter thought when he first met her. Always dressed elegantly, was educated and refined from a family of scholars in Düsseldorf. She was surrounded by suitors from the finest families. But Agnes took him, Gunter, a farmer. Way back, he could not believe his luck. That was at the turn of the century, when Ten Eicken was one of the richest estates in the district.

What a luxurious life they led during those years. Agnes employed eight maids in her farm household. She did not dirty her hands with common work. It was exhausting enough to give orders. Over the years her wasteful lifestyle emptied rapidly the accounts of the estate. And before the second world war, Gunter even cut five acres of his best oak forest to bring in some extra cash. His wife begged him to send their daughter Gisela to a Swiss finishing school. She did not find a husband there, as expected. But later married Fritz, the son from a smaller estate north of Cologne. A penniless gentleman farmer, lazy without interest in a good day's work. A perfect fit for Gisela, neighbors gossiped.

Yes, Otto knows all that. Farmhands talk and whisper when they mow the pastures. They have their fun while telling stories larger than reality. But not Otto, not in the fields where he keeps to himself. And especially today he feels pity for the old man and his son Ernst. Abused by those women, belittled by farmhands. In the evening, however, when thunder and lightening announce the disaster and heavy rain sweeps through the valley destroying the hay in the fields, Otto feels anger.

That stupid Eicken family.

Such a waste. Two weeks of work and nothing to show for but an empty barn.

Enraged Otto steps outside. What business is this to him? It's not his land, it's not his hay. Why should he care more than the owner? And yet, he must worry. He is a farmer from Pomerania. It is also his personal pride which feels blemished. How can he stay indifferent when the labor of so many workers rots in the fields, when the Holstein cows wait for their feed.

Annoyed by his anger, soaking wet from the rain, Otto finally returns to his quarters above the mill. He is done with worrying for others.

At least for tonight.

A cloud of shame lingers over Ten Eicken for days after the incident. Nothing new, just a repeat of waste meanwhile predictable.

Hilda is sitting on the corner bench in the kitchen, staring into the dark outside. Her son is asleep, her husband is upstairs visiting his parents. Of course Ernst won't complain to the old folks about that trip to the city which caused the hay to waste. He will not say a word, the effects of the war have made these occurrences a banality in comparison. Most people have seen worse. Methods of survival have taken on the oddest forms in this household.

"Enough for today Lotte, you work too hard," Hilda says while turning around. She looks at the woman who is not a maid but has become quickly a friend in this household. Like Otto and Albert, Lotte's face now shows color. She looks healthy and strong.

"But really, you work too hard," Hilda repeats.

"Not harder than you," Lotte replies while scrubbing the last pots of the dish load from supper.

It is the work, the tired bones which is the glue that ties these women. Hard physical tasks soften their thoughts, place memories at arm's length while keeping sanity within reach.

Not once these past few weeks Lotte has thought about her homeland in the east or the future in the west. She lives in the moment. And makes it last by scrubbing even harder the bottom of those pots. She feels needed and therefore content with her work on Ten Eicken. No, Lotte is not restless like her husband, whose thoughts wander along the trenches of dark rich soil when plowing the land. His solitary work in the fields is a dangerous task, creating pathways within the mind which overshadow the way forward.

Otto's sweat is like the steam evaporating above the belly of that tired horse pulling the plow. He is that horse. Although he walks behind that animal, he pulls the weight of those plowshares with invisible ropes attached all the way to Pomerania. Unable to forget, he is also unwilling to settle his desires. At times his unharnessed yearning for Pomerania angers his waking hours so much, that his nights above the mill become as restless as his days in the refugee camp.

Nothing has changed for him.

He remains a tool, a steal wrench or hammer in the shed. Used when needed, ready for disposal when broken. Only for moments, when he thinks of his wife and son, Otto mellows. But it never lasts, it just keeps him hungry for more than life can offer in these dire times. On Ten Eicken he is not his own master although no one patronizes him.

But this is not his real home or own land. He can't get used to the smell of the dark brown soil in the Rhineland. And at night under these Rhineland skies, even the distance to the stars seems further.

And he feels small and sad. Lost in space with those sparkling stars which are unreachable like Pomerania.

"I worry about Otto but even more about my son. He will be nine this year," Lotte tells Hilda while putting cleaned dishes into the cupboard.

"Nine years already and he hasn't yet seen a school from the inside."

The stillness in the house at this hour animates homely talks. It has become a habit after midnight, a familiar practice after a busy day on the farm. The women often sit here and chat another hour in familiar territory with soothing smells.

"Why don't we send Albert with Wilhelm to the village school?" Hilda suggests.

"I've heard some teachers give lessons again after all these years without regular schooling. The boys can bike to school together through the valley. It's only an hour away. Your son is older and stronger, he can look out for Wilhelm," Hilda says. "This arrangement could be practical for both of them." She talks in a business like voice, because she does not want to shame Lotte with another handout by the grace of the Eicken family. No, this woman deserves better, she earned it even before she set foot on this farm.

"So, how about it?"

"He is a smart boy that Albert. He'll learn how to read and write in no time," Lotte responds with eagerness. "He'll catch up with the others. When we left he was going on six. This would be his first year in school. That poor boy just didn't have the opportunity to start his education earlier. Oh those barbarians, those soldiers ..."

She stops talking, the words are stuck in her throat. Overwhelmed by memories, tears stream down her face. She is crying for Albert, Pomerania, Otto and for herself. Finally, it's been a long time but now her emotions surface. Uncontrollable. Delayed by fear and pride, they finally caught up with her journey. And arrived. For moments, Hilda simply sits there, uncertain how to react. But finally she reaches out for Lotte's hand.

"I know," she says. "No need to tell."

A week later the boys bike together to town for their first lessons. But after Albert comes home from school that first Wednesday afternoon, he refuses to go back the next day and the day after.

The other children called him a "stupid Pollack and potato beetle". Why doesn't he go back to where he came from? And what is he doing here in the west anyway? Isn't it crowded enough?

Little Albert just stood there. He could not interfere. The other children retained him while the boy from Pomerania got his first beating in the Rhineland. He avoided some punches by holding his hands over his head. But there was no escape from words, those terrible curses mixed with laughter by the other children.

"Mother, are we Polish now? And what is a potato beetle?" he wants to know while Lotte attends to his swollen cheeks.

Children. They can be as brutish as adults, she thinks. How so after all those horrible war-years? Haven't they learnt anything?

What did Lotte expect? As if war teaches something? But couldn't one at least expect greater compassion in the face of so much agony?

Keep on dreaming. No chance. War only releases the caveman in us, sets him free to handle his inferiors and reign, she realizes.

Caveman. That's right. Who is the strongest now? And you thought we lost that war. Not the children, they are training for the next conflict. Kids are exercising their fists to be ready when politicians call for battle. There is always a war around the corner, isn't there?

You have to learn aggressiveness early. Every generation anew. Isn't that what this is all about? Lotte contemplates. But the roots of aggressions lie deeper.

After the defeat and degradation of a whole nation, German children now practice war against themselves because there is no one else left to fight.

Lotte swallows her anger while looking at Albert's swollen face.

"You'll read," she finally says. "Soon you'll even read better than all the others. Don't you worry now. I'll teach you, we'll start right now."

While Albert still holds his burning cheeks his mother opens a fairy tale book and whispers with a gentle voice: "Once upon a time ..."

4

Yes, once upon a time. It seems like only yesterday when Lotte read those very same stories to me. I remember it well during my next visit, a Saturday when I find her in high spirits. She wants to talk. I can sense it. The further she reaches back, the clearer her pictures take shape. Her stories now fill the once empty frame.

"She has been waiting for you all morning," says Albert. "You are her link to the past, she remembers it well. Thank heaven, she is so much better today. She is her old self."

I smile at Albert. What a good-looking chap he has become. And always cheerful. When I was a child I told him to wait for me until I was a grown-up. I'd marry him one day. But then he fell in love with a refugee girl from East Prussia.

He was attracted to her by their common loss of eastern homelands. They bonded because of similar displacement experiences. When he announced his engagement I felt betrayed for a while. And jealous. He could have waited for me to become an adult. But willingly I later carried the traditional salt and bread toward the altar in the church.

On the day of his wedding I was almost five years old.

Albert is a trained mechanic presently working as a truck driver. A hard worker with street smarts. And also a good reader, because his mother home-schooled him. Albert never went back to the village school after that beating. Years later he attended some classes in the city. But it was too late then to pursue his dream of becoming a veterinarian. Albert loved animals, he had a special affinity for them. The boy would have made an excellent vet. But he was robbed of his future by postwar circumstances as many youngsters of his age.

The country needed workers in the Rhineland to rebuild the landscape. It didn't need preaching scholars. When the coal mines in Essen and Bochum became in the fifties part of the economic miracle of a new striving Germany rising from the ashes, young men and aging soldiers were sent underground to work.

Down there in the dark, that's were they also buried their dreams of a university degree.

Yes, Albert could have been a scholar.

We go outside to sit on the porch. The evening sun caresses the garden in the backyard of their house with rows of potatoes, rhubarb, raspberries and beans. Not a square inch is wasted with recreational grass. Albert carries a tray with cups and saucers, a pot of coffee and three slices of home-made strudel with russet apples from his own trees.

If not a vet, he would have also made a great farmer. But that was then. Way back. What's left are two stolen dreams, not just one, I think, because he also lost his family farm in Pomerania.

"You are not only self-sufficient but you can feed several families with the amount of vegetables you grow here," I point out. Albert laughs but it is Lotte who quickly reacts to my observation.

"My dear girl there will be a time, even during your life and not only in this country, when people will plow up their lawns to plant vegetables for survival. If they don't act early enough and prepare, they'll find themselves one day in front of bare supermarket shelves with empty stomachs. I know, I remember it well," Lotte warns.

"Trust me, even today with all this obvious abundance in the west it's not wise to feel too safe. Remember, after you climb up, there is only one way left to go. Down. Can't stay up there forever. I should know."

"During those postwar years we learnt the hard way that worse times often hide behind bad times. Whoever said it can't get worse was wrong. It can and it usually happens when you least expect it. Even during fat years it's never good to develop overconfidence."

She is sipping her coffee while pointing at her cup.

"How we missed this brew during the late forties, especially your mother. She just couldn't do without it. Hilda longed for coffee as if it was as essential as the blood in her veins. But ground coffee could not be bought during those years. It was seldom available and anyhow outrageously expensive. We couldn't afford to buy it. So we became inventive on the farm. We grounded a mixture of barley, malt, acorns and beechnuts. We roasted that to make *Ersatzkaffee* (Coffee substitute). What a terrible brew but with some fantasy *Ersatzkaffee* was the closest to the real thing," Lotte says.

"Years later when coffee beans became affordable again your mother and I would drink several liters of coffee every day. It wasn't only to get caffeine to keep us awake when we baked and cooked during our busy years in the business throughout the night. It seems to me now that we wanted to make up for all those years of scarcity." She giggles.

"The possession of coffee became such a fixation for your mother, that she always kept at least forty to fifty pounds of coffee hidden in the storage room."

"Today you would probably call that behavior a form of sick hoarding but during those years, when uncertainty was a daily companion, it seemed an intelligent foresight. You had to hoard essentials because money couldn't buy much any longer. It wasn't worth the paper it was printed on because prices soared and in addition the shelves in stores were almost empty. Just imagine, a loaf of bread was 150 Reich Mark. The black market blossomed during those first years after the war, it was goods for services and item for item. A dozen eggs was traded for a pair of leather shoes, a winter jacket for a sack of potatoes."

"You had to have goods to trade for survival. Lucky Strike cigarettes became the most valuable currency during that time. You could buy almost anything with them. City kids followed American soldiers in hordes to pick up thrown away stubs. With that tobacco kids rolled new cigarettes. A Sisyphus task but extremely valuable for trading."

"As banknotes lost their value more and more, people parted with family silver and jewelry. Some women even traded their golden wedding rings to buy bread. Black market wrangler showed no empathy. Their business was striving."

"Effects of hunger mirror the faces of beasts. Dear girl, may God help you that you'll never see such desperate times." While listening intensively I dare not interrupt her story.

"Don't ask me about compassion. Compassion is a luxury reserved for full stomachs," Lotte says. "And even then it's not guaranteed. Each man and woman fought for themselves. Survival can be a brutal affair when you have nothing left but hunger. There were stories about butchers in the city, who did not only catch and slaughter pets in those dire days to make sausage. Horrible times, extremely bad in the cities."

"During those first two years after the war the German police and Allied Military Police were helpless, they could not control the overwhelming excesses which desperation created. The traders of the black markets ruled like the Mafia. They organized quickly across the country. Some said the city of Munich was their headquarter. From there they brought supplies in bulk loads across the country. Heaven knows where they got the goods. I suspect many of those traders befriended allied soldiers to tap into food reserves of the army. That's how those hustlers made a fortune from starving civilians."

"If you ask me, when wars end the greatest crooks surface," Lotte points out. "During postwar years lots of wealth was made with little labor by the most scrupulous Germans. That's how it is after every war. Don't kid yourself. It happens in every country. The scum surfaces. Don't we know it. What about those poor people, the general public?"

"They survived the war but were now threatened to demise by peace. Even food stamps, many of them faked, could barely fill supper plates. Most items were simply not available. Oh dear, those times were rather gruesome. It got so bad that sheets of toilet paper appeared more valuable than *Reich Mark* banknotes."

Lotte pauses. "I should not complain. We lived on a farm and ate better than most city dwellers. We had a roof over our head, work and full bellies. Everything else we could do without. You'd be surprised how little else you need when your only concern is the next meal."

"Those poor people in the cities suffered a great deal more. They were so pale and thin, their faces ghost like. Skin folded. And the clothes. So bad. I saw one man who was wearing a jacket tailored from a dusty potato sack. You felt like crying with him."

"In bombed out cities like Mainz, seventy per cent of the population lived after the war in cellars. The roofs of most houses were gone. Surrounded by rubble, nothing but debris, they had nowhere else to go. They lived like outcasts of a lost civilization. Inhuman like rats."

"Can you imagine so much suffering and agony in a country which created such greats as Goethe and Beethoven? What few living quarters survived the war in cities were shared by several families. Not out of compassion but pure necessity."

"No use to ask me about morals and virtues and how everyday life was led. Those first years of hunger and overcrowding left little space for sensitivities. What about the lost war? Yes, what about it? Nothing. Shame, guilt? Not then. There was only hunger. The only question on anybody's mind was, where is the next meal coming from. Yes, we were lucky to live on Ten Eicken during those hunger-years."

"Mother," Albert says now, "there were also curious episodes, moments which made us laugh. Why don't you talk about that as well? Remember our first Christmas on Ten Eicken? I am certain you do. Hilda sent me into the cellar to fetch a loaf of bread. You know in those days there were no fridges and everything perishable was kept in the cool cellar of the estate. The basement looked like a huge dungeon. I had never been down there before."

"In the dim light I spotted rows of shelves with sealed glasses of cherries, peaches, raspberries and other fruit. I counted at least ninety one-liter jars. How I would have loved to open one to taste the sweetness of fruit again."

"Come on boy, get us one of those jars," I heard Hilda. She was standing on top of the stone stairway to the cellar grinning. "Why not, it's Christmas, we'll make an exception."

Now Lotte laughs out loud, she was the first to taste the valuable goods stored for the black market from the cellar.

"But the cherries tasted bitter. They were rotten, spoiled," says Lotte. "I spit out a mouthful into my hands. It was just awful. How old are these, I asked Hilda. When she explained the cherries had been in the cellar since 1939, we laughed with tears in our eyes."

"You see," Lotte adds, "your mother always created something for an emergency. And since those glasses with fruit were still in the cellar eight years later, life appeared bearable because no one was starving yet. Smart, rather clever. You never knew what tomorrow had in store for you, not in those days even if you saved food or money. Especially money," Lotte says.

"Not that anybody had much, but what little we earned we saved and kept hidden under the mattress. For the future, for better days, we believed. But it was all in vain as we found out by surprise in the summer of 1948."

5

The crops in the fields look promising; it will be a good harvest this fall on Ten Eicken. They need the income as their resources are nearly exhausted. A few thousand *Reich Mark* are left in their bank accounts are set aside for new machinery on the farm and taxes. Although not many people make a special effort to pay them these days. But despite hard times, German bureaucrats who are still under the control of western allies, try to enforce new strict tax laws with vehemence.

Not that people have anything to share.

How can bureaucrats dip into the pockets of a naked nations? Despite all the paperwork even taxation officers have to shelve their efficiency when devastating news rocks the nation that summer. No one expected such news. The nation is stunned.

"It's all gone. Wiped out, all our savings in the bank and whatever anybody has under their mattress," Ernst is shouting into the kitchen. He is in a fury.

"What are you saying? What's gone? Our money? I don't understand," Hilda says. How can her savings have vanished, she has been hiding them in a safe place even out of reach for her husband.

"Turn on the radio," Ernst says, "they've been announcing it all morning. Dear Lord, help us. The worst is yet to come." Hilda doesn't need to find a particular station on the radio, they are all reporting the same story that Friday, June 18, 1948.

The extend of the announcement seems incomprehensible. Impossible. There was no warning. Didn't anybody know? Hilda now holds her hands over her face, the words of the government newscaster feel like lashes. Her body is shaking while listening to the voice on the radio. The monetary reform is in place and effective Monday when the *Reich Mark* will be gone. Practically useless. Devalued.

A new currency which is called *Deutsch Mark* will be installed.

"But what does it mean?" Lotte asks. "We've saved every penny for the future these past twelve months ..."

"What it means? We are being robbed in broad daylight of our savings. That's the essence of this story," Ernst says. "They won't exchange Reich Mark at full value for Deutsch Mark – meaning one on one. That would be fair. But no, they are getting rid of too much money on the market. It's going up in smoke, burning holes in our pockets. Starting Monday, 100 Reich Mark will be worth 6.5 Deutsch Mark. In essence, money saved won't be worth anything." He pauses as if listening to his own words to fully understand what's going on,

"Have the authorities totally lost their minds?" Ernst complains. "You want irony? Father will be happy that debts will be downgraded ten on one. I bet mother will have a fit that she didn't buy more useless junk now that her waste will be almost forgiven. How is that for justice?"

Hilda looks pale. All that money she put aside, banknotes which have the stain of sweat and agony. Money she has been hiding for a future nest egg. What will happen to her family now?

They have tax obligations, expenses and employees to take care of. With a country still in rubble cautious beginnings are shattered. Stopped dead in their tracks.

Won't there be riots, perhaps looting again? The war is over yet the distress escalates.

"And yes, because we are such good Germans and endure every nonsense any official shovels down our throats, we are also getting a present on Monday," Ernst says now.

"Every person gets a handout of 40 Deutsch Mark. That's what we are worth these days. Forty Marks for every *Kraut* in this country. Doesn't that make me puke? Government alms for a nation of beggars who just lost all savings ..."

Ernst has swallowed his last words, he is choking on the bitterness of his own remarks The awareness of reality is settling in.

Is this another punishment by the victors?

A people already on their knees take additional whipping personal. He leaves the women standing there and goes to the living room to pour himself a schnapps.

"The government can't do that? Can they?" Lotte asks with tears in her eyes.

"What government?" Hilda says with resignation in her voice. "We are politically incapacitated, we live in a vacuum. They can do what they want, trust me. And they'll have plenty of help from Germans. There is nothing worse than a German handling a fellow German, history has taught us more than once. It's our Teutonic nature. Typical German."

"Yes, true to our nature. We either lean toward total determination or fatalism. That's us, alright. What to do now? How to carry on? We have to think. Come on Lotte, let's put our heads together," she adds now with encouragement in her voice for Lotte's sake. But silently she thinks this news marks the end.

Hilda suddenly feels the need to peel off her own skin in order to breathe. It's an urge which is not new to her. It was there before several times during the war and nearly unbearable when the Red Cross informed her of her husband's death.

That darn feeling called hope. It's elusive. Useless. And what about faith? Gone, lost many years ago. What's there to believe in with all those injustices and atrocities around you. A God up there would not stand idle to witness such inhumanity by his own creation. Or would he?

"I wonder where Hubert is right now," Hilda suddenly says. "I don't even know why I am thinking about him today?"

"Who is Hubert?" Lotte asks.

"My brother, he's been missing since 1943. He is a pilot, he flies the Junker 52. Stalingrad was his last assignment, transporting supplies to the 6th Army. We last heard from him five years ago. He could be dead or a prisoner of war in Siberia. We don't know. My father is convinced that Hubert will return on day. They say, every eighth man died during the war. But the loss is much higher, especially for those born in 1920. Forty percent of that generation died. Just imagine, nearly every second man. And then those missing on the eastern front, millions. Several million men."

"May God have mercy on him," Lotte says. "I lost two brothers on the Russian Front. When they left for the east, we knew we would never see them again. We just knew." She stops talking. What else is there to say? It's her private pain. She cannot even phantom the sorrows of Russian, Polish or British families who lost their sons in this war. And their anger of having been drawn into battle.

Death only hits home when it comes to family members raised under the same roof.

What are numbers, statistics after the fact? Both sides do the math in vain. And what about the living?

Who counts dead souls hidden in bodies still alive? Hilda reaches for Lotte's hand and pats it gently. "I think we also need a schnapps. Ernst, do you hear me? This is no time to drink alone."

They sit in silence. There is nothing more to discuss about the new monetary system. It's coming on Monday. They may as well accept what's real and keep busy.

Praying won't help and hoping is a waste of time.

Work is the solution.

Tired bones rest well.

The mind must be numbed to endure the pitfalls of life.

"We'll be bankrupt before we can cover those losses with farming after the conversion of our funds," Hilda says.

"We have to find new ways to make money. Maybe we could … Perhaps it's doable. After all, people always need to eat. Why don't we open a restaurant on Ten Eicken?" Hilda suddenly says.

"We are wasting all this space in this huge house. The living rooms and saloon are not being used, they only collect dust. They need people, guests. We would be self-sufficient because we have the vegetables, fruits, meats and especially potatoes. Lots of potatoes. I know more than fifty different meals we could serve. The cupboards are bursting with dishes, although the cutlery is missing." Hilda laughs.

Is this the beginning of hysteria? Lotte thinks.

"Yes, I am convinced we should open a restaurant for city folks. What do you think, Lotte? A restaurant, that's how we'll make money.

They also said on the news that eventually we'll see an economic miracle in Germany. It will take time, of course. But we have to give it a try. This is the moment to initiate diversity on Ten Eicken. We won't make enough money by growing wheat and barley, we never have."

Lotte looks dumb-folded now. Has Hilda lost her mind? People have nothing, most still lack a roof over their heads. In addition they just lost all their savings. Didn't Hilda hear the news on the radio? Who wants to dine in a restaurant in the country when basis food supplies can't even fill bellies in the city?

"You must think, I am crazy," Hilda says. "But how much lower can we fall. It will go uphill from now on. You'll see. And don't forget the forty *Deutsch Marks* everyone will be getting next week People will spend that money right away. Then they'll work harder to earn even more. People need to reward their efforts, they'll go to a restaurant for a treat. Guess where they'll go?" Hilda says.

"Into the country, to our restaurant. Oh come on Lotte, that's how it's always been. After every war. We should get a head-start and be ready for their spending frenzy. So why not open a restaurant, it will be as easy as looking after this large household. Actually we are sort of running a country inn already with so many mouths to feed."

"But listen, please Lotte, look at me. I need your help. I can't do it alone. I need a strong woman to be my wing-man," Hilda says. "The two of us, what do you say? If we can cook for twenty we can also cook for fifty or a hundred persons. It makes no difference. It's an easy task; we'll just need bigger pots."

Needed, wanted. Did she hear those words? Suddenly Lotte is overwhelmed by emotions, tearing up. But Hilda won't allow it.

"You can do that later, partner. Let's get busy right away. We'll make an inventory of dishes and spare chairs we have in those living rooms and in the library. There is so much to do. Let me think. I'll go to the town office on Monday and check, what permits we need for our restaurant."

After Hilda gets up to leave the kitchen, she turns around at the doorway and smiles.

"Lotte, I think we'll grow old together."

6

The women map out their preparations in secrecy and with increasing urgency. But when Hilda drives to the city that Monday her plans clash with reality. Her inner convictions of success dwindle. She didn't anticipate it was still that bad in the city.

In Düsseldorf the world appears upside down. Over the weekend shelves in stores have been stocked with merchandise, goods which were not available three days ago. But prices increased by more than seventeen percent overnight.

What abundance, Hilda thinks. But who can afford to buy anything now? The Reich Mark is invalid. Grocery stores charge up to one Deutsch Mark per egg.

Jawohl (Yeah), bake a few cakes and then eat stale bread again. How far can you go with forty new Deutsch Mark?

It's a new world. A visible change within two days. The lack of money and the sudden abundance of goods mocks window shoppers. They gaze in amazement at the merchandise and then turn their heads with disgust.

People are screaming and lifting their fists.

Betrayed again by those who run their affairs.

Anger lingers in the streets as British soldiers and police are watching and waiting. Hilda walks on the sidewalk of Bolkerstrasse. No, she won't step aside for that British soldier as the laws of the victors require. It's still her city, isn't it? The grim look on the British soldier's face softens at the sight of Hilda.

Such beauty within this mess. He smiles and makes way for her on that narrow pathway by stepping onto the street. That law for Germans to clear the sidewalk when strolling allied soldiers use the lane seems ridiculous anyway, he thinks.

Suddenly a stone smashes a window. More follow. The rubble is ammunition at hand for the mob. Anger guides the crowd while Hilda is pushed into a side street by a wave of meanwhile uncontrollable hordes of people.

"In here, quickly," she hears a woman yelling. The small coffeehouse is crowded with British soldiers and a few German civilians. They watch the spectacle through the window. In silence from a distance without uttering comments they observe the revolt.

"Ah yes, it's always about the money, isn't it? Devaluating the currency at this point in time. Ridiculous. They organized this one in secrecy. Nobody saw that coming. Clever. They want to keep us small and down on the ground," a young student whispers into Hilda's ear. He is standing behind her while pointing at the mob in the street.

"Hah, first there was lots of money but nothing to buy. Now the shelves are stocked to the ceiling but who has cash? The monetary reform has bankrupted people. They can't afford to buy what's displayed," the young man continues whispering while watching the street.

"It's like holding a carrot in front of a donkey and beating it with a whip on his hinders to run quicker. I have a feeling the so-called *denazification* after the war has become a joke. The same crooks, the same scum runs this country. Have they no shame collaborating with victors who orchestrated this?" His voice has become louder now.

Two British soldiers step closer. Did they hear anything? Do they understand German?

"He's with me, he's my cousin," Hilda says quickly while pulling the student onto a corner bench.

"Are you mad or only suicidal?" she whispers. "People have been locked up for less. You have to be careful what you say in public." The student nods but will not calm down. His name is Augustin.

"Thanks, but you are wrong. Let me buy you a cup of ground coffee, the coffee that has beans with caffeine. Remember?" he invites her.

"May as well spend our precious new Deutsch Mark. The government hand-out won't last long anyway. But don't despair, we are supposed to get an additional twenty Marks per person in the fall to jump-start the economy. Ha, Ha. Mustn't spend it all at once. Big deal." He looks at her for a comment but Hilda remains silent.

"Say, you must be from the country, haven't you heard? They are laying off people everywhere. No money, no jobs. Can it get worse? You bet. But let me assure you, lots of politicians and bureaucrats will be rich by the time this is over. It's like the twenties. Different time, same thing." He laughs out loud now at the irony of the situation. Other customers are turning their heads. If they could hear his words, most people would definitely agree.

They remember the time after the First World War when their parents wheeled thousands of devalued Marks on carts through the streets to buy a loaf of bread. When banknotes were burned in fireplaces to heat living rooms. Yes, many have seen it before.

"History always repeats itself. Come on, can't you see that? The similarities are obvious. Most people cannot connect the dots, they lack the wits to see the bigger picture or are simply not interested. So the frame of the larger picture is shrinking when the belly screams for essentials," Augustin says.

He sound like an communist, Hilda thinks. If he isn't careful, they'll throw him in jail. Fearing for his safety she moves closer to his right side to whisper in his ear.

"Psst, be careful. You don't know who is listening. Here, if you should ever be in trouble or need anything, come to this place in the country." She has written down the address of Ten Eicken on a beige paper napkin and pushes it across the table.

"Listen, perhaps you are right. Heaven forbid , what you say is true. However, try to be clever. Some words are better kept as thoughts right in there," she points with her index finger to his head. Augustin grins at her while placing the napkin into the right pocket of his tweed jacket.

The streets are empty when Hilda steps outside the café onto the sidewalk. People have grown tired looking at stuff they cannot afford. They left to go home.

Despite her observations of a desperate people who certainly have no means to visit soon a restaurant in the country, Hilda makes her way to the town office. Her feet just carry her in that direction. She does not know why. Nothing to lose, she thinks, may as well give it a try. The permit she needs for a restaurant maybe useless today but perhaps not in a few month from now.

The hallways at the municipal building are lined with people. Heads bend down, eyes fixed to the stone floor. There are no benches for the elderly to rest while waiting. No talk. Not even a whisper.

Like children they wait to be scolded by parents. The depressing silence is only interrupted by the harsh comments of officials.

Der Nächste (Next), the clerk yells. Hilda steps into an office and walks toward the desk of a clerk. No courtesy of a chair. But she won't make a comment. What's the use? So Hilda simply waits standing in front of that seated bureaucrat. She stands tall and beautiful. With great expectations and words to package her ambitions.

The officer listens to her request as if she is speaking another language. He shakes his head in disbelief when she outlines her plans.

"A restaurant? In the country. Ha, don't make me laugh. And anyway, first of all you need a certificate of *denazification* if you want to run a public restaurant under your own name. We don't just hand out permits to anyone coming off the street," the clerk says, anticipating he can get rid of this woman as quickly as she appeared.

Hilda locks eyes with the man. His request is no surprise. She expected that and hands him the required paperwork. When her husband Ernst filled out those twelve pages with 133 questions requested right after the war by the British, they both decided to go through the process of clearing their names.

But what a joke that attempt of *denazification* was, she remembers.

Active Nazi or just bystander? Who could tell? Right after the war the occupiers intended to separate wheat from chaff. In vain. Many Germans filled out the forms to their own liking and presented sworn affidavits of innocence to authorities. Granted, many were blameless and simply lumped together with real perpetrators.

But it also happened that big shots of the *Third Reich* now declared in writing their innocence by using the same pen and ink which in prior years was utilized to bring death and agony to thousands of people.

The white-washing of many culprits in government, schools, churches and universities was repulsive to Hilda. But during the war not everybody intermeddled with politics. They couldn't care less. And why go after farmers. Why did they need to be *denazified?*

Could plowing the fields be suspicious? Perhaps. There were some suspicious cases. Even in the country the odd farmer turned out to be a big shot in the party. A participant of the system, not just a bystander. You never knew for certain. Not then.

The result of the process in general was astonishing. Ninety-five percent of Germans who filled out the forms were *denazified*. They received a clean slate after the white-wash. Not even two percent were later put on trial as perpetrators.

The Allied Forces could not put a whole nation in jail, the new system needed leaders who knew their way around departments. That's why the Allies used old brooms to clean the house. For them those Germans were useful because they were familiar with the system.

But old brooms never sweep well. Pathetic, Hilda thought. That was an outrageous and degrading handling of affairs for Germans who sincerely had nothing to do with Nazi crimes.

"Are you listening? So what are your qualifications? Have you ever run a restaurant?" the clerk interrupts her thoughts.

"If running an estate with over twenty persons to feed every day counts, I'd say yes," Hilda responds quickly. The clerk shakes his head, ready to reject her proposal but not without giving her an earful of his own opinion.

"This application stinks. It's crazy. Did you not see what's going on in town? And you want people to come to the country to dine. Incredible, rather stupid. Ten Eicken is way out of town, by horse carriage more than an hour from Düsseldorf. What? You really think people will come by car to get there quicker? Keep on dreaming, nobody has fuel yet, " the clerk objects.

Excuses, objections, accusations. The butter on the bread of bureaucracy. Peasants are pleaders. They have to obey. Haven't they heard, they are not running the show. Hilda has, but she will not succumb. That clerk will not get rid of her with such ease. Hasn't she just lost her savings as every German citizen? Is there no need for innovation to make money?

"I thought it's your job to encourage new ideas to rebuild the economy. Instead you are lecturing me in business affairs and wasting my time. Is this how it's going to be?" Hilda asks with angry words but a calm voice. An elderly superior has watched the encounter, admiring the courage of that tall blond lady.

"Enough already," he finally says to the clerk.

"Give her that permit. Let her have a go at it. Her business is not your risk. What's wrong with you?"

"But I thought ..." the clerk now stutters, "I thought it should be handled all orderly. And we should only give permits for a certain number of restaurants in every district. I am only following the guidelines. It's written right here ..."

"Always the paperwork, paragraphs and rules. Haven't we had enough of that these past nine years?" the superior says while Hilda just listens. She won't comment to embarrass the clerk. He surely was not in the war and never saw the brutality in the field. Doesn't he look like the kind of guy who hides behind a desk in a cozy office? He was perhaps a privileged party member pampered behind enemy lines while others fought in the war. Obviously, Hilda thinks.

Nothing ever changes she contemplates while looking into the empty streets. Nothing new in essence. Only names, faces and circumstances appear different.

But so many people are playing musical chair in postwar Germany, aren't they? People can't help it. And therefore they cannot help. Neither themselves or others. Hilda suddenly feels overwhelmed. How she misses her first husband Walter. He was a courageous man, gone too young at age twenty three. If he was still alive he would have come along to this office with her to say a few words. Yes, Walter was different. Outgoing and brave. Not wary like his brother Ernst who always hesitates before danger even surfaces.

But what does Hilda truly know? Both brothers fought in the war. They kept their horrific encounters to themselves. Who is Hilda to judge anybody?

"Here you go, Frau Eicken," she suddenly hears the voice of the superior. He hands her a restaurant permit, signed and valid for three years.

"Good luck. But wait a moment. You may want to check back with me," he adds, "they are talking about sending busloads of children from orphanages to be feed in the country. It's a relief program by the Americans. Most of these children we help lost their parents in the war, they are hungry and malnourished. You can apply for one of those government contracts. It won't bring in much money, you'll earn just a few pennies per meal. It's considered more of a charity. But it's a start for your restaurant."

"How many? I mean, how many children are we talking about?" Hilda asks.

"There are thousands but you'll only have to deal with eighty, sometimes a hundred kids at a time. Once a week every Thursday. Can you feed that many?"

For a moment Hilda feels breathless but she regains her composure and smiles.

"Not a problem. We'll be ready for the children, I'll be in contact," she says before leaving the town office. And while she walks back to the tram station, she can hardly bear to witness the agonizing pictures of desperate people in the streets. Such suffering. They live on Ten Eicken with only essentials but they eat well enough, have dresses that fit and shoes without holes.

"We have become a nation of beggars, vagabonds and black-market traders," she says to Lotte after her return to Ten Eicken. "Such agony in the city. Wasn't it enough to lose the war?"

Lotte keeps quiet. She witnessed enough sufferings, perhaps more tragedies than Hilda can imagine. But she will not talk about that. Especially what she saw three years ago when chased by the Red Army toward the west.

Lotte will not unearth hidden thoughts to reveal memories which still cast frightening shadows each evening before sunset. Lotte's mouth is sealed for the sake of sanity. She still is uncertain about the future of all those displaced Germans. And she is one of them. The land under her feet is not her own, the roof which shelters her family's sleep belongs to others. Granted, Lotte feels at peace in this house but it is not her own home. She has to watch and wait while keeping her mouth shut.

Displaced Germans. What are they anyway? Aren't they only visitors on foreign pastures by chance and not choice. How can they feel safe in the Rhineland or Bavaria? Their lives were not even secure in Germany's east on their own estate in Pomerania were generations of Marlows plowed the land. Therefore Lotte's empathy with the tragedy of Germans in the West has its limit.

These people still have their land, their homes. And in the countryside few brick houses were damaged. Lotte's only possession is her worn-out brown leather suitcase. And heaven knows what she is hiding in that old piece of luggage.

She won't let anybody take a look. Not even Albert has permission. That suitcase is locked anyway.

7

Soprano voices echo through the hallway. Ever since Lotte came to Ten Eicken the women began singing while working. Today they are cutting boiled red beets for salad while arias from Franz Lehar's 'Merry Widow', *Vilja* and *Lippen Schweigen* fill the air. Hilda's voice is full and clear. Lotte has learned to follow her lead.

Singing is therapy, another form of escape. Perhaps also the avoidance of talk. Music uplifts and speeds the completion of their tasks in the kitchen.

"Do you know this one?" Hilda says with encouragement, "it is my brother's favorite. From Wagner's Tristan and Isolde. The aria is Isolde's farewell song *Liebestod*. You will love it." And she sings with a strong and sweet voice. Her soprano echoes down the hallway and travels across the fields. She sings loud and beautiful as if her brother could hear her. Somewhere. Perhaps in a Siberian labor camp or in an unmarked grave outside Stalingrad? Hilda abruptly pauses.

Maybe Herbert was wounded and suffered amnesia? There have been cases. Many missing soldiers are returning home these days. The British and French released another four hundred Germans last week. The Red Cross revises lists of the missing every day. They are posted at town hall. Must not give up hope, anything is possible, she tells herself.

The morning chores are interrupted when Hilda's husband Ernst runs through the yard waving his arms in panic. He yells from afar for assistance.

"We need help, townsfolk are about to raid the fields again. This time they are after the potatoes. Where is Otto? We need every man, the police is already there," Ernst shouts. Three workers are rushing toward the entrance gate with pitchforks in their hands. They hop on the wagon while Ernst drives the horses toward the fields.

It's a pitiful sight. Hundreds of people, most of them women and children have lined the east side of the large field. Five acres of potatoes ready for harvest. But not by the farmer this time around.

Hordes of desperate people are waiting with baskets and pails, sacks and carts, shovels and pitchforks to charge and dig in. They are driven by hunger.

Meanwhile three policemen are guarding the edge of the field while Ernst and his workers are standing back. This is no situation for arguments, sunken eyes and determination speak for themselves. These people have nothing to lose. But still, they wait in silence and anticipation for the police or farmer to make the first move. Ernst waives at an officer, who quickly runs over to him. They whisper for several minutes.

"Order please," the officer now yells. "We don't want a stampede where people get injured. Listen, please. Herr Eicken has given permission to dig out those potatoes. Take as many as you need."

Permission? How do you permit survival of starvation. Consent to eat for another day. That's laughable. But not to the hungry. By the time the last words find listeners, women and children run onto the field and start digging. In haste they harvest the crop. And two hours later the fields are stripped empty. As if grasshoppers invaded and cleared the land. When three weeks later the maize crops on Ten Eicken are raided by hungry city folks, the police and Ernst do not even stand guard.

Hunger is mightier than a gun. At the end of the war, the Allied Forces collected all weapons from the Germans, but they forgot the most dangerous weapon - desperation. And hungry people are desperate.

"There is only so much we can do," Ernst says to Hilda.

"You did the right thing today, I am proud of you," she praises her husband.

"But it might get worse. Ever since the Deutsch Mark was introduced, factories and businesses are laying off workers," Ernst says. "In addition they are dismantling factories to keep production down in Germany. The Allies want to punish us a bit more. There is no end to this. Have you talked to our neighbors lately, the Bergmann Family? They want to immigrate to America. I suppose, they have relatives there. Leave Germany and turn their back on this country? Disgusting."

"Why is that repellant to you?" Hilda asks. "Anyway, the Bergmann's cannot go there. It was in the paper, the New World doesn't want them. America and Canada take everybody from Europe, except Germans. They won't allow us to come. What does that tell you? They are making us collectively guilty for the war."

"America? That's a joke. I wouldn't want to go there anyway," says Ernst. "This is my country, this is our land. And it will get better one day, you'll see." But he cannot convince Hilda, not for some time to come.

As the Allied Forces see a nation of perpetrators, Germans wear the racks of postwar victims. Many indulge in self-pity. Especially men. However, most children and women do not suffer in silence. They pick up the fight for survival. Children form gangs and raid loads of coal from slow moving trains. The border between Holland and Germany becomes a haven for smugglers.

Coffee and chocolate are the most precious items on the black market. And the currency to get them are cigarettes. You can get almost everything for a smoke.

But most desperate people lack vision how to go about survival. They simply steal to provide the basics for their families. These poor souls don't rob stores. They become petty larcenists of food.

And who counts the chicken anyway? Well, Hilda does. She has a mathematical mind. Lately she has noticed that the daily amount of eggs collected from the barn has been decimated by nearly fifteen percent. But is it the eggs or the chicken?

"It's the eggs, it the chicken. It's both," Otto reports two days later.

He has caught the thief, a fifteen year old boy. He is the son of a new Ten Eicken farmhand. And his father does not know. So Hilda talks to the teenager alone.

"This is between the two of us," she says to the boy when he is brought into the house. And she listens somewhat ashamed when the kid tells her of his sick siblings and hunger in the village.

Hilda does not report the incident to the authorities. Only the father of the boy is baffled when his son volunteers without pay twice a week to shovel manure out of the hen house. There is not an evening he leaves without a huge package of food to take home. Hilda makes sure of that.

8

Such kindness and free lunches are uncommon in the city where women age fifteen to sixty-five are ordered to remove the footprints of war. No exception of name and family status is permitted when the control committee lists their names for assignments.

Former maids work alongside their mistresses in the ruins of bombed out houses, scavenging remains of a war lost and carefully gathering materials for the reconstruction of Germany.

They are scraping mortar from bricks with knives and scissors and any other tools they can find. With small kitchen buckets they load debris on carts and later pull heavy loads with boney bodies.

Rubble women. That's what they are called. And there are thousands of them in every city across the land.

Day after day they work like ants to clear and clean the mess created by men. Dusty faces and bleeding scars brand their task. Bent backs exemplify the weight this war has left. Known for their endurance, sometimes perhaps motivated by anger, at least rubble women eat better. They earn seventy pennies per hour and collect an extra hundred grams of meat as well as a pound of bread per day. Enough to also fill the bellies of other family members in the city.

How they envy country folks during postwar Germany. On farms at least stinging nettle and dandelions picked in pastures to make salads don't bear the dust of scraped cement from these ruins.

Country folks. They lead a make-believe existence without the rubble as a daily reminder. Setting those pictures aside on Ten Eicken, it is possible to forget the war for moments while fixating the eye on pastures in blossom.

But how do you stop thinking at night?

Hilda and Lotte rearrange the furniture on Ten Eicken. Keeping busy helps to suppress memories. At least during the day while setting goals and tackling tasks. They'll do almost anything to outrace the dangers of idleness.

The women lift tables and chairs, placing them here and then there. For the start, the restaurant will occupy three separate rooms with a total of sixty-eight seats. Adjoining doors are removed to allow for customer flow throughout the ground-level of the estate. Otto has used his carpenter skills to build a bar in the library. The existing kitchen is large enough to accommodate additional cooking. They only invest in extra cutlery and dishes, which are easy enough to get for five loaves of bread and four smoked sausages on the black market.

While cleaning the windows in the saloon they are singing merry tunes. Soon word of mouth will bring their first guests, they hope. They create menus and special recipes with the meager supplies available to them. Seeds have to be purchased to expand the vegetable garden next year. It will be more work but also fun to participate in the future instead of aimlessly recalling unwillingly the past.

Yes, life is bearable in the country. And it is tempting to feel a sense of normality once again. But perhaps too soon. An angry voice interrupts their work. They listen.

"You can't play with that boy. How often do I have to tell you? Don't you understand me? That boy is not your kind, " they hear grandmother Agnes shout at Wilhelm as he comes racing down the stairway. Chased by the harshness of the old woman's voice. Lotte's son Albert is waiting at the door. He hears every word, while his head is bend down. He pretends to tie his shoes.

"I won't have it in my house," Agnes screams. "Enough with them.

What are they doing here anyway? And there are more coming each week. It was in the newspapers. Now they are also deporting those Germans from Russia, Poland and heaven knows from where else. Can't you see, nobody wants them. Why do we have to take care of them?" Agnes mumbles, before she shuts the door to her quarters upstairs with a loud bang.

But it is not quiet yet. Her words linger and echo in the hallway like lashes. The damage cannot be undone. Grandma Agnes has dismantled her face in a moment of fury by simply verbalizing thoughts out loud.

"Come here Wilhelm. Come to me, don't cry," Hilda calls for her son.

"Grandma won't allow me to play with Albert but I want to, he is my friend. Why can't I play with him? He is German too, isn't he?"

"Now you listen, it doesn't matter if he is German or not. He is a good boy," Hilda says while hugging Wilhelm. "Go now, go outside and play with Albert." She feels embarrassed and looks at Lotte.

When does it end? Or has it only just begun? We are one nation, but damned by ignorance branding a second-class citizen stamp on newcomers to the west. They are Germans too. Have people lost sight of their own geography?

She won't have them insulted. Not if she can help it. Not under her roof. Hilda has brewed coffee and invites Lotte to take a break.

"It's real ground coffee with caffeine. Just for the two of us. A bonus from the black market when they delivered the cutlery for our restaurant this morning."

"Our restaurant? Is that what you said," Lotte says with indifference in her voice. What can she call her own? A brown worn-out suitcase. Nothing much else.

"Yes our restaurant. We'll do this together. It can only happen with your help. Here look," she says while pushing a sheet of paper across the table.

"Read this, fifteen percent of all income for you as a start. And I will carry all the costs. You don't have to put up a penny." But Lotte isn't listening any longer. She is lost in her own thoughts. The harsh words of that old woman from upstairs still ring in her ears.

"Believe me Lotte, it will get better," Hilda says. "People aren't as bad as they sound. She is old and frustrated. Her son Walter died in the war, it has made her bitter. But you are right, she should not say those things, especially in front of the children. She poisons everything that is good. She can't help it. So simply ignore her." Soothing words. However Lotte is not entirely convinced. Perhaps Agnes is simply honest and says aloud what many Germans in the west think about displaced people.

"What about the others? It's not just Agnes. They all talk like her. I've heard them in trams and grocery stores, " Lotte says. "They don't even whisper but call us names in front of everybody. Our dialect triggers their aggressions. Why do you think I keep my mouth shut in public?"

"Now listen, I understand your pain. But don't sulk in self-pity. You are smarter than that and stronger. People are stupid. Out of fear they act rude," Hilda says. Fright, that's what it is. Everybody's future is still uncertain. We all lost loved-ones during this terrible war. Most people are still without jobs, homes or perspective."

"It's like this. The battles are lost, the opponents have gone home. You understand? People now focus on new enemies within to feel better about their meager existence. Call it the tragedy of human nature or whatever. At present most people in the west are mentally as uprooted as refugees from the east. They don't know what to expect. Have some empathy with their ignorance," Hilda pleads.

Lotte's eyes are fixed to the kitchen floor. Some words sink in. Hilda is right, Lotte thinks, but the well-being of her own family has priority. For her, Albert and Otto come first; they rate even above forgiving other people's ignorance.

"Will it ever change, will it get better?" Lotte finally asks.

"It has already. Right here in this house. At this very table, with us," Hilda responds.

9

"You know in hindsight it feels as if Ten Eicken became an emotional free zone for past memories. That place helped to keep shadows locked up in closets. It made us feel safe. It was Hilda's doing. What a special person your mother was," Lotte says to me a few days later. She wants to talk, needs to tell.

"Your mother, God bless her soul. She always found the right words and took immediate actions. In those days it wasn't easy to find a German in the west who would openly defend us. We were called *Rucksack Deutsche* (Backpack Germans). Hilda was different, she was an exception, always kind and fair. What about your father, you may ask? Grandmother Agnes controlled his life. He adored but also hated his mother. But mostly he obeyed her because he lacked the strength to stand up to her authority. She raised him that way to keep him small"

"When grandmother Agnes interfered with Wilhelm, Hilda knew she had to take action to protect her child. She needed to rescue him from the claws of that woman. Years later Hilda sent her son to Westphalia to live with her own parents. She had no choice." Lotte closes her eyes. It's enough for the day, she wants to rest. And I quietly leave the living room.

"She sent him away too late," Albert continues in the hallway. "Grandmother Agnes had planted already her evil seeds before Wilhelm left Ten Eicken. You see, she had the opportunity to spend time with the boy while the other women worked rock around the clock with little time to spare for the child. So naturally, Grandmother Agnes became Wilhelm's teacher. Not just for math and piano lessons. She also influenced his thoughts and manners by becoming his only confidant."

"No wonder the kid became a carbon-copy of her. He went with his grandmother everywhere, and even stopped playing with other kids on the farm. All of a sudden we were not good enough any longer to be in his company," Albert remembers.

"To Agnes displaced persons were inferior. She treated us with indifference in rather arrogant ways. But she was also cruel to some of her own family members. Just how vicious she was we only learned several month later after that accident, that terrible day in the city. I'll tell you about it so Lotte doesn't have to go through that again."

"It was in the fall of that year, a Friday. I remember it well, because the restaurant was to open the following week. We didn't have a functioning automobile on the farm as fuel was a luxury and not easy to come by," Albert says.

"What a magnificent sight your mother was that day. She was wearing a white costume and blue hat with a yellow trim. Grandfather Gunter who adored her, offered to drive her by horse carriage to Düsseldorf. She wanted to buy a roll of checkered linen for the restaurant tables. Gunter was proud to drive her. He was exited to be seen with his beautiful daughter-in-law. To show her off and perhaps escape for the day the endless bickering in his own four walls. When they left they were laughing and waving at us at us like children until the carriage was out of sight."

"Waving and laughing one moment. And then this tragedy. It happened within a few hours. We later learned that a British officer honked the horn of his jeep on account of Hilda's beauty. No offense, just a gesture of admiration. He even waved at her. But the noise of the horn scared the horses. They went out of control, smashing the carriage into a huge chestnut tree right in front of the city's hospital on Lindenstrasse."

Albert closes his eyes for a moment. "Dear God why? Everybody was just getting back on their feet. And then this. Grandfather Gunter was killed instantly and Hilda only survived a double scull fracture because the accident happened right there in front of the hospital. The doctors could help her immediately and thus saved her life," Albert shakes his head while talking.

"It was such a long time ago but I can still feel the shock and devastation of that day. It paralyzed our thoughts and left us with utter sadness and helplessness. But the work on the farm needed to be done. We carried on in silence. And although there was no one in charge to assign jobs, the chores got done because we did it for Hilda."

"What about your father Ernst? Of course he was devastated. He became a shadow of his own appearance. Too shattered to take command of everyday affairs on the estate, he went to the hospital every day for the next two months."

"After Hilda returned home it took another four weeks before she was her old self again. Only a small scar on her upper forehead reminded of the accident. Because she was so long in the hospital, she could not attend the funeral of grandfather Gunter. He was brought to rest in the private family cemetery of Ten Eicken," Albert recalls. He scratches his head.

"You know what's weird about those postwar years? During that time people seldom got sick. They just died or carried on without lamentation. As if time didn't allow for anything else in between. It did not seem strange after the war. Everybody was preoccupied with survival. No one had time to get sick and rest. Yes, you lived or you died. Like Hilda and Gunter."

While talking we reach the fence of his large vegetable garden. "You should take some salad home, you can't get that quality in any supermarket," he says to me.

"It's painful to think about days like that," Albert suddenly adds. "There was death and devastation in the family and that old woman made life even worse for everyone. Agnes became a real bitch. Sorry to call her names. But after the accident she became furious. She yelled for days, saying it was Hilda's fault that grandfather Gunter was dead. Wasn't it Hilda who suggested that trip to the city to buy linen? She carried on and on, until Ernst told his mother to stop those accusations and shut up."

"And then there was silence, Agnes did not talk to her son for eight weeks. You had to admire Ernst, he finally came to the aid of his wife. That speechlessness among family members however was only the prelude of a much nastier story. It began with the arrival of a letter from a law firm."

"You see, after the death of grandpa Gunter apparently his testament got lost and a new document was presented by Agnes. She maintained, the old man had rewritten his will a month before the accident. But nobody truly believed in the authenticity of that new will. It was typed, not handwritten as all his other notes. Gunter's signature could easily be forged. Although it's the law in the Rhineland that the youngest son inherits the farm from the father and other siblings have to be paid out with a certain amount of money, the new testament claimed the disinheritance of Ernst, apparently signed by his father."

"Initially Hilda and Ernst did not react at all. Let the old woman play her silly games. What else has she got to do? The law, nothing but the law will count. And in the Rhineland it states that the youngest son is the sole heir of the land, while in the province of Westphalia the oldest gets the estate. Oldest, youngest, it didn't really matter, Ernst was the only male left to inherit Ten Eicken," Albert explains.

"The letter sent by the law firm was registered and addressed to Ernst personally. It contained a written statement by his mother Agnes. The first line read 'My dear son', and then continuing in harsh words she informed him, that he had one week to pack his suitcase and leave the estate with 'that wife of yours'. If he does not conform, Agnes will consult the police. His mother wrote that Ten Eicken was now under her management until spring, when the estate would be handed over to his sister Gisela and her husband Fritz."

"She wrote: You married Hilda, a woman not only unfit but also the cause of all troubles on Ten Eicken. I am only the executor of your father's testament. It was his last wish." The letter was signed mockingly with 'Your loving mother.'

"Can you believe it? She signed this note with Your loving mother," Albert recalls.

"What hypocrisy, what falsehood. That's how she was. I sometimes wonder if there was any goodness in her. Not that I saw any empathy during all those years. She hated Hilda all along. First that woman married her oldest son Walter and had his child. After Walter died in the war, she married her youngest son Ernst."

"Agnes went mad with anger, she openly belittled Hilda for her charitable attitude toward staff and townsfolk. It got worse in time. Her hatred spilled over in her old age, when she witnessed how her young and beautiful daughter-in-law Hilda was adored by everybody on the farm."

"Yes, we all worshiped her. We worked hard because of Hilda. She never made us feel like servants. She did not play the boss, didn't have to. Hilda was loved. Of course our admiration was also noticed by grandmother Agnes, it increased her anger. I believe that old woman was envious. Yes, jealousy that's what it was. And that's why she needed to punish her son in order to get to her."

10

Ernst throws the letter on the floor. My own mother, he thinks. His left arm is hurting. Shrapnel from a hand grenade itches beneath his skin. It's tearing nerves while inching further up inside his flesh. The doctors could not remove several of those metal shell splinters which are now part of his body. Over time those splinters will travel toward his heart. It's not life-threatening yet but could be in the future.

There is a sting. He constantly feels pain in his arm since his injury during the last days of war. But that's only physical pain. It is bearable compared to the wounding words in that note.

Ernst wants to run upstairs, scream and disown his mother. Then hit her, perhaps even choke her. Ernst pauses. His anger is out of control. Mother brings out the worst in him. Although he did not kill anybody during the war as a soldier, he now appears capable of harming his own blood. Those thoughts suddenly frighten him. He has to control his temper or all will be lost.

If Agnes has her way of removing him from the estate, where could he go? What could he do? He only knows farming. It is his life, the edge of the valley marks his horizon of possibilities. Ten Eicken, the land, that's all he knows. He was raised as the heir of this estate, to carry the torch for future generations. He cannot become a servant like most of those displaced people. But now his mother wants to take it all away from him. Has she no mercy? And what about those years of obedience? Don't they count? Ernst feels betrayed but most of all powerless. He is no match for his mother. That he knows.

Again it is his wife Hilda who has to take the lead.

"We have to get a lawyer," she says insistently. "You must take this matter to court. And what about Wilhelm, the boy is entitled to at least a third of the estate when he is twenty one. He is Walter's son, a rightful heir of the next generation on Ten Eicken. The inheritance law is clear about his entitlement."

"Take my own mother to court to make our private affairs public?

Are you insane? I'd rather kill her," Ernst yells. "What will the neighbors say if we battle in front of a judge? We have a standing in this community." He shakes his head in disbelief.

"Listen, the courts have to settle this. Put it into their hands. Agnes won't get away with her intrigue," Hilda says. "Who cares about the neighbors? When was the last time anyone came over here to help us? I haven't seen a neighbor for ages. I believe you can expect more loyalty on Ten Eicken from Pomeranians and Prussians. They care, that's why we have to think about the future of those people as well. They depend on us with their jobs." Hilda is now shaking her husband's right shoulder because he simply sits there motionless and obviously drained of any visible energy.

Is Ernst even listening?

"You want to help or not?" Hilda asks.

"What will it take to keep Ten Eicken?" her husband finally utters. "What should I do?"

"First of all we have to get an injunction to stop this eviction which is without grounds or reason of any sort," Hilda explains.

"How do you know all this?" Ernst asks.

"Reading, lots of reading. The library on Ten Eicken is well stocked not only with fiction," she says to her husband.

For two hours they talk. For five days they wait after filing an injunction. A week later the court's initial reaction comes by telegram. It reads: Hilda and Ernst can stay for the time being. But the living quarters of the fighting parties on Ten Eicken will be separated by law until a trial date is set.

Two families under one roof but confined to their own space. That arrangement is not new. They have lived like that ever since Ernst married Hilda. But now it's official.

For Ernst this decision also means grabbing a box of nails to pound some permanence into that court decision. He hurries up the stairway and seals the access of the living quarters of Agnes and Gisela to the downstairs exit with long nails and a chain. His mother and sister can use the former servant door of their upstairs wing if they want to leave the house.

When the pounding of the hammer meets the nail, the echo sounds like gunfire similar of a battle in progress.

Neither Agnes nor Gisela check the source of that commotion. They too received the court's decision today with the stipulation that neither party can intrude the space of the other. Any provocative behavior can and will be used later in court.

They whisper and tip-toe around the house. Upstairs as well as downstairs. Distance, not time is of the essence.

One family still in the same house but now worlds apart by hatred.

Neither is willing to talk. Silent pride is mightier than the word. The authorities will have to decide on the question of entitlement to the estate. The missing testament of grandfather Gunter will be the key to a fair decision.

Over the next weeks lawyers come and go to Ten Eicken to consult with both parties and map out their strategies. Otto drives to the village every Monday to meet the advocates at the railway station. Two lawyers for Agnes, one for Hilda and Ernst. Although representing opposing sides they seem to be best friends, chatting like buddies in that carriages on their long way to the farm. Otto catches bits and pieces of their conversation while driving them to the mansion.

But what are they saying? Latin phrases are not part of Otto's vocabulary. And anyhow, this is a family affair, an internal fight of no concern to others. However, there is static in the air, sensed during long hours of work in the kitchen and bakery. Hilda stops singing, while Lotte keeps to her chores in silence.

An invisible space settles between both women.

"What's that song again from Wagner's Tannhäuser ?" Lotte finally asks to break the awkward silence. "You know the one where the choir marches in?"

"You mean the pilgrims song. Yes, lovely. But not today Lotte. I don't feel like singing," Hilda says while cutting the cabbage on the kitchen counter. "I am sorry but my mind is preoccupied these days. Maybe tomorrow we'll sing again." But her voice stays silent.

The music has died on Ten Eicken.

Sometimes at night, when Lotte finishes her chores, she sees Hilda alone in the library bend over books. She is reading and taking notes. It's not for the restaurant, Lotte knows that much. They stopped talking about their business venture since the accident. And anyhow, money is scarce all over the land. A restaurant seems an illusion.

Who wants to tackle the future now when even the present is uncertain.

When Lotte asks Otto if he knows what's going on, her husband keeps quiet. He has heard this and that but he will not gossip or draw the wrong conclusions.

"We are still working and eating, aren't we?" he says to his wife. "There is nothing else that should interest us. This is a good place to pause before we'll return home to the east. Let's keep it that way."

It's Pomerania, always Pomerania. Doesn't he know about the tremendous geographic westward shift? The borders have been redrawn by the victors.

While the Soviet Union has annexed 70 000 square miles of eastern Poland, the Polish borders have moved further west, covering 40 000 square miles of former German territory. Lost are nearly all of East Prussia, Danzig, Neumark, Silesia and Pomerania. Those Germans who did not flee before the Russian Army moved in were expelled later.

Pomerania, she thinks. Their homeland. Now Polish farmers plow their soil, sleep in their beds and milk their cows. The Marlows will never return. Lotte knows that but she won't say it out loud. For too many displaced people, that hope of returning is the last straw of sanity.

Especially for Otto .

I cannot talk to him anymore, Lotte tells herself. He lives in the past. The present does not exist and the political reality of the future might kill him. I must watch him, I fear for him. These unbearable times have stolen my husband from me.

Where is he now? Otto has gone to bed and pulled the covers over his head. It's harvest time. So much work is waiting out there.

Satisfying work.

At night he will be too tired to contemplate about anything. And life will be bearable for yet another day in the west.

11

Late sunrays of summer accompany their efforts when they harvest their crops. It's a hard job which requires many busy hands while bringing in the abundant harvest. Despite several raided fields by hungry people from the city, on Ten Eicken the cellars fill with enough potatoes, red beets, cabbage and maize for the winter. The thrashing machine in the barn runs ten hours each day. The dust of this work covers faces of men grinning. Content with the results of their labor they smile at each other.

While cleaning up for supper at the well in the yard they sing familiar folk songs. Their shirtless bodies gleam in the evening sun. Lust for life. As if the war never happened and memories can be washed off. It feels good to be alive, have a place to work, sleep and fill the belly. They eat well enough, Hilda and Lotte make sure of that. Despite hard work, it is a comfortable life for them. They feel secure and cannot see dark clouds lingering over the farm. That nearing storm is only visible to the inner circle of the Eicken family.

"Lotte, we have to go to the city today, Ernst and me. We'll be back very late," Hilda says. "Can you look after Wilhelm. He has not been eating well these past few weeks. Have you noticed it too." Oh yes, she has. When the boy tried to go upstairs to visit his grandmother, the door was locked. The child did not notice the nails which sealed the door to the frame. He banged his little fists against the entrance, but there was no answer. Lotte watched him, as he later sat on the stairway for the longest time. Convinced, that grandmother did not love him any more.

"You come here boy," Lotte finally said. "Your grandma is not feeling well. She has a terrible cold. You'll see, she'll be better soon and then you can visit again."

Behind the door Agnes is listening. Not entirely unmoved. She wants to react but cannot utter a word. How she loves her grandchild. If only she could control his education. That boy looks like her firstborn son Walter but has the sensitivity and talents from her side of the family.

Wilhelm could study to become a doctor or judge. Not a farmer. Those rough people in the country with their square edges. She does not despise them any longer. Agnes only feels pity for them.

Land as far as the eye can see but their intellectual horizon ends right there where the valley meets the hilltops. That's what Agnes believes, because she reads novels. Not those by Tolstoy, Dostoevsky, Hesse or Goethe as Hilda prefers. No, Agnes reads the love stories of French authors who know of courting and romance. She reads them in their language. In French. Those writers understand her world contraire to farm life with Gunter. May he rest in peace.

When Agnes lived in the city she had plenty of suitors from families with good names. But most of them lacked what she needed most. Money for her lavish life-style. Her father was delighted when she announced her engagement to Gunter, the heir of a fine estate with plenty of money to finance her personal expenses.

As always, even with this upcoming battle in court, Agnes feels content. She has lived in some form of abundance all those years, despite two world wars. Her only grievance was Hilda. That woman came at age nineteen during the war to her estate as a *Haustochter* (house daughter). She was raised on a small farm in Westphalia and studied law for a short time at the University of Soest until war preparations interrupted her education.

Agnes welcomed the extra help during the late thirties in her household. The girl was no bother. She ate and slept with the servants and kept to herself. Agnes made sure of that. Granted, the girl was an extremely hard worker. But also dangerous for young blood.

Why, Agnes questioned many times, why did both of her sons have to fall in love with her. First Walter, then Ernst. What was the reason? To punish their mother? Contemplating about the past, Agnes considers this thought a possibility. But she decides, it must have been Hilda's fault. Yes Hilda, the seducer. Not her sons. That's why Agnes needs revenge. She will have her way now that Gunter is dead. The courts will side with her, she is convinced. Hilda can count her last days on the estate, resign her reign as the mistress of the valley.

Let her return to Westphalia. She is not wanted here any more.

Upstairs the old woman gets dressed. She chooses a black chiffon dress. Very appropriate as she is still in mourning. Isn't she? The judge will notice her grief and surely emphasize. Her daughter Gisela with husband Fritz will accompany her to the city to support their common cause.

Downstairs, Otto waits at the entrance. The carriage is ready for the trip to the city. He will drive Hilda and Ernst. And then wait. But not idle in front of the government building. Two Pomeranians have invited him to a coffeehouse nearby. Those *Landsman* from home want to talk to Otto.

While Hilda places her paperwork in a black leather case, Ernst has already boarded the coach. He is anxious, fearful, impatient. What, if his mother gets away with her intrigue? He has lost his belief in justice and fairness.

"We'll be late," he calls to Hilda. "please hurry." His wife hears him without rushing her final preparations. She must not forget to take along those bills grandpa Gunter once gave her. They are silent witnesses on paper, testifying overspending close to bankruptcy. And those checks he issued for his wife. Thousands of Reich Mark were spent by Agnes on personal items such as jewelry, mink coats and evening gowns when the till was already empty. Funds were wasted when money was desperately needed for a new roof on the barn.

"Coming," she calls while running out the front door.

The ride through their property is uplifting. Workers in the fields wave with their caps. Has there ever been a war or was it simply a nightmare imagined? A dreadful dream which does not fit into this moment.

However, reality is closing in when they reach the outskirts of Düsseldorf. Otto glances at hundreds of shacks with displaced people along Goethe Strasse. He remembers that place well. He used to live there. Across the street he spots piles of rubble of bombed out buildings. He is looking at the slums this war has left behind and the people who are still waiting for new beginnings.

Otto bends down his head somewhat ashamed considering his own fortune of living somewhere better than that. He feels Hilda pat his shoulder gently. Ernst nods in approval.

This pain all around them makes them equals for a brief moment.

"Maybe help is nearing. The airlift to Berlin is still in full force since the monetary reform," Ernst says to Hilda while looking at the shacks. She knows, she read about it in paper. Americans are breaking the blockade imposed by the Soviets in the eastern zone of Germany by flying in supplies. Day and night. An American plane lands every three minutes with food in the free western part of Berlin. Some care packages are even thrown out of planes during their flights over Berlin.

Help from the sky. But not in the Rhineland. Not yet in Düsseldorf. In this city old women and children pull wooden carts with metal scrap to black markets in exchange for milk. They are regulars on a black market which with the introduction of the Deutsch Mark officially does not exist any longer. As food prices in stores keep rising, the black market has gone underground. It's the women who know those locations because that's where they do business.

Ernst touches his arm. The shrapnel inside are itching. But he does not mind today. His injury was fate. It spared him from suffering in the east. It saved him from deportation to a labor camp in Siberia.

Otto has stopped the carriage in front of the town hall. The courthouse was bombed by the Allies and totally destroyed during the last days of war. All cases are now heard in the city chambers. A busy place these days. Hallways are lined with people. Many have lost all documents, paperwork which tells them who they are. They need a new copy of their birth certificate, confirmation of their land title or a duplicate of a last will and testament. But hopes of retrieving documents are dim. Official archives burned down as well when bombs rained from Allied planes over German cities.

12

Otto is whistling a happy tune while making his way toward Rosenstrasse where he meets his fellow Pomeranians. How does he recognize them in that crowded café? What a question. Your own kind always sticks out. They hug each other like lost brothers although he has never seen these men before. But memories of a common landscape and their dialect force eyes to tear up. Hasn't he heard? They are forming clubs now for displaced Germans from Pomerania, East Prussia and Silesia. They'll meet once a month in Düsseldorf. What do they do?

"They can help you to find jobs and trace down missing family members," says one of the men.

"We have work, it could not be better," Otto says. He is suspicious. Another organization? A group? Isn't it each man to his own? Nobody ever helped him when he had troubles. But then again, he was too proud to ask for assistance. But groups? That's not for him. The dynamic of people gathering is repulsive to this farmer who has always worked alone in the fields. Too often he has seen during the war what men will do when they come in groups. Feeling mightier and taller than their height. Looting and raping. No, Otto wants no part of a club.

"We heard they'll also help us to go back east. Home," the other man adds.

Home? Really? Otto can suddenly sense the smell of his home soil like familiar perfume. How an odor can linger in your mind triggered by a simple word? he wonders.

The men talk for hours about familiar places and customs in the east. Not a word is spoken about the circumstances and excesses of their expulsion.

They keep silent about that like raped women who often believe the assault is partially their fault. That's how they feel about expulsion. They had to run away. But wasn't that an act of cowardice? Should they have waited? They know better now. Those who stayed and waited for the Red Army to arrive were taught that lesson. The remaining people were deported in a chaotic and brutal manner. Many German civilians were also sent to Siberia as extra labor. Thousands died during those later treks. Western Allies did not interfere even when American newspapers like the New York Times called the undisciplined deportation of Germans from the east by the Russians a "catastrophe of inhumanity".

The men in the café will not talk about any of that today because they feel like those raped women. While Otto spends the day with his fellow Pomeranians, the Eicken family is gathered in a small chamber at town hall. No one really wants to be here. Not even the judge whose workload knows no end. For two weeks he has looked at this case. A mother disowning her son, another killed during the war, a dead husband and a forged testament. The latter was easy to detect. Even the signature was a poor match.

The judge is not impressed by so much hatred within one family which lives under the same roof. Three generations scarred. Bridges burned. No chance of reconciliation. Three lawyers have told him so. Such lack of compassion, the judge thinks, after all those agonies experienced during that terrible war.

"What is wrong with you people?" he now mumbles in frustration. He glances at Agnes, Gisela and Fritz who staged their entrance well rehearsed. Next his eyes are fixed on Hilda and Ernst, a young couple which simply wants to work, make a living and perhaps raise a family.

Quiet, all rise. The judge has reappeared after a brief recess. Eyes are fixed to the ground. Last hopes and prayers. The moment of fate is near. But not today. A final decision will be handed down in four weeks from today, the judge announces. Court closed while the case remains open.

Hilda and Ernst stay behind with their lawyer, uncertain what to make of today. The advocate looks pleased, reassuring the couple that all will be fine. It better be, they paid him a large enough fee. When they step outside the town hall, they spot Otto. He is waiting to drive them home.

"I feel much better about this now than earlier in the morning," Ernst suddenly says. He cannot pinpoint his optimism, it is simply a gut feeling. Hilda agrees while squeezing his hand. She feels close to him. Perhaps she should tell him now. This seems like a good moment. But she has to explain it to him gently.

Start at the beginning. She recalls that day of the accident, when Grandpa Gunter was killed and she suffered life-threatening injuries. She is in a coma, but she can see and hear everything around her.

Hilda feels awake. But is she alive or dead? She can spot two doctors and the nurse. But they are not in her room. They are standing outside in the hallway discussing her case while she is waiting in the operating room. The door is closed. This is crazy. How can she hear what they say? She can. They are saying that Hilda will die. There is nothing more they can do. A double skull fracture with possible brain injuries. They cannot tell for certain. This is postwar Germany, the hospital lacks medication, surgical instruments and qualified staff.

Dead then, *ach ja*? she thinks. It does not frighten her at all. She has been there before emotionally. In particular when she was told of Walter's death. Her first husband. Her dead husband. Walter. But he is there now with her. Hilda can see his face and hear his words. They are in a foreign landscape. Together, holding hands and talking for a long time.

Gently now, she tells herself while looking at Ernst in the carriage on their way home. I need to tell him, Walter is his brother.

"He is alive," Hilda now whispers at Ernst.

"Who?"

"Your brother Walter. I saw him, I talked to him. He lives, he'll return." She pauses to wait for a reaction.

"Stop it," Ernst screams in horror. He grabs Hilda by her shoulders and shakes her upper body violently. Otto has stopped the carriage. "No, not you Otto. Please hurry. We must get home," Ernst demands.

Although apologizing for his uncontrolled behavior, he pushes Hilda deeper into her seat. He cannot calm her down, he is incapable to even dampen his own temper. So he just watches her while tears are running down her cheeks. Hilda's now husband will not believe that her then husband is still alive. Come again? Yes, first husband alive, second husband also alive. It sounds incredible but more curious stories have happened during and after this war.

"Have you gone crazy?" Ernst finally remarks. "Walter is dead, the Red Cross showed us his death certificate. Have you absolutely lost your mind? You had a double scull fracture. Perhaps when you were in coma for eight days you fantasized about Walter."

"It was not a dream, I know, because I saw him in a prison camp. A camp somewhere in Russia. He is there with thousands of other Germans, most of them were with the 6th Army and captured in

Stalingrad. It was him, I am certain. You'll see, Walter will come home one day," Hilda says. "They will release our soldiers from Siberia soon. I heard it on the radio. Every day more and more men are coming home. It won't be long now."

"Listen to me Hilda," her husband says with determination but a much softer tone in his voice. "For your own sanity and mine, don't go there. My brother is dead. We have to live with that reality. I don't want to go through this again. We've been there before. Wasn't that painful enough? Let it go. I won't plead again, this is not a request," he says.

He is angry now. His harsh words linger. Don't you dare talk about that again. Hilda is getting that message, although she is convinced her encounter was real. But she has no witnesses to her conversations, except Walter. But Walter is dead. Isn't that what Ernst said? The young woman feels confused. Must not dwell on the past. Leave those shadows in the closet. Work is my only prayer, she thinks, while getting out of the horse buggy.

They are home and Lotte is waiting with Wilhelm at the front entrance. The topic is closed. The day is done. However, later that night Hilda looks for the longest time at the framed photograph of Walter above the fireplace in the library. Studying the black and white picture, she looks for shades or a hint. Something looks different, she thinks. Yes, of course. It's the uniform. He was not wearing it, when she saw him during her coma in the hospital. Walter was dressed in brown rags. Emaciated. Without a smile. That's how she saw him. She is certain.

13

Shorter days and colder nights settle over the valley of Ten Eicken. Hungry people still wander the countryside in search of shelter and a warm meal. They know, country folks eat better than city dwellers. The odd time barns have burned down because a new breed of Germans travel the land and stay wherever they can find a roof. They are not hobos but simply people who are destitute. Among them old men and young veterans, war widows and orphaned children. At night they secretly crawl into barns and sheds. They go wherever they spot shelter and suspect food.

It is fall and many farmers see them coming. Not seldom the dogs are send to keep them off farmyards. Vagrants quickly know where to go and what places to avoid. The open barn on Ten Eicken has many visitors that night. Sleeping on a bed of straw is better than resting on the damp ground in the forest.

"He'll see you and get angry again," Lotte whispers. But Hilda is already outside with a basket of bread, cheese and apples. She did not expect eight homeless people in the barn and quickly returns to the house to get more food and a large pitcher of milk.

The people in the barn stare and chew. And eat some more. No time for talk, for those who talk can't fill their mouth and eat. Hilda sits on a bail of straw and waits. This has to be the last winter of scarcity, she hopes. It will soon get better. Perhaps next spring but nobody can tell.

They are still dismantling factories in the cities and shipping those parts for reparation payments to France. The Allies are afraid that Germany could soon be strong again, produce weapons and start another war. But keeping this country on its knees economically makes no sense, not to Hilda. With empathy she looks at the homeless in the barn, among them two girls. Not eighteen yet. The brunette looks pregnant. How to help? What to do? So many in need. Hilda decides to bring the two women into the house.

"It's only for the night," she points out because anything else would be in vain. Ten Eicken cannot carry the whole load of postwar Germany. When she hands them blankets to sleep in one of those large empty living rooms, tears tell their story. Villagers call them names: Whore, prostitute, collaborator and Negro lover. Gaby and Elsa admit that it wasn't love. But basic human instincts kicked in. A form of survival prostitution followed. The benefactors were American and British soldiers. For the girls willingness to be with them, the soldiers gave them chocolate, coffee and cigarettes. Valuable items for trade-ins at the black market to help their families in Düsseldorf.

"What would you have done?" they ask Hilda. "Starve to death? The soldiers treated us well, like ladies." They keep silent for some time. And then Gaby points to her friend's belly because Elsa is pregnant. The father, a colored American soldier won't stand by her side. He knows but will not acknowledge or believe he fathered a child. In three months he has to return to the US, to Kansas. He has a wife and two children there. And no extra space for a German *Fräulein* (Girl).

With the dilemma of an unwanted pregnancy Elsa is therefore on her own. It will get worse when she gives birth. A black child is a *Schande* (shame) in postwar Germany. Sleeping with the enemy will become visible once that child is born, and brand Elsa as a whore, perhaps even a collaborator forever. She is not an exception, her child will be one of nearly ten thousand war children fathered by allied soldiers during these years of occupation.

"So I ask you, what would you have done," she says to Hilda. "Starve or trade goods with soldiers? I had nothing to give but my youth and body."

"I honestly don't know what measures of survival I would have taken. I don't condemn you or judge what you did," Hilda says. "Rest now. I understand what you are going through."

She tip-toes out of the living room toward the kitchen where Ernst is waiting for her. He looks angry, betrayed. Why is he, her husband, not Hilda's priority? Why always others? Hilda cannot tell him or make him understand. When Ernst was gone during the war, she took matters into her own hand for her first husband Walter. She was in charge as all women were during the absence of men. So why back off now only because some men are back from the battlefields? Taking care of business become a matter of survival, like Elsa did in her own way.

"So, feeding the hobos again, are we?" Ernst mocks.

"Those people are homeless and hungry," Hilda responds. "Do you think they choose life as vagabonds? Can't you see, they have nowhere else to go. We have to show some compassion."

"Why us, why you?" Ernst queries her.

"Who else if not us?" she snaps back. "We have more than we need."

"It's always us and never them. Maybe my mother is right at times when she complains about your exaggeration for charity," he says.

"You should bite your tongue speaking such nonsense. Or have you forgotten the letter and court case against your dearest mama?" She realizes the harshness of her words and walks toward her husband, patting him on the shoulder. He needs to understand why she helps those hobos.

"Perhaps somewhere in Russia at this very moment a woman is feeding my missing brother. Yes, call it selfish. Maybe I am feeding those hungry people in hope, that my brother won't starve to death either. Helping others feels like an attempt of saving him."

Those words bring tears to Ernst. He spontaneously hugs her and swears he will never complain about her charity. She mentioned her missing brother when feeding the homeless, but he still doubts that was all she was thinking of. A cloud of secrecy lingers between the couple. A shadow which is always there. But neither of them touches the topic.

It's about Walter, her first husband, his brother. Always Walter. Yes, what about Walter? Is she not also feeding the hobos to nourish her hopes of reawakening him from the dead?

14

I have brought Lotte a box of Swiss pralines wrapped in colorful paper. He eyes shine when she carefully unwraps the gift. She folds the paper and puts it in a cupboard which is overflowing with sheets of paper for every season and holiday occasion. Waste goes against everything this Pomeranian stands for. Her son Albert acts the same. She taught him well.

"This form of recycling you do today is not new," Lotte grins. "Only the motivation is different. We did it out of necessity, you recycle for the sake of the environment. In my days every bit of scrap, every cardboard, shoes or old clothes were kept. We mended what was broken and reused it until there was nothing left of the material. I even stitched shoes out of a ripped leather jacket for Albert and Otto. When you have nothing, the mind becomes inventive. You rise above your imagination." Lotte looks at me with intensity.

"I don't want to lecture younger people, I am simply recalling how it was." She glances into her garden where Albert is digging out potatoes. "The meals we made out of anything we found in nature. Incredible. Most people have forgotten, that dandelion and pine-comb are healthy and nutritious. We even used stinging nettles to make salad. Very tasty. I can give you some recipes if you want. We wrote them all down during those years. They'd make an interesting guide to healthier living in today's affluent and abundant times."

Lotte pours two cups of coffee. "You look just like her," she now points out. "Just like Hilda. Except for that scar on her left upper forehead. But no one could really see it, her blond curls covered the reminder of that tragic accident. When she came home from the hospital, we became even closer friends. It's not only that Hilda was very grateful that I had looked after the household and Wilhelm during her hospital stay. No, it wasn't just that. We suddenly talked on a more personal level, like sisters. I did not feel like an employee any longer but a confidant. She spoke about her first husband Walter and the love they shared for one summer. Did you know that Walter wanted to become a lawyer?," Lotte asks.

"Really? They never spoke about him when I was a child. At least not when we were around. They just told me he died as a young soldier during the war. That's all they said," I point out.

"A lawyer. Yes, that's what he wanted to be. And he would have made a fine advocate. From what your mother told me, Walter despised injustice. He couldn't wait to leave Ten Eicken because of his mother Agnes. In addition, he was not the heir of the farm, his younger brother Ernst was to get the estate as the law stipulates in the Rhineland. Meanwhile his father had set up a trust fund to cover Walter's university fees." Lotte explains.

"It's not that Walter didn't love the land. What he wanted most was to be his own man. Watching his mother's lavish life-style and especially how she handled her husband Gunter was repulsive to him. He was not willing to raise a family in that hostile environment. So he prepared to leave Ten Eicken with Hilda. But the war stopped them," Lotte says.

"The war killed plans for the future before it killed men."

71

"Why didn't he just refuse to become a soldier?" I want to know.

"My dear girl," Lotte says, "the history lessons they teach in school nowadays. My, my. Refuse? You had two options as a male in Germany during the war, march into battle or line up right there against a wall and be shot by your fellow German superior for treason as a war resister. In essence, men did not have a choice. It was either to be killed later on the battlefield or right away at home. That's the reality of fascism."

"German war deserters were on top of the country's enemy list. Some 30 000 German soldiers were caught as war resistors. Two thirds of them were shot, the rest deployed to the Russian frontline during a *Himmelfahrtskommando* (ascension command). Today you may call them heroes because they saw through the web of lies the fascist government told them. But that awareness did not exist during postwar years. People pointed fingers at them, called them traitors and cowards. Do I need to say more? The system controlled people. I cannot stand listening to opinions today by people who weren't there."

"Many accuse their parents of cowardliness now and argue, that they would have opposed the system and deserted. Easy to say fifty years later. Those know-it-all would have been dead and unavailable to tell the story to their offspring." Anger lingers in Lotte's statement.

"In hindsight it's easy to criticize. I tell you girl, I know. I was there. Nobody ever wants war and take the life of another human being. No one. Ever. Understand? Why we remain the perpetrators of the world today for other nations I even understand in some ways. Just think about some of the atrocities."

"But why was there no tribunal against the guilty to bring justice for millions of displaced German civilians who where killed by Russian soldiers in the east during expulsion? Nobody talks about that. And that makes me angry and sad, " Lotte says.

"Let's not forget that even today the fate of over one million German men still remains unknown. What happened to them, where did they die? The archives in Russia remain closed."

"It's a depressing world at times, isn't it? War. Atrocities, they are still happening as we speak," Lotte says. "Look around, watch television.

It's still going on and will never change. I know it is the right of victors to write history to their liking but the iniquity and massacres against Germans after the war should have been stronger acknowledged. You are a journalist. What do you believe?"

Lotte looks exhausted. She is tired of remembering the past and those shadows I lure out of her closet. Quickly I guide her to another topic of her days on Ten Eicken.

"As you said earlier, your relationship to Hilda changed. You became sort of sisters. What happened after that accident?"

"Your mother was the same. Friendly and kind to every stranger, yet she was also different. An air of secrecy surrounded her. Nobody outside the family knew what was going on. I didn't know about the inheritance battle on Ten Eicken. No one did. Hilda kept that a secret until the courts decided her family's fate." Lotte points out.

"She also acted somewhat peculiar when nobody seemed to watch her. Ever so often she would dust her first husbands photograph. Mumble and remain standing there in front of the fireplace in the library. It occurred to me she wanted to be close to him. As if the picture was somehow alive. Strange, very strange. I asked her, and finally she told me about her visions of Walter during her coma in the hospital. She maintained that she saw him alive in Siberia."

"It spooked me, you can imagine. What did I think? I told her that I once knew a woman in Pomerania who could talk to people by just thinking about them. There was also gossip at the time that Russian scientists were experimenting with this phenomenon of communicating without the other person's presence. One rumor was, that during the war, commanders sent troops to the frontlines without giving a verbal or written order when exactly to attack. They did it apparently by telepathy. Must be a special gift if it's true, I told Hilda."

"It was simply weird," Lotte continues. "The mystery of the mind. That was a topic I definitely was not familiar with. I was not as educated as Hilda, so I could not help her with reasonable explanations. I told her to forget it. Yet Hilda was convinced, she saw Walter during her coma. For many months she kept that conviction alive and would not let go. We talked a lot during those long working hours in the kitchen. Our singing days were done. We now spoke. And so I advised Hilda to contact once more the Tracing Service of the Red Cross about Walter's death certificate. Ask them if it is authentic, I said. It was the only way to find out. Maybe bureaucrats made a mistake, it happened rather often during and after the war. People declared dead would suddenly appear again. No wonder with all that chaos."

"The answer to Hilda's new request came by telegram two weeks later. They reconfirmed that Walter Eicken was killed in Russia, a few miles west of Stalingrad. The Red Cross pointed out that two separate reports by unrelated eye witnesses were filed at the time. There was no mistake. The man was declared dead and the file was closed," Lotte says.

"Hilda seemed indifferent about the result of her inquiry, it was just a repeat of the news she heard years ago. Did she believe it? I could not tell. She never talked about her first husband again. Not to anyone. Late at night I often saw her sitting there in the library, reading a book. With Walter smiling in that photograph right above her. They looked content, perhaps happy. Both of them."

15

The stillness in the house at two in the morning is soothing, a relief from everyday worries and banalities. Hilda is cuddled up on the couch in the library while reading Pushkin's *Postmeister* (Postmaster). Diving into the story, she can forget her surroundings. And travel with the author deeper and further into Russia, becoming one with the heroine Dunja. She can feel the pain but also the hope of redemption. Yes she is in Russia, in a landscape which places her closer to Walter.

"Why are you still up?" Ernst asks. He suddenly appears out of the dark. His silhouette fills the door frame. She cannot see his face but the tone of voice is harsh. Commanding.

Is it possible that the living can be jealous of the dead? It can. Ernst feels envy. All the time. He married Hilda but she does not belong to him. She puts her book down and smiles. But not at him. That grin is inwardly. It's a joyful gesture which does not go unnoticed.

"Come to bed, we have to get up early to go to town. Or did you forget?" he points out.

She has not. Tomorrow their fate will be decided by a judge in Düsseldorf. Hilda is confident. No need to worry, she is certain. But she is tired of thinking about those fights with her in-laws. That's why she came here to read that book. Why can't he leave her alone?

"In a while, I'll be there in twenty minutes," she says while turning another page in her book. But the moment is spoiled. It takes her away from Walter and back to reality. To Ten Eicken with Ernst.

Not tonight, she thinks. Ernst wants his wife by his side to exercise his rights as a husband. Rights? Hilda contemplates. This marriage was over before it began. She exhausted her love years ago. Ernst seems like a brother, not a husband.

The lack of emotional attachment on her part has constructed a brick wall. The sign says: Don't step closer to me than I am to myself. When she feeds the hungry, the homeless, when she is kind to strangers, it feels safe. Those people don't know her and cannot overstep boundaries. Hilda will always be there for others, except for Ernst. War has written that chapter in their private history.

Scarred from the battles fields the fight simply moved into their private quarters.

So she reads for another hour before leaving the library. He will be asleep by now. She'll have her peace. Tomorrow, she promises, they will take the future of the estate into their own hands. The judge will be on their side. A new wind will blow across the valley. The women will pick up the pieces to labor for a prosperity, Ten Eicken has yet to see.

That next morning judgment is quickly passed down by the court. The decision is final and favors the young couple as the inheritance law in the Rhineland requires. But Hilda and Ernst leave with a dent in their victory.

"Frau Eicken," the judge calmly says to Hilda. "The debts on this estate are beyond imagination. It will take a miracle to reverse the mistakes of the past. There are outstanding taxes which need to be paid. From what, I ask, your accounts are empty?"

That news cannot devastate Hilda. She knew, as everyone else in the family.

"It's nothing we did not expect. But I'll promise, not only will we put a stop to wastefulness, we'll bring Ten Eicken back to riches," Hilda says. The judge nods. He does not doubt her courage. What would this country do without the strength of women? the judge thinks. Our smallness would shrink even further.

Later that afternoon all workers and family members of Ten Eicken are called into the living room. Hilda and Lotte have prepared barley-coffee and sandwiches. They wait for an announcement. Even Agnes, Gisela and Fritz are there. A notary will speak for the court. He explains that one third of the land will be under the supervision of Agnes until her grandson Wilhelm inherits that part of the estate at age twenty one. The other two thirds of Ten Eicken will go to Ernst.

"Living quarters are divided as follows," the notary points out. "Ernst and family receive the entire main house. Agnes and family will move into the foreman's cottage. The mill, blacksmith building, barn as well as cattle and farm equipment will be equally divided for usage. Employees are free to choose for whom they want to work in the future."

Silence in the living room. The news of the estate division was not expected by the workers. Nobody has touched a sandwich. Farmhands glance with uncertainty around the room. What's next?

"We'll make this quick and simple," Hilda says now. "Those who want to work for Agnes and family, please step over to the right side. The left side here beside me is reserved for workers who choose Ernst and family."

Silence again, followed by mumbling. Footsteps on the parquet can be heard. When all is done only one woman has stepped to the right side beside Agnes. Nobody else wants to work for her. Not even Friedrich who labored for husband Gunter some thirty years. Yes, farm folks know by nature that you reap what you sow. Except Agnes but she is from the city and still rejects the rules of nature. She steps forward and looks with a grim face at three of her former maids. Ungrateful common folks, she thinks.

"This is a set-up, ridiculous. It's a trap to undermine my authority,"

Agnes complains. "Let's ask every worker individually where he wants to work. Let's do that, then we'll see." But nobody moves, the result stays the same. The farmhands know who treats them well. Hilda sighs. We'll be overstaffed, she thinks. But not for long. Not if we open the restaurant soon. There will be more than enough work for all.

An hour later Lotte and family move into the staff quarters of the main house. Their days above the mill are done.

And Agnes? Moved out, right after the vote. Not just out of courtesy Hilda's farmhands carry furniture and suitcases from upstairs and through the yard into the foreman's cottage. They cannot get Agnes quickly enough out of the mansion.

16

The division of the estate is in place, but the battle is not over. It's as if some people did not get enough war action. Only two days later Otto reports that two Holstein cows are missing from their section of the barn. In addition farm equipment from the shed has disappeared. They don't suspect that homeless people stole those items to sell on the black market. Those people travel light without material burdens.

They have to find out what's going on. Therefore Ernst and Otto will watch tonight to catch the thief and teach him a lesson. They bring along two dusty potato sacks. Their wait is short. An hour later they spy a lone figure behind the barn.

"If it isn't Fritz, my sister's husband," Ernst whispers. "Stealing from his own kin, how low can you sink. I am not even surprised. I would have put my money on him as the culprit beforehand." Both men wait until the thief reappears, carrying a heavy load of stolen goods. Noisy merchandise. The thief can hardly handle the large bag, it is being torn to the left and then to the right. Otto and Ernst do not wait. They run behind the man and put the potato sack over his head. When the thief's bag falls to the ground five chicken run scared into several directions.

"We should just drown this package we caught tonight into the lake and drown it," Otto says in a loud assumed voice to Ernst.

"Yes, I know a deep spot," Ernst plays along. The words make the hooded man scramble and scream.

"On the other hand, if a thief like this could replace all the goods stolen we could pretend that we never saw him." Otto points out. The potato sack bends several times forward.

"Looks to me like an affirmative," Ernst says. They drop the man, not without smacking his head for memory of his promise.

Like a miracle the Holstein cows, the tools and other stolen goods reappear within eight hours. After that night nothing ever goes missing again from the farm. As Fritz did not see who caught him, he now has the habit to greet every farmhand with courtesy on the estate. Wondering, always marveling who caught him that night.

Although Agnes lives merely two hundred meters away from the main mansion, it's far enough for Ernst to avoid any contact. He is done with his mother, unable to forget her betrayal.

But in some ways it helped him. Since the court settlement Ernst is a changed man. After escaping the claws of his overwhelming mother, he now pays serious attention to the business of farming. He leads his workers with a firm but kind and fair hand, working long hours himself. His consideration for Hilda even alters. He lets her be, undisturbed in the library at night reading now that winter settles upon the Rhineland.

Meanwhile on the other half of the farm, new refugees from East Prussia arrive. They applied to Agnes to lease land. Ellie and Dieter Karstov, a family with two sons and a daughter, have moved above the mill. Their sons Achim and Siegfried, age thirteen and fourteen will work the fields with their father. Although daughter Trudi is only seven, her childhood ends in the Rhineland, she has to help with the cleaning.

The Karstovs are hard-working people from a small farm in Prussia. That's why Agnes hired them. She is not interested in managing the estate. Her job is to keep the land in trust until her grandson Wilhelm is twenty one. What then? The boy will most certainly sell his inheritance, Agnes has bigger plans for him. Fourteen years from now. Her daughter Gisela and gentleman farmer Fritz are useless, even Agnes knows that They are young and strong, but refuse to run this part of the estate. That's a peasant's job, they argue. They scaled down their affluent lifestyle, now living in the foreman's cottage but the rent from the Karstov family will support them just fine. To the delight of Agnes her grandson Wilhelm visits nearly every day after school. He spends more time with her than at home with his mother.

"You have to watch what you say when that kid is around," Hilda says to Ernst. "Her goes to your mother every day after school."

"He can repeat whatever is being said in this house, I really don't care," her husband says. "If my mother wants to use a child as a spy, let her. We have nothing to hide." But it is the child's behavior which disturbs him most. He rejects his uncle's authority.

"You cannot make me do anything, you are not my father. My real father is dead.," Wilhelm yells more than once when Ernst scolds his manners.

They are losing influence over the boy. He is turning against them. Even Hilda feels helpless. She has little time to discipline the child during these years. Survival is not a private affair. There are twenty persons in her household. She will not treat Wilhelm like a little crown prince.

Postwar Germany has no place for extra servings of attention.

What to do? Hilda's father in Westphalia has asked to educate his only grandson. His farm has no heir since his only son Hubert went missing on the Russian frontline. Males are rare in postwar Germany. But the fields are waiting to be plowed. Most often the only workforce available are women, children and refugees.

The farm in Westphalia needs to be secured for the next generation. Tradition requires a heir. Little Wilhelm is family, he can be taught and molded. The estate has been in the family for over four hundred years. The soil is part of their bloodline. They need that boy to come soon. There is no other alternative as they will never sell the place to strangers. It just isn't done. Pride forbids such thoughts. Send Wilhelm, he is needed in Westphalia.

"Not just yet," Hilda begs her father. "He can come and live with you when he is a little bit older. Let's wait a while. He is only seven and not ready to leave home. It's too early."

When Wilhelm finally moves to the farm in Westphalia at age twelve, Hilda realizes she waited too long. Grandmother Agnes has made the child her own. Nothing, neither kindness nor strictness will reverse the child's mannerism. He is spoiled and unkind to other children. Where is that little boy Hilda loves? He talks like an adult, reproving others. Even Lotte, who is loving to everybody, avoids now being around that child who does not show an atom of his mother's compassion.

17

He is lonely and cruel. Or alone because he lacks kindness. Wilhelm learned the absence of love and compassion from Grandmother Agnes. And soon it's payback time for the old woman. Her tool is her grandchild. Even if her long arm needs to reach from the grave.

Although her daughter-in-law Hilda secured the inheritance of one third of Ten Eicken for her son Wilhelm, it's the grandmother who will keep control of the whole valley. Just wait and see. She'll have her revenge on Ten Eicken with the help of the boy. He doesn't realize it yet, but he hates farming. His interest in the land is only the value in Deutsch Mark. Yes, Agnes made sure of that. Her little boy is superior to the rest.

Wilhelm can't help it but those displaced people are not his kind. They are scared and obedient. Nothing like those other strong Germans. Of course there was a time he liked Albert as a playmate. But he despised where that boy came from. The east. And now that Karstov family who farms the land of his future inheritance. Also from the east. What is it with those refugees? They can work, but can they also think?

"Hey you, where is your backpack?" Wilhelm teases Trudi, who is scrubbing the stone floor in his grandmother's kitchen. The little girl keeps working without looking up while responding.

"Why would I bring a backpack to work. We live on this farm?" the girl says. "What a silly question." She has not heard that expression or other names people use for her kind. The Karstov family was expelled from their land in East Prussia only six months ago. They did not taste the bitter life in camps or insulation of Germans in the West yet. When they arrived in the Rhineland, the regional agriculture committee offered them the lease of two hundred acres of land on Ten Eicken within a week. Call it luck, but it was not. The Karstovs lied. They told the authorities they had three grown-up men to work the estate. That's why they got the contract.

Children working became a necessity to survive during postwar Germany. The years of childhood were cut short everywhere. Many youngsters supported their parents. They worked like adults to bring bread to the table.

But what does Wilhelm know about scarcity or the tragedy of others? Pampered by his family and undisturbed country life, he simply repeats the talk of adults.

Backpack Germans is one of his favorite expressions. Grandmother uses it all the time. To him it means these people won't stay, their backpacks are ready anytime to continue their journey. They are simply people passing through. But what about Albert? He is still here after more than a year. Isn't he also one of them? Or is a Pollack different from backpackers? Grandmother Agnes doesn't explain. She uses words he has never heard from his mother.

"You mean, you live on my farm," Wilhelm corrects Trudi while stepping on the tiles of the wet kitchen-floor to go outside. Hours later Wilhelm watches Albert and Trudi at the creek behind the mill. They are talking and laughing without paying attention to the young master.

"All this land will be mine one day," Wilhelm now shouts at them. Aren't they listening? Can't they see?

"Wait up, I'll come with you. I don't mind, if you play on my pasture," he adds quickly.

Albert and Trudi giggle while slowing down. He is after all Hilda's son. And they respect the mother of that little weirdo.

"If you want, I'll share a secret with you," Wilhelm says now. Those words find listeners. Trudi runs toward him first. A secret? He must tell. Where and what? Even Albert is now exited. Expectations ignite in the monotonous daily routine. Wilhelm points to the blacksmith shop. It's hidden behind that building. He parts the long grass and they look at a dented metal cylinder.

"So what?" Albert says, "scrap metal. You can get three Marks for that on the black market. "Big deal. Is that all you've got." He pulls Trudi's arm gently in order to leave.

"But wait," Wilhelm says, "there is more to it. I've heard it from the adults. I'll get a hammer from the shop and then you'll see."

"See what? More dents?" Albert says with sarcasm in his voice. But Wilhelm is already back. He smacks the hammer on the metal. Nothing happens. Then again and again. Perhaps Albert wants to try it, he is two years older and physically stronger. Why not? It's just a game. Isn't it? By now Trudi feels bored and sets off to walk home.

"Hit it again, perhaps a bit closer to the front," Wilhelm urges Albert. He labors with might. But then it happens. A swift push slams the hammer out of his hands. He falls to the ground and is pulled backward. The last thing he sees are Wilhelm's fearful eyes. But they are not fixed on the metal cylinder, his eyes look upward at uncle Ernst.

"Over here, both of you. Right now, hurry," Ernst yells. The boys follow his command. All is still. "I swear, we did not steal it," Wilhelm says now. "We were just playing." He looks at the pale face of Ernst, awaiting punishment. But instead, the boys hear a soft voice.

"It's a hand grenade from the war, if it explodes you're dead," Ernst explains. It would not be the first time. Hundreds of children and adults have triggered by accident unexploded war ammunition. If lucky they only lose limbs, however, most civilians get killed. *Blindgänger* (dud munitions) people call those bombs.

It was common toward the end of the war that soldiers threw bombs out of planes without unlocking the primers properly. They got rid of ammunition on their flight back to base and thus leaving time bombs all over the countryside.

Ernst knows from experience. Last summer when working the fields, his plow hit an object in the soil. At first he thought it was a huge stone, but when Ernst realized he had unearthed metal, a bomb, he quickly unhitched the horses from the plow to bring himself and the animals to safety. In the afternoon a disposal unit scanned the field with metal detectors. They found another three bombs and defused them right there on the field. Farm workers were informed. It was not uncommon that bombs were even found in the woods on Ten Eicken. Disarming ammunition from the war became an extremely delicate task. More so in the cities where often bombs were found during construction of buildings and roadways, endangering thousands of people.

"You did nothing wrong. I should have told you about the danger. How could you know?" Ernst says to the children. "It's my fault. That darn war. In the future never ever touch or move any metal container you find. It could be another hand grenade or bomb," he says.

"Understood? It's a deal then?" Albert nods. Wilhelm is shaking but for the first time he looks at his uncle with admiration.

18

Missing soldiers are returning. Not all. But some of them. Lucky are those who were captured on the western front and North Africa by the Allied Forces. Hilda checks the list of released German prisoners of war once a week at town hall. And when they arrive by train she goes there. She looks at tired faces hiding exhausted souls.

Disillusioned, awakening from a lie. Trying to cope with a new reality.

Since the end of the war they worked as forced laborers in France, England and even as far away as Canada. Young men now look aged beyond their years but they are fed well enough. None of those released fought on the Russian front. Hilda needs not to ask. She can read facial expressions. The branding of years in the desolated countryside of Siberia has different marks.

German soldiers are coming home. But to what? Their own children don't recognize them. Wives act estranged. A new beginning at home looks like the end. Two words mark this time; divorce and suicide.

While women committed suicide at the end of the war because they could not bear the mass raping by Russian soldiers any longer, returning German men choose years later the ultimate way out because of shame. Ashamed of losing a war and returning home to nothingness, including the loss of authority under their own roof. A dilemma, which infests itself and stays for years to come.

But shame is not a topic up for open discussions. It remains hidden in every family. Lingering first with fear and is later paired with guilt.

Dishonor drowns in silence.

Nothing to talk about.

The past was in another life.

Let's start all over again. Look at those men, at least some are back. Their return feels like a small victory after all those years.

Among those released from a prisoner of war camp is Dr. Mertel. He is Ten Eicken's veterinarian. Caught by the British in North Africa where he served under the famous desert fox Rommel, Dr. Mertel was shipped to a prison camp in Canada. Initially to Kananaskis in the Rocky Mountains and later south to Lethbridge in Alberta. He looks well nourished upon his return. Strong and lean as if he never left Germany.

"They treated us well in Canada. I suppose we were lucky," he says to Otto and Albert in the barn while tending to the birth of a foal.

"Here, hold this needle," the veterinarian says to Albert. "You are my assistant today." A bright smile develops on Albert's face as he watches the men attending to the mare. They talk about the time after the war, avoiding to recall years in trenches, faces of comrades who died in their arms and enemies they killed from a distance.

"Those Canadians are something, unbelievable how kindly they treated war prisoners," Dr. Mertel says. "After our release they even offered us immigration to North America if that's what we wanted. Incredible."

The veterinarian is full of praise. He will not share other stories he witnessed abroad. German-Canadian farmers held as war prisoners in their own country while their offspring, born in Canada was abroad fighting Germans in Normandy. Or those stories about Ukrainian-Canadian who suddenly during the war were suspected of sympathizing with communists in Russia and therefore locked up in Canadian prison camps. Or those Japanese-Canadians who were stripped of possessions and dignity before herded like cattle behind barbed fences in camps.

"Depicting logic, war times perhaps ask for different measures? Do they need to?" Dr. Mertel asks. "But who am I to place judgment or even utter an opinion?"

The former soldier carries his own mark simply by being German. His opinion would be taken as an excuse to minimize invasions into foreign territories. Others would call him a Nazi, a man who didn't learn anything from history. His personal opinion is unwanted.

Therefore the returned soldier stays silent. He'll never talk about his experiences. Not even to his children.

"Good job, excellent," the vet now says to Albert. A healthy foal is born. "Here, take a handful of straw and rub. Yes, just like that. He'll be cold if you don't rub quickly enough." The boy works with all his might, following the veterinarian's instructions. "When the foal gets up, you are done. The mare will do the rest and lick him dry." Back in the house, the women later listen to Albert's exciting afternoon.

"I want to become a vet," the boy says. Hilda smiles and nods. Albert would make a wonderful vet because he loves animals. But he will never become one, she knows. His lack of schooling cannot catch up with the requirements of that profession. What a shame, a stolen opportunity by time and circumstances.

But she will not kill Albert's dream by telling him the truth. She sends him outside to tend to the cows to get more practice for his future job, while Lotte is reading the newspaper at the kitchen table.

"How terrible and sad. Read this. Another soldier killed himself. Senseless, after all those years. Absurd," Lotte says to Hilda while putting down the newspaper. Richard, the neighbor's oldest son did not leave a note when he died. He could not even pull a trigger because all weapons on their farm were confiscated after the war.

The young man hung himself in his room. No explanation needed. No alternative in sight. His two younger brothers were killed at the Russian front; the guilt of surviving was unbearable for the oldest.

What will now become of his aging parents? Compassion comes later in the form of two loafs of bread Hilda baked for the old folks. But she knows, it won't do. Kind gestures can ease the pain but not heal.

"I feel sorry for his parents, so wretched," Hilda says. Secretly however she understands the suicide of their son Richard. A late act of bravery, she thinks. Or is it wrong to believe that?

Giving up and giving in makes sense in 1948.

Being done with overbearing struggles which mount each day anew.

Yes his act is understandable. It even has appeal.

How often have her own thoughts gone there? Haunted by memories of her first husband Walter and her brother Hubert.

Their shadows have tripled in size by the distance of years. Shadows which have partnered with her existence. Not only at night.

Oh yes, Hilda understands her neighbor Richard rather well.

"I know where he's coming from," Hilda says.

"Yes, so do I," Lotte responds. "I only pray our children will have it easier one day. Dear God, what a world we live in."

Lotte still prays? Will it help? She is not convinced any longer. But it calms her nerves to recite the prayers her mother taught her as a child in Pomerania. When she recalls those lines late at night they are like a mantra. Lotte feels comforted and safe. At home with herself, in a cocoon where *angst* and shadows stay outside. She learned to create this safe place on the trek to the west, during moments of human insanity. What to believe, who to pray to and what to expect? She doesn't know any longer and only mumbles lines. And she wonders if such an approach of religion is a sin. Hilda looks up from her paperwork.

"Lucky you, if you still can pray. I wish I could. It would make life so much easier," Hilda says. Existence without that religious safety net to her is a balance act. You are always on the edge. One day at a time. Up that hill a few meters and then back into the trenches. It's exhausting. Perhaps she battles in spite. She is a born fighter. Her pride prevents her from giving in. Embracing life is her form of religion.

"It's more out of habit," Lotte says.

"What?" Hilda asks.

"This praying we talked about. It's a routine and it seems to help," Lotte explains. "To be honest, I have no idea what to believe any longer. Perhaps it's also this time of year. These long winter nights are dangerous. They play tricks on the mind, giving us too much time for idle thoughts. What do you think?"

But Hilda is now somewhere else with her thoughts, contemplating about the restaurant and money they need to keep Ten Eicken safe from bankruptcy. She does not want to burden Lotte with finances. It's her private problem. Their common topic is the practical development of the restaurant. They have to keep going. The opening is set for spring.

Now that fields are covered with snow, farmhands are building tables, chairs and benches for a large garden restaurant. Hilda is aiming for a seating capacity of at least one hundred outside and seventy within the mansion. They will open in March. A time for new beginnings not only in nature.

Winter will be soon be over. Shortened by intensive work inside the house. The women are pickling vegetables, butchering and smoking sausages as well as brewing fruit wine. Huge wood barrels with a brew of apples, raspberries and cherries are stored in the cellar. The recipe is simple, add water and sugar for fermentation, allow time. Lots of weeks. When it's done, serve at cellar temperature. Hilda anticipates that wine will be a winner.

"Quality, simplicity and affordable prices are the key to a successful business in the country. But seriously, Lotte, we cannot put rutabaga on the menu. People are sick and tired of that vegetable. That's all everybody has been eating. Turnip, turnip, turnip. Used for food, as tobacco and even coffee. I know it's nutritious. But forget it for our restaurant. I like those dishes you mentioned, *Pomeranian 'Caviar'* made out of goose lard with onions and lots of spices. And how about my idea of serving a Rhineland *Sauerbraten* (Roasted pickled beef) marinated with red wine and vinegar, bay leaves and juniper berries."

"Ah well, I am fantasizing. We don't have the spices or enough meat yet. So there. Let's start with good old German potato soup, served with smoked pork sausage. People need calories on their plates. And how about *Himmel und Erde* (heaven and earth), mashed potatoes with onions and apple sauce," Hilda asks.

19

They talk about the moment. And maybe a short way ahead. In postwar Germany a whole country lives in avoidance of looking back. Call it mental survival. They have no concrete expectations of the future yet, they literally live in no-man's land like children under supervision.

The Allied Forces run their radio stations, newspapers, schools and bureaucracy. But something is changing. You can read it between the lines of words printed in papers. The Germans in the West are not alone any longer with their future fears. Since the monetary reform and Berlin blockade, the Allies see a new enemy. It's the Soviet Union which occupies nearly one third of Germany in the eastern zone beside all those lands they stole in the east.

But in the new Germany the communists are now going their own way. They are splitting up from western powers. Slowly they are running their own show, introducing in their zone a form of socialism Germans have never seen on their soil.

Communism made in Russia has arrived in East Germany. Who saw that coming? It's too late to reverse history. And before the opportunity of freedom is gone a new stream of German refugees makes a run from Saxony and Mecklenburg to the Rhineland and Bavaria. They escape to an area which is still occupied by British, French and Americans forces.

It's better to have Coca Cola in the West than Karl Marx in the East, the Germans say of their now divided country. It's an expression of resignation because they don't really have a choice.

The victors of the war make that decision. West and East. They watch each other with suspicion. Smiling and spying. Distrusting anybody who plays left field. Birthing the cold war before the ruins of the Second World War are buried. Lucky for West Germany. The occupiers are now the protectors. They need this part of Europe as a buffer-zone against the spread of communism.

Those stories the folks on Ten Eicken hear from Augustin, the young student Hilda met in the city last summer. She gave him her address and now he is here. Still outspoken and rebellious as if trying to make up for all those years of silence, of suppressed opinions in his home country.

"I am not a student any longer although I should be," he explains while eating supper with the family. "They made me a teacher without further studies thanks to *denazification*. Another joke. They kicked out over seventy per cent of the teachers because they were party members. Yet, here I am using classroom material from the Weimar

Republic. We have no other schoolbooks. How is that for reeducating a nation? On the other hand, the daily radio broadcast in school is under the military regime of the Allies. So we have Weimar philosophies in books and American propaganda on the airwaves. It has to make some students schizophrenic." He laughs out loud.

"Classroom size? About fifty children, but I've seen as many as seventy in a single room," Augustin explains. "We try to feed them at lunch. They have to bring their own spoons and plates. But there are shortages everywhere, especially a lack of food and volunteers. It's hard for the kids to concentrate on Goethe's Faust when their bellies are rumbling. It's an agonizing picture, I tell you. Do you know what some kids do? They scrape part of their lunch onto pages they tear out of books. That lunch portion they take home for their younger siblings. I pretend not to see. Many of those books are useless anyway." Augustin leans back and closes his eyes for a moment. No, he is not tired. He is angry and disgusted.

What will become of those children when they grow up? What shadows are passed on to the next generation? There is not one face in his classroom which looks its age.

He is teaching children whose eyes look like old men.

Hilda and Lotte glance at each other. They don't need to talk to decide. They just nod in understanding. Yes, that's where they'll start. Feeding the children. During the winter the women will volunteer their cooking skills at least twice a week at that school.

"Maybe we'll rise again from the ashes. Perhaps one day, I hope sooner than later. For the sake of the children," Augustin says when the women reveal their plan.

"Augustin, we want to help under one condition. We'll bring old newspapers to wrap lunch leftovers. We don't like that the kids use book pages," Hilda points out. "Think of Goethe's poetry. I am not talking about social science books from the Weimar Republic, but we must preserve the literature of our thinkers and poets. It would be sacrilegious to destroy Goethe's *Sorrows of Young Werther* or the works of Schiller. Those authors were not political. Their philosophies are timeless. We can't just toss out everything German and put it into the garbage. It's insane that nowadays the love for Wagner's music and even German Shepherd dogs mark us as Nazi-sympathizers. Ridiculous, just because Hitler liked the same music and adored those canines?"

She looks at Augustin but he makes no comment.

"Don't you think we are overdoing this self-loathing? Isn't it getting too much?" Hilda asks. "It would be different if there was a critical debate about the past. But this? Being ordered to spit at ourselves constantly? It's fruitless. It won't change the past and doesn't help the future."

No answer. Silence. Heads are bending down over empty supper dishes. Thinking. Wondering. Does collective guilt include future generation? Will they be held accountable as well?

"It's difficult to follow new ways. You hear this and that from the occupiers on the radio in comparison to what our ancestors taught us. And how can we forget the propaganda chatter of the past? How can we delete that from our minds?" Hilda says.

"You have to ask yourself what you truly want," Augustin says. "Is it mainly coke, jazz and jeans? It's your choice, maybe. But perhaps not. I know for certain, it's not mine. I may leave the west and go to the German East Zone," he suddenly says.

Mumbling is heard around the table. Is he insane? Germans are running away from the Soviets who are in charge in that part of the country. There is even talk that the German territories Saxony, Brandenburg and Mecklenburg will be lost soon and form a separate state under Soviet protection. Is Augustin out of his mind?

"Why go there? Don't you see that in a divided Germany this eastern zone will get a communist puppet regime? Come on, you are smart," Hilda says. But Augustin shakes his head.

"And what will you have in west Germany? An imperial greater state of the Allied Forces?" Augustin asks. "What's the difference. We'll be marionettes on either side of the fence, one way or another. Yes, I have heard we'll have our first free elections next year. Officially it will end the occupation. I know, they promise the western zones will be sovereign soon. But at what price in the future? What will the concessions be?" Augustin has talked himself into a rage. He is losing some of his listeners.

For most farmhands this discussion is far too political. They get up and leave the table. Not in open protest. They retreat politely. Perhaps they cannot follow the young man's line of thought. But they know one fact for certain.

If you loose a war, your bartering days are over. You take the crumbs and chew them carefully and very slowly. So they will last for a long time.

Losers cannot ask for cake as dessert. It's that simply. Except to Augustin. He wants more. That Augustin. He demands a glass of milk with cake. But he better be careful. The Cold War is warming up. Spying eyes hide everywhere. German socialists and communists are as suspicious to the allies as former fascists. He better watch out. These are complicated in-between times. You never know who is listening.

But Augustin is not afraid of denunciation. Why should he care? He has nothing left to loose. His parents died during the bombardment of Cologne, two of his brothers are missing on the Eastern front. His rebellion against any form of authority esteems from patronization. Blah, Blah, Blah. That's all he was ever told, all he has heard. And what did it amount to? Suffering here and there. Agony everywhere. Nothing gained for anyone. All lost for most. Silence is mightier than the word history has shown. That's what this young intellectual believes. Nobody will shut him up. They'll have to use force before he retreats into silence.

20

"That Augustin. What a man. I must admit we admired him that night when he came to Ten Eicken," Lotte tells me during my next visit. "A danger to himself, a dare-devil. He lacked visible scars from the war, but his emotional damage was beyond repair."

"When you have nothing to lose you can afford to risk everything. That was his thinking. And that's what he did. We later learned he went to East Germany before the elections, which split this nation in two. He tried a career in politics but even the communists did not want him. Too radical, we heard. When the east fenced its people in with barbed wires and later that cement wall, when they created that Iron Curtain, Augustin tried to escape back to the west. That was in the sixties. By that time thousands of east German soldiers patrolled the borders and shot at people who wanted to flee. Augustin idealized socialism but then he got that reality check."

"Did they kill him?" I want to know.

"I don't think so but we never saw him again. Friends claim he arrived safely back in the west. And that he then became a spy for the Americans. They even said he later arranged escape routes for east Germans into the west. You've heard about tunnels underneath that Berlin Wall, haven't you? Well, apparently Augustin developed the most curious ways of getting people out of that eastern imprisonment. But many lost their lives trying. What an historical irony during those years. Germans shooting at Germans," Lotte says.

"There are times I cannot believe all this was real, in hindsight it looks like a tragic comedy of sorts. We don't know what happened to Augustin. Stories circulated that he was a double spy and the Americans found out. Anyway, he just disappeared one day. Some said, he was killed, others believe he ran off to Argentina."

Lotte pauses to straightens her green apron. I have never seen her without an apron. Different shapes and colors. At least a dozen are in her dresser. She wears them like an armor over her fine dresses, always ready for a task. The apron embodies her readiness to work. Anytime. Anywhere. She does not wear it any longer to protect her dress. Out of tradition, this wear has become a habit, like putting on her shoes in the morning. And although her daughter-in-law cooks all her meals, Lotte won't be seen without an apron. They might need her in the kitchen, perhaps even ask for her help one of these days.

"I am getting ahead of my story," Lotte says. "Where was I? Ah, yes, that Augustin. There he was in the kitchen on Ten Eicken in the winter of 1948. He talked and talked, we mostly listened. Until we heard the sound of a car. A jeep, definitely a four wheel drive. Two officers jumped out of the vehicle, wearing helmets and American uniforms.

They did not even ring the doorbell. Quite rude. They just stormed in. During those years we did not ask questions. These men had the authority to go where they wanted and do as they saw fit. Although I think a little politeness at times would have been in order. So here they were, in our kitchen. We stayed silent, wondering who would be picked up."

"You never knew which German denounced another German in order to score points with the Americans. It could be a neighbor or even your friend. So we just waited in the kitchen with anticipation. You see, having lost the war, all our faces looked somewhat guilty. We showed obedience with little self-confidence," Lotte says. But now she laughs.

"Fear? Submission?. No way, not Hilda. Not her. Wasn't she the mistress of the house? Certainly. What about those soldiers. Yes, what about it? Hilda asked. Can I help you? You gave us a good scare, thank heaven you are Americans, she told them."

"Were her words a mockery? Perhaps, but the officers did not notice. The language barrier. The men were simply charmed by Hilda. She asked them to sit down and warm up at the kitchen stove. Such a cold night out there and fresh snow. So how are the roads? Did you have problems finding us in this blizzard?"

"Your mother talked like a radio announcer without pausing. Clever, as long as she talked, the officers could not ask their questions. Even Augustin did not interfere. Secretly he probably feared they had come for him. Meanwhile your mother was hilarious. She just kept those officers cozy beside the kitchen stove. In an entertaining way she spoke a mixture of German and English. I am certain, they didn't know what she was saying. But they appeared mesmerized. Twenty minutes passed. It was snowing heavy now."

"They had to go back to headquarters, the soldiers suddenly said. Only when Hilda escorted them to the door, they seemed to remember why they came here. If there was a Fritz living in this house, they asked. A Fritz? Hilda responded. Fritz? That is a common German name, we have at least three men by the name of Fritz working the fields. Fritz Becher, the officers specified. Is he living in this mansion? And if so where is he?"

"Let me think, Hilda said. In this mansion? No. There is no Fritz Becher living in this house under my roof, she told them. The courts kicked my brother-in-law Fritz out, you can check that information at town hall. The officers nodded politely, hopped back into their jeep without asking her where that Fritz might be living now. Hilda closed the front door with a sigh of relief. Let someone else tell them where Gisela's husband is. Probably hiding under the skirts of Grandma Agnes, Hilda said later. But I'll be damned, if anybody tries to make me a collaborator for their own purpose."

"What an evening that was. It saved the night but not Fritz," Lotte says. "Two days later he was picked up by different officers. They did not step into the mansion to query Hilda. After all their Fritz Becher was living in a totally different part of Ten Eicken. Well, sort off."

"What happened to him? Why was he taken?" I ask her.

"He was gone for only three days. A neighbor had denounced him. During *denazification* Fritz apparently forgot to answer the question of party membership within his family properly. You see, his older brother Norbert was a big shot in Berlin during the war and now on the naughty list of the Allied Forces. They wanted to put him on trial."

"Too late, what could the Americans do? That brother of Fritz was dead; killed on Russian soil. During the last months of the war, even his high party rank could not save him from being used as cannon fodder on the eastern front. Therefore case closed for the Americans. No use to unearth what's buried," Lotte explains.

Her statement sounds factual without emotional attachment, because such endings were no exception under a totalitarian regime in Germany.

Was Norbert's death in Russia as a soldier a personal victory over the proposed trial by the Americans where he surely would have been sentenced to hang? Sometimes I wonder. Can different forms of demise be a worse death than others? And what about an honorable death? Would hanging from a rope in Nuremberg have made that brother of Fritz a better person?

If so, for whom?

For the soldier himself?

The judges?

The victims?

Many cases were reopened later; in the early sixties by a generation who was too young when crimes were committed to be guilty. The question of culpability drew trenches within the nation. It divided families when old men and women were dragged in front of judges.

21

Tired, so tired of politics. They turn the radio off most days. Few want to hear another word. Nine years of German propaganda are followed by constant broadcasting of the victors, leaving a nation politically apathetic. No news is good news for most. All thoughts are directed toward the next moment. How to carry on and if so, with what strength?

It's like being on remote control, Ernst thinks while pouring oats for the horses into the wood trough. Just functioning. Mindless routines to burn daylight and time. And later? What then?

A stolen life for his generation. Wounded inside out. Now with fuller bellies but stripped of honor, dignity and perspective. Nights haunt his memories. He knows until the day he dies his mind won't rest. A life-sentence brought upon a nation by a dictatorship. What about his brother Walter? Wasn't he sentenced to life as well? Not to live but to die. Ernst will never tell Hilda, it would kill her. She would not be proud of Walter? Or would she?

Ernst pats his thoroughbred Theresa gently on the neck Smart animal, smarter than people. Especially than that brother of his, Walter. His sense for justice. Look what it got him? Opening his big mouth during the raid of Poland. Opposing commands, refusing to shoot at civilians. The village was not saved, other soldiers finished that job. They pushed Walter to the ground, ripped the Iron Cross off his uniform and disarmed him. They wanted to shoot him right then and there where bodies of dead enemies lined the ditches. But he was a lieutenant, so he was tried and sentenced to death as a war resister. They did not kill him, which would have been mercy. Instead, Walter got front row on a punishment battalion at the Eastern front. Without a weapon to defend himself as thousands of other Germans who resisted gruesome orders, he was sent as cannon fodder deeper into Russia.

Soldiers can die, deserters must die. That was the rule in those days.

No, Ernst will never speak of the circumstances of that deployment. Let it remain a family secret to be judged in time. There were millions of fateful stories on both sides of the battlefields. Enough with individual stories. No one is willing to listen.

In the aftermath most Germans call those war resisters and defectors cowards, traitors and communists. They spit on sidewalks, when they recognize a man whose compassion saved enemies. Few are interested in circumstances of humanitarian acts during times of war. Justification denied. Always. Ernst knows why? Those who now gossip perhaps think, that's why the war was lost. Ernst simulates in his mind: Even if war resisters survive the impossible, the harshness of Siberian winters and cruelty of Russian prison camps, returning home and settling into a normal life is nearly impossible.

There is no pardon or peace treaty for defectors.

The archives list them as dead and dishonored.

Why is compassion shameful, particularly after the war? The *Schande* (shame) is with defectors. It has to be so for the mob, those mindless followers. Standing out of the crowd, being different is a crime. Individualism is on the same page as opposition.

But what about the past? The war? Wasn't thinking prohibited when following orders? Perhaps understandable for career soldiers because they choose their profession. But not for a whole nation which is forced by superiors with pistols to pick up a gun. Ernst stops his line of thought. To be honest, he tells himself, nobody forced crowds to cheer the *Führer* before the war.

Minds on a merry-go-round, telling themselves stories to fit cause and effect. Attacking and battling details with precision. Like soldiers marching forward with numbed senses. Leaving thoughts behind with distance. Resting the conscience later. Or perhaps never in the aftermath. Always in silence, never out loud.

On his way back to the house Ernst spots a white Mercedes-Benz in the yard. City folks, his cousin Bernhard with wife Frida. From the clan of his mother Agnes, the intellectual city slickers. How can he afford fuel when food is still hard to come by these days? On Ten Eicken two motor vehicles, an Opel and a DKW are collecting dust in the barn. Auto parts and gasoline are not yet readily available. That's why farmers still use old horse buggies for transportation in the late forties.

Ernst looks at his in-laws. He knows what to expect. Wars cannot change attitudes, personalities or characters for that matter. These people present themselves as always, carrying their calm faces snot-nosed. Consequential without remorse when eyes are lowered by those they address.

"Where did you get fuel," Ernst asks.

"Easy task. You simply need to know who to be friends with," Bernhard says. Yes, buddies. Bernhard knows how to befriend important people. He is a slick man, his aunt Agnes adores her nephew who became the dean of the University of Aachen at age thirty. He speaks seven languages, including Russian. Impressive. A studied man. But without education of the heart.

When greeted by little Albert, Bernhard turns his head arrogantly to the left without responding to the boy's friendly gesture. His wife Frida complies with Bernhard's mannerism. She is just a silent collaborator without an opinion she can call her own. When they enter the house, Hilda and Lotte only briefly look up and then continue their work in the kitchen. That's how it is done on the farms. Visitors wait or help while talking. Work only rests after completion. Two dozen bottles are lined up on the kitchen table.

"Try this, Herr Eicken," Ernst now hears Lotte. She has filled a glass with a dark red liquid. Perhaps juice? He takes a sip and feels warmth spread through his body. Tasty, a bit sour, but rather becoming.

"It's cherry wine, it needs another three weeks. We are tasting and testing recipes for the restaurant," Hilda says. She fills the other glasses on the kitchen table. Cousin Bernhard empties his glass with one gulp. When he leaves, he will ask to take a dozen bottles home for the family. And of course potatoes, some sauerkraut and a box of apples. They live in abundance on Ten Eicken, don't they? In the city, he points out, there is still so much scarcity.

"What do you think of the European Recovery Plan, better known as Marshall Plan?" Bernhard wants to know from Ernst. But he doesn't wait, he answers his own question.

"The new Deutsch Mark was printed in New York and shipped to Germany in secrecy. Did you know that? A kilo of coffee is now 32,50 Marks. The wage of two full working days for a laborer. I remember drinking coffee during the war, lots of coffee, and it was very affordable." Ernst recalls that as well. Despite those terrible years they could purchase almost anything on food stamps.

"I understand there will be some relief like those Care Packages and the mass-feeding of schoolchildren," Ernst says. "They are setting nearly 14.5 billion dollars aside for the European Recovery Program. That should help."

"Really?" Bernhard says, bragging with inside knowledge. "Germany will get 1.4 Billion dollars, repayable naturally in reparation costs to all those countries we invaded. We'll have to make a lot of other payments, the final invoice hasn't even tallied up yet. The bill is always given to the losers. I'll tell you what else I've heard. Okay, some money will be used for hunger relief but the biggest piece of the pie will be given for fighting communism. Not only in the German East Zone run by the Russians but also against communism way beyond Poland. That's were the money goes. To fight communism, the political bogeyman for the next generation."

"Got to have an enemy, don't we? The cold war is in full swing. The recruitment of spies underway. So don't just believe what you hear. The Marshall Plan doesn't just feed the hungry, that's only a small part. And let's not forget, the money used for a quick recovery of European economies will also secure future markets to sell merchandise to. Ah, well, I am only an academic. I should have been a merchant. The future belongs to those who wheel and deal. This is their time. They'll make lots of money as they always do when the soldiers return home."

Hilda and Lotte have left the men alone in the kitchen. Always the same, talk and more chatting. Politics and assumptions after the fact.

What does it matter to the women anyway? The bread still needs to be baked, the potatoes peeled, the cabbage cut and cooked. And these men certainly won't help with the chores. They need to talk. When wars are done the next conflict must be discussed, analyzed and later exercised. Too much peace needs battles sooner or later. Human nature. Unnatural to all other beings. But man? His kind? The same dilemma over and over. Who ever fantasized a world without wars? A peaceful place where young men and women can choose their own path and walk it toward the end?

"You will see the day soon, when Germans will be armed again. First they disarmed us, soon they'll order us to wear uniforms once more and carry weapons," Hilda hears Bernhard call after her. He will not shut up, he is pouring his visions like molasses into the hallway, slowing down escape from his speedy flow of words.

"It will be the west against the east," Bernhard points out. "The victors decide about new enemies, they'll need us too for their cause against communism. Our participation won't be optional, trust me." Hilda pauses for a moment. Is that possible? Germans again with weapons? If so they'll reintroduce a compulsory military service. What about Wilhelm and Albert, these young boys who already saw so much cruelty? No, Hilda won't allow it. They won't get her son. She'll keep him out of any army.

This family has lost enough men for generations to come. Isn't it her duty to shield the son she birthed from the madness of war? Must she not find ways to keep him away from battlefields? Such are her thoughts. But Hilda knows better. Is it ever possible? During the Roman Empire when people lacked initiative to reproduce, the state encouraged birth by introducing a child allowance. A first, as far as she learned. But clever. Money always talks. So mothers got busy bearing children. The idea of cannon fodder did not come to mind.

No, Hilda thinks, my boy will not become a soldier.

An hour later cousin Bernhard and Frida leave Ten Eicken. Their car is loaded with food supplies from the farm. He stacked two sacks of potatoes into the trunk of his Mercedes. There is a war widow in his apartment house who looks after five in-laws. A poor woman. A person who needs help.

Naturally Bernhard will share those potatoes. Anything else would be inhumane. Bernhard's promise sounds believable. And Ernst is easy to convince. He tells him his aunt Agnes now lives in the foreman's cottage, while pointing to the house across the yard. Right there, see. The lights are still on.

Won't he visit her? But Bernhard is suddenly in a hurry. Useless to go there, the nephew thinks, Agnes won't even offer him a glass of water.

22

Still hungry at home but not so much at school.

The children attend classes in the village now regularly. They come for the pea and pork stew to fills their bellies. They don't attend for food of thought. During recess hundreds line up in silence, holding on tight to their tin plates and spoons they brought from home. They don't have pencils and paper yet, their focus is on lunch utensils. Education can wait, hunger can not. The awakening of curiosity comes with a full stomach much later.

For more than eight weeks during the winter Hilda and Lotte volunteer twice per week in the school's soup kitchen. Often they bring vegetables from Ten Eicken to add to the still meager meals. But the supplies by CARE (Cooperative for American Remittances to Europe) and CRALOG (Council of Relief Agencies for Operation in Germany) are coming on a regular basis now. Empathy from across the ocean, food from America. Not because of politicians but because of women.

American women demonstrated in front of the White House in Washington for weeks, forcing President Truman to finally let the ships sail from New York to Bremerhaven. The circumstances are not common knowledge in Germany at the time, Hilda and Lotte hear about the battle for kindness from across the ocean when an American reporter arrives one morning at the school.

"For nearly a year those ships were not allowed to leave the harbor. Inhumane. I was there, I covered those stories." Jacky Baumann tells

Hilda and Lotte. "Politicians? Aren't they the same everywhere?" Jacky is a journalist in her mid-thirties from New York. She is on assignment in Germany for Life Magazine, reporting about the distribution of food by American volunteer organizations. She points out, that help from America began with CARE packages soon after the war. Those brown cartons contained canned meats, sugar, powdered milk, flower, chocolate, coffee, chewing gum and cigarettes. They called them 'ten in one packages', because they were the ration per soldier for ten days. People in France were the first recipients, she explains.

The chronic hunger in Germany however found no immediate relief. When people were literally starving to death even the church tried desperately to help. In vain. When the Vatican in Rome organized food supplies from Chile to be shipped to Northern Germany the Americans did not allow it.

"It took another year before CARE packages made it to Germany," Jacky says. "A few newspapers in the US wrote about a conspiracy of silence. They named the delay of helping a crime against humanity. I mean, after all, why starve women and children in Germany after the war, when countries like Sweden and Denmark had food stockpiled? It wasn't necessary; it just didn't make sense. Perhaps it was only political payback?"

Jacky shakes her head angrily. She knows, that none of this news has reached this country yet. It is hidden from history for the time being. Especially in Germany. Jacky pauses, looking at the women. But they make no comment, they have no questions. They don't dare to fully trust. Anybody, any news.

"Finally, perhaps thirteen months later, the first packages were sent to specific addresses over here. Mostly to relatives. You know, more than twenty percent of Americans can trace their roots to Germany. Naturally they wanted to help their aunts, nieces and aging parents in the old world. German charities and churches also received those packages for distribution. I know, for many children and women this help came too late. They starved to death, I am quite aware of that."

Jacky pulls out her *Leica* camera. She wants to take photos of Hilda and Lotte with the children to document their efforts in the soup kitchen. But Hilda turns away and Lotte follows her gesture. It's a no, they don't want to be the center of a story.

It's the malnourished children and the *Trümmerfrauen* (rubble women) in the cities who should be featured. Show their faces, capture their skin in folds with the camera. Report about their hands shaking as though they suffer from palsy.

"*Bitte* (please). Just one photo," Jacky begs. But the women's expression rejects her plea. Finally the journalist points the camera at the long row of waiting children, she also takes a close-up of the meager meal on their tin plates.

"Where did you learn to speak our language?" Hilda asks.

"My grandfather was German. He came to America from Hamburg in 1892. I still have relatives in this country," she says. "We grew up in America with the German language. That's all we spoke at home. Would it surprise you that many traditions made it to the new world? Even the *Oktoberfest.*"

Parties, dancing, laughing. How long has it been? Hilda looks at Lotte. They cannot remember. Staying alive has been their daily celebration for the past eight years. Oh yes, America. They would like to see that continent one day and thank the women there. Talk to all the women who feel like mothers, sisters, aunts and grandmothers and congratulate them for their understanding beyond political dogma.

"It is amazing, those council of relief agencies are feeding meanwhile more than three million German children and youth in schools each day," Jacky says.

"In the Rhineland the elderly also get additional food from army stocks, supplied from fat and meat of German livestock. It is getting better now. Isn't it?" Jacky asks.

It definitely is, Hilda tells herself. She will never forget the kindness of the American women who made this possible. They sent aid across the ocean although many of their men were also killed in this war. What a forgiving gesture.

"Maybe we too can go to America one day and start all over again," Lotte says to her husband Otto that evening. Go west all the way across the ocean to that land of golden opportunities. Why not? Germany is over-crowded. There is not enough housing or space for all those displaced persons from the east. Yes, America or Canada. Even Australia sounds great.

"Be quiet woman. That's enough," Otto says with anger in his voice. "If we go anywhere it will be east. Back to Pomerania. That's our home, that's where we belong. Forget America. We are Germans. I will never leave this land." When Lotte tells him that many Americans have German roots and are making a good life in Montana, Oregon and California, her husband shakes his head in disbelief. He is convinced a German will never be fully welcomed anywhere again. Not after this war. Not his generation. Even his son will carry the torch of collective shame. Not by free will. But that's how it will be. Otto is certain. America? That woman of his, what is she thinking?

"Stop fantasizing and get some rest," Otto says with a change of tone in his voice. "You look exhausted. How much longer will you work in that soup kitchen at the school anyway?" He hears a loud snore. Lotte's answer to an ignorant question. She has closed her eyes pretending to sleep while her mind is racing in circles. I have two children, she thinks. Otto and Albert. Pomerania, always Pomerania. Such nonsense. Wishful thinking, illusions spiked with hope. Isn't hope like prayer? You never know what you'll get. Otto is unrealistic, Lotte thinks, he is hiding behind his hope to find blame somewhere else. And yet he needs that thought of going home like a prayer. If I'll take that perspective away from him he will vanish one day. Dissolve in spirit and soon in body. She needs to feed his illusions for the sake of his survival.

"Yes, why not? Perhaps Pomerania again someday soon," she says out loud while feeling the gentle touch of Otto's hand resting on her left shoulder.

23

For the time being Otto is not going anywhere except to nearby Düsseldorf to dismantle factories. Not by free will but the Allied control council orders him to report to the city. They argue, there is not enough work on farms in the winter. He is dispensable on Ten Eicken with three other farmhands who will work during the winter in those factories. Not to produce anything but to take machines apart for transportation to England, France and Russia. Equipment, which the Allied Forces consider part of the reparation payment.

Along university professors, teachers and bakers, Otto is one of thousands of forced laborers who are now ordered to destroy what's left of German infrastructure instead of rebuilding the nation.

Otto is equipped with wrench and hammer to take apart valuable Gutenberg printing presses to be loaded on trains and shipped to Britain and France. The empty building will be demolished after the job. The Americans however show little interest in dismantling German factories. They know already that this part of Europe will soon be needed as a stronghold against Russia. A fact they learn during the Potsdam Conference at the end of the war.

The Berlin Blockade opened their eyes considering the Soviet's agenda. However, the French are hungry for machinery in their occupied German zone, dismantling four times as many factories as the British. The worst are the Russians, Otto learns. Ten times the amount of equipment is put on railroad wagons headed to Moscow where they never arrive. Abandoned on the way. Most of those expensive machines will rust and degrade to scrap. Wasted, never reassembled to run again.

As if there is not enough destruction and rubble all around them, every day numerous factory halls are simply blown to bits and pieces. The Allied orders are clear. Manufacturing has to come to a dead stop. In addition billion of dollars worth of German patents are confiscated. Many scientists are jailed and later transported to Russia as well as to the United States. War has a price-tag, not only in millions of human corpses.

"Are they afraid we make bullets and grenades with these Gutenberg printing machines?" a plumber asks Otto and grins. "Reparation equipment. They don't know a thing about these machines. Somewhat idiotic the way they go about punishment. See what I do to make this work?" And the man puts a few essential nuts and bolts from the dismantled machines into the pockets of his pants.

"That printing press will never work again, you better believe it," he says while spitting on the floor. Otto just shakes his head, he has no interest in sabotage or questioning orders. He follows any given task. The quicker he is done, the sooner he can go back to the country. This is not his world?

"Well, you should be interested in what's going on here," a former teacher working alongside Otto complains. "It's that lack of concern which got us here in the first place. Don't you agree? Too many people kept their mouth shut before the war. Where were you when all this started?" He slams his hammer awkwardly on the side of the machine, cracking the cylinder which holds the motor. Looking carefully to the left, he spots the back of an American soldier who is smoking a cigarette in the yard. But no one has noticed. The now worthless machine is quickly loaded onto an army truck.

"What I was doing during those years? I was milking my cows in Pomerania, if you are interested," Otto says to the teacher. "Minding my own business. No one asked me for my opinion. Or was there a plebiscites to decide to invade or not invade? You talk nonsense. What's real? Look at that machine you just broke. That's real."

They are fighting among themselves. It's frustration against the occupier, the lost war, their own unknown fate. It's not about their difference of opinion. Degraded to forced laborers in their own country alongside four million former German soldiers who are still imprisoned in Britain, France and Russia, they have to obey orders.

Here in the city, scraping the bottom off their tin plates, at least they eat well while dismantling those factories. The Americans make sure of that. Even canned meat and peanut butter are on the menu.

German workers are not allowed to take any food outside the factory. But many try. Like Otto. He never tasted peanut butter before. What a delicious heavenly food. His son Albert has to try some. Carefully Otto scrapes three tablespoons into the left pocket of his jacket. It's cold enough. Minus eight. When he is patted down at the end of the working day, an American soldier hesitates for a moment. He suspects. And now he knows. But looking at Otto who has lowered his eyes to the ground, he spots deep scars on both hands. He feels ashamed, perhaps the young soldier thinks about his own father in Colorado who worked his hands to the bone during the thirties.

"He can go, he's good. Next," the soldier says to the relief of Otto. That same evening Albert gets his first taste of peanut butter which came all the way from America. But Otto will never try to smuggle anything out of that factory. He was lucky, other soldiers are not as forgiving when they catch a worker for *Mundraub* (petty larceny of food).

The German owner of the printing factory Meier & Söhne is still on site. Ordered to stay, he has to oversee the proper dismantling of his company, a business his great-grandfather founded in 1823. He knows those machines better than his own children He prepared the typesetting of thousands of pages for novels and school books with his own hands. Later his company also printed propaganda leaflets as ordered by the Nazis in Berlin.

What could he have done? He did not write those words, he only printed them on white paper. Those lies and defamations. They were not his thoughts but the printing presses belonged to him. He should have known better, that's what the Americans say when denying him to clear his character during *denazification.*

Now Meier's name stays tainted, he is called a collaborator. And although he may get away with a large money fine instead of going to jail, his business is ruined.

The work of four generations is being destroyed.

Wiped out. Finished as the man.

He is done here too.

Through his office window on the fourth floor Meier watches the loading of the last Gutenberg press. And then he jumps. They can take it all, may as well load him up too. Nothing left to live for.

Director Meier is not the only owner of a dismantled factory who becomes a postwar casualty by his own desire. In three other companies of the neighborhood five workers kill themselves. The dismantling of their workplaces shows a finality without hope for the future. What's to become of them? Where will they work? How can they rebuild a life when dismantling is ordered?

With relief Otto finally finishes his forced labor time in the city by March. The snow has melted, British soldiers allow him to return to Ten Eicken to plow the fields. After all, growing wheat is essential because forced laborers in the city need to be fed well. They have to stay strong when dismantling those remaining eight factories in the city. The occupiers will see to that.

For desperate families this destruction is beyond comprehension, a paradox to common sense. These days cities become dangerous places for sane minds because this form of constant punishment is visible everywhere.

And what about those monotonous sounds when the hammer meets metal.

They feel like horsewhips on human flesh.

Bang, smack without an echo from the skyline visible because the roof is missing. A day's work destroys another hundred jobs. With one last tremor the rest of the factory is flattened by dynamite.

24

"What a hopeless time. In addition to all the rubble from the war, the destruction of factories only increased our anger and tendency of self-pity. It may sound hypocritical today that Germans saw themselves as victims. But that's what we did during those postwar years. Perhaps civilians on both sides are always victims of wars?" Lotte tells me during our next talk. I want to hear more and have brought a tape-recorder. But she objects when I turn it on.

"Listen and remember. What can you capture with an electronic devise? Certainly not the depth of emotions. Read my face while we talk," she advises. And then she speaks for hours, picturing the city landscape with still hungry people begging for work and rubble women picking up additional stones from dismantled factories. I can visualize her words, but I cannot fully fathom the depth and totality of the picture. And I tell her so.

"Neither could we," Lotte says. "It didn't make sense to add rubble to ruins. Perhaps that's why we seldom talked about the war or the occupation by the allies which followed. We kept silent, suppressed our true opinion. Even within families. And in public? Beware. We didn't dare say anything. Call it a form of paralysis. That's what it was, I am certain. At that point in time, questions of quilt or shame didn't even cross our minds."

"We were a nation decimated to nobodies. I know, this sounds again like self-pity. What can I say? That's how we felt. Of course it was easier to cope in the country if you stopped listening to the radio and avoided newspapers. Perhaps avoidance is an ally for survival. As you numb your senses today with game shows on television and endless hours surfing the internet, we simply kept ourselves busy. We worked to exhaustion as we didn't have those games you have today for distraction. Work kept us occupied fourteen hours a day, and late at night I knitted socks while Hilda read."

She looks at me. Yes, I remember. When handicraft was compulsory during my first years in elementary school in the early sixties, I was useless with yarn and wool, preferring to rather use my fingers for turning pages in books. Lotte finished all my school assignments in the evenings at home. Proudly I would later show her the top grade for that blouse she stitched or the scarves she crocheted. The teachers never knew about our secret arrangement.

"If we only would have known then, what's being disclosed today," Lotte points out. "The Americans suddenly were keen to befriend us. Everything got a little bit better, although after the monetary reform wages were very low and prices for food incredibly high. But the Allies began to treat us better. Out of the blue, we thought. Today we know the cold war was based on real threats and showed it's claws beyond our shadows. The Americans were afraid that eventually all of Europe would fall to the communists. We read about the communist takeover in Czechoslovakia and Hungary. Politicians in the US were afraid not only east Germany was lost after the Berlin blockade but the whole west would soon follow socialism. And that, they could not allow."

"Only today we fully know that West Germany was a pawn in the chess game between Russia and America. Propaganda was hailed from both sides for years. In the late forties we didn't have television yet. We were never fully informed. Only bits and pieces of information, carefully selected by authorities, made it to the public. Where there was no theater, the Americans created mobile cinemas and showed movies they created especially for Germany. Even Hollywood actors like Ronald Reagan participated in these propaganda productions. Dear child, there was so much disinformation from both sides. We did not know what to believe any longer."

"Bad Russians, good Americans. Communism versus capitalism. Both sides truly believed Germans were ignorant and needed to be taught how to think after the Weimar Republic and years of fascism. But it wasn't only politics. Even in everyday life Americans instructed our nation: How to organize your kitchen and how to speak to your neighbors. All directions included topics of reeducation. It was really manipulation and another form of brain-washing."

"Come on already, German culture created the likes of Schopenhauer, Gutenberg, Kepler as well as Bach long before fast food became an imported culture from overseas. Their methods of making us function again was at times laughable." Lotte shakes her head.

"Such underestimation. Reeducation? They believed the individual needed to be taught democratic manners not only in politics. Adults were treated like children but it felt better than being despised by the allies. It also gave us some space to focus on our own future, our own lives although interference into our privacy was not excluded from propaganda. You want to see some letters? I still have them. They called them truth letters, sent all the way from America to private households in Germany."

Lotte opens a black wooden box and hands me an envelope. "See, this one is from Twin Falls in Idaho from Mister Caldwell. I had to look it up on a map. This new pen friend was a carpenter with his own shop and very successful in America. In a communist country like the Soviet Union, he wrote, he'd be working for the state with a small salary. No shop of his own, no car or his own house. But in America you can have it all. And in Germany too if you oppose communism."

"When we got those letters we were impressed. Mail from the new world, from people who wanted to be friends with us. It made us feel good, we didn't know why Germans were bombarded by those truth letters. Today we do. Yes, history can be much better understood in hindsight."

"When you live through those times it's like being in a darkroom where the film hasn't been fully developed yet."

For moments it is silent in her living room. Only the humming of the refrigerator disrupts this moment. She looks at me with so much compassion, knowledge and love that I lower my eyes. Overwhelmed by the history of a nation whose roots we share.

"During postwar years the entrance of Valhalla had a revolving door. Often we did not realize how far or close we were to the *Götterdämmerung* (Dawn of the Gods). We lived in the ultimate of reality with all its unpredictability. Every moment counted because the next minute could be the beginning of an end," Lotte says. "It was real, alright. You could see, you could touch what was there. Not like today."

"Oh dear, this abundance of nothingness today. What a culture of denial we live in. I like it less than the memory of my worst days. Let's see what stands out today. Denial of death and the illusion of immortality where people want to reflect perfection. It's all about appearances and little bravery to tackle problems at hand.," she says with disgust.

"During the worst of times we grabbed the bull by his horns so to speak. Without fear. Nowadays many people run away from the bull or worse, most don't even see the bull and the dangers which are dawning upon their fate. I tell you, if we continue this road of self-indulgence, we may end up exactly were we were before that terrible war. Dangerous. A thin line separating us from disaster. There is always that tipping point. Isn't there? It's like the place you'll find when you travel beyond fear. Callous, benumbed and ice-cold. A safe place where feelings are deadened in a land of indifference. There is only one way out. Reality. Those years I told you about. Do you understand?"

She pauses. Although I grasp in-between the lines the pain she carries hidden, I secretly envy her memories, the depth of endurance and experiences. Of a real life instead of mirror images from television and the internet I unwillingly pull behind me as my carry-on luggage in the twenty first century. It feels shallow in comparison, decadent in essence. The shame is on my generation not on hers, I believe. She did not have a choice regarding the larger picture. We have that luxury now, but do we use it to our full potential? Perhaps we are incapable of doing so. It's too easy.

Does choice need a prelude of hardship and nothingness?

It's the frame, always the frame. That's all I can see clearly. For the picture is still fogged within. Hidden by shadows. Fragments become visible here and there but it's like in a jigsaw puzzle. I need to take a step back to gain distance in order to clearly see what I am looking at.

25

Hilda is browsing through a pile of tax bills. They need to be settled Some nine hundred Deutsch Mark are due by April 12th. Third notice. Why not ten thousand? May as well. Despite tight budgeting there is not enough money to pay the tax man. Maybe three hundred Marks are left in the safe for emergencies. That's all.

Owning property is a curse these days, land a liability for keeps not revenue. There is no speedy way out of this dilemma when the season dictates plowing instead of harvesting. Ten Eicken is on the verge of bankruptcy, Hilda realizes. Postwar times are not a valid excuse for outstanding taxes. Even the interest on debt accumulated by her mother-in-law is soon due. Sins of forefathers leave the next generation liable. They won the court case but inherited the land with all those debts. Their victory feels like punishment.

When collecting taxes, bureaucrats refuse to look at painful circumstances. They go after the last man standing to confiscate what's due. Hilda's husband Ernst is aware of the financial urgency and fiasco at hand but acts helpless as so often before.

Withdrawn he curls up within memories of childhood. He goes to that time when he learned to play the violin at age five and studied Latin a year later. Those were good years, times when he was pampered and carefree. Ernst goes to those places worthy of revisiting when reality bites. Like today when the mail arrived. Let Hilda take care of it. She is in charge, isn't she? He seldom submits a solution but he has an opinion. That counts too. Or?

"Relax. What are they going to do? Confiscate the plows if we don't pay?" Ernst says with irony. "The country needs food, the government won't close down Ten Eicken. We are valuable to the system. You worry too much." When she hears those words, Hilda looks at her husband for the longest time. A dreamer, always on the defensive. Rejecting reality like a child. But without that innocence because he knows better.

"If we don't pay the government they can force us into bankruptcy, the estate will be auctioned off. New owners will plow the fields. Bureaucrats don't care who pays those dues. If it's not us it will be someone else on this land of your ancestors. This would not be the first farm to become a postwar casualty." Hilda's voice echoes desperation. "It's urgent. We have to find a way to get the money within the next fourteen days. What are we going to do?"

Money. It's always about money. Or more precise, the lack of it. First he had to listen to the quarreling about Reich Mark now it's constant disagreements with Deutsch Mark.

Their lives are run by the currency of changing times. It is like the current of ebb and tide. Never restless, always trying in this household. As if money is everything. Not to Ernst. He avoids those discussions, remembering well how his mother Agnes and father Gunter battled over banknotes all their lives. And now his wife. She continues the tradition on Ten Eicken although for different reasons. Hilda is a saver while Agnes wasted money. To Ernst, it does not matter. It's about money. Coins and banknotes embody arguments. Endless hours of debates. And he is tired of battles. Ernst wants his peace and quiet. Wasn't the war noisy enough?

Not for Hilda, not for the women. Drums are beating a new pace during trying times after the fact. Their echo lifts the dust out of rubble, fogging the air, blinding sight and clouding the path. But steps must be taken. Forward or sideways. Any way. We have to open the restaurant, Hilda thinks now. And we need paying customers. Think harder, she tells herself while watching her husband leave the kitchen as is his habit when the topic gets too hot for his liking.

Alone with her task she sits there in thoughts, glancing into space as if wishful thinking can wipe out debts and make government notices disappear. Hilda knows better. She is a realist who lives by her father's philosophy. Help yourself and God will help you. Not once in her life it rained bread from heaven without labor. Not for her, as time is her witness. At least not until tonight. Ghostlike Lotte appears in the frame of the kitchen door. She knows, as every farmhand on Ten Eicken. People hear, listen and talk when thick walls cannot harbor secrets from daylight. Without a word, Lotte steps forward to place a small leather bag in front of Hilda on the table. An offering, a gesture of friendship. Just enough to help, not too much to embarrass.

"It's from all of us, just a loan until times get better," Lotte says matter of fact. "You better get some rest if we are to open the restaurant next week." And before Hilda can even react, Lotte disappears again.

Hilda counts the money in the bag twice, then a third time. Freshly printed Deutsch Mark in small banknotes, collected from the farmhands and Lotte's family.

Six-hundred-eighty Marks from the workers toward the tax debt of the master. They have given every last penny from their meager savings. The expression of devotion and love is a humbling moment for Hilda. She is not alone. And for the first time in years tears stream down her cheeks. Unexpected and cleansing. She'll make up for their generosity, she vows. No need to say, they know because she made them part of her family and home.

Within days all government dues for the year are paid. A fresh breeze not only marks the first days of spring in the valley, but also purifies the air within the stonewalls of the estate and replaces the weight of secrecy with a revived lightness of openness. An intoxicating relief from a long winter. Work becomes play, singing voices echo once more in hallways. And when the first group of orphaned children comes from the city for their Thursday meal into the country, Hilda and Lotte double the portions on their plates.

The Ten Eicken Restaurant quickly becomes known for generosity, for hearty large servings but low prices. A strategy, which is rewarded later when their first dinner guests are American soldiers stationed in Düsseldorf. They come in a convoy of jeeps, not to requisition the estate as at the end of the war but as customers who marvel about Hilda's and Lotte's food and home-brewed fruit wines.

The women often work two days and nights in a row without much sleep. Baking breads, cutting vegetables, peeling potatoes and butchering pigs. Restlessness and anticipation keeps them awake. Strong coffee, the real stuff with caffeine is consumed by the gallon. They are more than ready, when the doors open for the public and over a hundred guests are seated.

Shiny black leather boots, uniforms decorated with medals, chatter in English and mostly young faces expressing anticipation in the dining rooms of a German estate. Glancing, waiting. Five farmhands wear white aprons while serving meals, offering hospitality with a welcoming smile. They are doing it for Hilda and Lotte, for their business success.

Don't ask what some German farmhands truly feel while placing plates in front of American and English soldiers whose uniforms trigger memories? Not enough times has passed for either side to allow ease and create familiarity to diminish awkwardness. Not just yet. But beginnings are made that night, aided by home-brewed cherry wine which animates to songs and loud laughter.

"We'll have to get even bigger pots," Hilda notes while scraping the rest of the stew from the bottom of a pot. Like Lotte, she is overwhelmed by the positive response during the opening of the restaurant. Who would have anticipated such a success?

"They want to know, if we take US dollars for payment?" Lotte says. When Hilda tells the soldiers, she'll take any currency except Russian Rubles for the time being, the echo of laughter is even heard in the yard where Ernst is returning from the barn. He won't have anything to do with the restaurant. And especially those foreign soldiers singing and clapping their hands while his wife Hilda sings for the second time tonight *Lili Marleen*.

Has she no shame serenading the former enemy? How can she be cheerful while looking at those uniforms? And what about keeping distance? Yes, what about it?

"You want distance?" Hilda asks Ernst later. "Perhaps fifty kilometers away from Ten Eicken, working in a factory after we lose the estate. Is that the distance you want?" She knows how cruel those words sound but she cannot stop herself from trying to argue the arrogance right out of his constant prejudice. And his pride, a terminal family disease. Ernst cannot help himself. How can he, when awareness is missing?

"Those soldiers are just boys far away from home. Americans, Brits, what does it matter?" Hilda points out. "Of course, I will also sing for Germans once they have enough money to come to our restaurant. It's a business, a stage on which we perform to make money. It's to avoid bankruptcy. You surely know that, don't you?"

Ernst shakes his head without willingness to understand. Pride forbids agreement, a trench which will secretly separate them for all times. No, he won't take that step, it's dark down there and treacherous like those trenches he remembers from the eastern front. But what do those women know about war? Nothing. Absolutely nothing. They cook and sing as if there was no yesterday. But there was. Soldiers remember it well. Too many yesterdays haunt waking hours, recalling horrific memories.

Perhaps the simplicity of the moment explains the rage Ernst carries around much better. His jealousy has no room for sharing. Watching those American soldiers boils his blood. In his house, under his roof. But let's be honest, where is the root of such jealousy? Of course, with his dead brother Walter. Ernst knows how Hilda still feels about her first husband. The closeness of distant memories she cherishes is a disturbing part of this union with him.

What marriage anyway? Isn't it rather an alliance of convenience for his dear wife? How Ernst adores her. Can't she see? And what about that friendship with Lotte, like sisters they run the estate, sorting money on the kitchen table way after midnight.

"Count it again," Hilda says to Lotte. After only a few weeks she repays every penny of the loan she received from the farmhands. The

115

money was earned thanks to their fine meals and the generosity of the soldiers who left large tips for Ten Eicken's hospitality. Lotte smiles, she has also earned her first share of the restaurant profits exactly as Hilda promised. The women giggle while stuffing the banknotes into their large apron pockets. Their earnings manifest a revival of self-esteem and new-found usefulness.

"You were right with what you said last year," Lotte whispers to Hilda, "I believe now as well, that we'll grow old together."

26

Finally it feels like going forward. Prosperity also nurtures self-confidence despite political dependency on foreign nations. But that changes in May of '49. It marks the official formation of the *Bundesrepubik Deutschland* with a constitution and Konrad Adenauer as president of a parliamentary commission. They call the former mayor of Cologne the old man, because by the fall when he is elected as first chancellor of Germany, he is already 73 years old. An ally of the Americans, Adenauer will reign fourteen years with his Christian Democratic Union party. The east German sector under Soviet rule forms a socialist peoples democracy in October of that year. A nation divided once more until reunification in 1989 when the Berlin Wall falls.

"Crazy, crazy years. From one day to the next we were supposed to politically be someone again," Lotte recalls during my next visit. "Mind you we voted. Nearly seventy-nine percent of the population went to the polls. We did not miss the chance to be part of that historical moment. It felt uplifting. But not for long. Within a year, the unemployment rate rose to two million people, prices climbed forty percent. We even closed the restaurant for two months when workers demonstrated in the streets. Ah yes, up and down. During that time thousands of Germans turned their back on the land of their fathers. It seemed impossible for them to believe that Germany could overcome this never-ending poverty. Immigration to North America and Australia was now an option."

"The new world lifted the immigration ban which excluded Germans for nearly seven years after the war. Hundreds of ships sailed from Bremerhaven to Halifax and New York. Better to go west than in circles, immigrants thought. Only a year earlier, North Korea invaded the south and the Americans went once again into war. They feared the separation of a country similar to Germany. That split eventually happened anyway. So you see, the fear of communism was everywhere. Again Germans hoarded food supplies. And then there was this talk about remilitarization," Lotte recalls.

"Remilitarization, do you believe it? Dear God, the dead weren't even counted and here we talked about rearmament. We truly feared we could be drawn into a fratricidal war with East Germany. Propaganda from east and west hailed over Germany. Communism against capitalism but most of all our nation again with weapons."

"Germans demonstrated against those plans. Didn't they just lose a war and turn in their guns? Now the victors wanted them back in uniforms. It seemed somewhat schizophrenic. But America's role changed meanwhile from occupier to protector. They needed German soldiers for their future alliance. Left, right. Weapons, no guns. We felt like a football in a soccer game of two powerful nations," Lotte says. "Well, as you know from history classes, it all ended in East Germany with an uprising of the people which was ended by Soviet soldiers."

"That incident showed the ugly face of communism. No further propaganda was now necessary," she explains. With the help of the Americans, West Germany donated food worth fifteen million dollars to the east. That was also a stabilizing factor for internal politics. Socialism was suddenly a threat, voters switched to the right during the next election which kept Adenauer in politics and made way for the economic miracle.

"Germans rose again from the ashes. Spreading their wings, trying to fly higher and higher in terms of economics. As if to make up for all that went wrong. To prove something to themselves and to the rest of the world."

"In a way it took forms like recanting. Apologizing for hidden sins," Lotte says. "If we thought we worked hard on the farm, you should have seen those factory workers. Double shifts, even on weekends. Money was made in abundance and quickly spent, consumption of meat and liquor doubled within two years. Eating and drinking was exercised with just as much enthusiasm and passion as working."

"We dulled our war memories with fried sausage, sauerkraut and beer. Wine was called *Sorgentöter* (wrecker of sorrows). People became *Fresser* (over-eaters). It was at times rather disgusting. But the Ten Eicken restaurant flourished, we added some two hundred seats in the gardens. We baked bread and made sausages at night. And we earned a lot, we made so much money. Those years were a miracle. Who would have thought? Everybody got a generous slice of that Black Forest Cake so to speak. Suddenly there was so much work and new prosperity. Minimizing talk about displaced people stopped dead in their tracks. They were valuable laborers now, part of the economic miracle. In addition thousands of Pomeranians and East Prussians opened their own companies to create jobs. With millions of men killed during the war Germany now even experienced a worker shortage. The first permits for foreign laborers from Italy were issued."

"By the end of the fifties unemployment was down to 2.5 per cent in Germany. Unheard of anywhere. It was a miracle. It truly was, also creating the baby-boom during those years. Suddenly people could afford to have children again. Your brother, sister and you were born during the early fifties. One after the other and the third child, you, three years later. Your father called that a true miracle, extraordinary regarding his relationship with Hilda," Lotte says. And then she stays silent. She has said enough and refuses to utter another word, leaving me alone with my thoughts.

27

Hilda looks pale again like last week, when Lotte begged her to lie down for an hour to catch some rest. Long working hours, an abundance of guests are tearing nerves and robbing sleep. But miracle years must be utilized and turned into cash. Who knows what the future will bring? Mustn't lose the momentum. But Hilda feels weak, unstable on her feet. Twice she threw up last night.

Could it be? Of course, she is pregnant again with her second child from her marriage to Ernst. Naturally she loves children but not the morning sickness which comes before birth. It's an inconvenience interfering with her work which has developed into a full-time business venture. Beside being a partner in the restaurant, out of necessity Lotte takes on the role of a second mother to Hilda's offspring. Wilhelm, Hilda's firstborn is not on Ten Eicken any longer. He moved to her father's estate in Westphalia. At age twelve she finally sent him away, out of reach of grandmother Agnes.

"If I could only choose again, start our private relationships anew as well. I'll tell you, I would never get married again," Hilda laments to Lotte that evening. "Too late for me, I have to concentrate on those children and teach them independence so they'll never marry out of convenience or need. If I could do it all over again my choices would definitely not include marriage. It's not for me." She is right, Lotte thinks. But only because of Ernst.

Would she talk like this if her first husband Walter was still alive? She loved him more than her own life. What a couple they would have made in later years, with a family founded on love. Pure love and devotion. History would have had to be rewritten within the Ten Eicken family. Too late now, the new pregnancy acts like a reality check.

"Does Ernst know yet," Lotte asks.

"You know, that's all that counts," Hilda says, continuing her kitchen work as if hard labor can lower the odds of bearing new fruits of the loin. But she is strong and hardy like the boy who arrives seven months later. No need for a hospital, like Birgit a year earlier, little Manfred is born in a bedroom on Ten Eicken. A midwife helped during that easy task. Five hours later Hilda is back in the garden picking beans as if nothing in particular happened that day.

It is Lotte who tends to the new arrival on the estate. And Ernst admiring his offspring. While Hilda bits her tongue to suppress her pain in the garden, she vows this was the last time. Never again will that man touch her. And it's not the long weeks of pregnancy she thinks about this time. It's Ernst. He constantly needs to be the man again, a feeling he lost on the battlefield.

While blood slowly triggers down her legs, Hilda decides right there and then that this relationship will only continue on paper, with separate bedrooms starting tonight.

Enough already with pretensions. Life will be so much easier without a lie. She bore him two children, she has nothing left to give to him.

The new arrangement of two bedrooms only reflects the distance within a marriage which never was close to start with. She tied the knot during the war out of desperation and necessity, not to bond with the younger brother of her dead husband Walter. The war, a thief of true destiny. A robber of free will. That is the story Hilda tells herself over and over. But she is too smart to even convince herself of such a tale. She chose the high road because of the view. And that remains the truth. A self-inflicted reality which haunts and punishes over and over.

Meanwhile daily routines on the estate remain unchanged. While Ernst minds the farm she runs the restaurant. They are a an unhappy couple without an option of divorce. Separation would bankrupt Ten Eicken. Responsibility means staying together for the sake of the estate. And so they live unhappily ever after. Like brother and sister with much greater ease, without this constant tension and sparks of aggressions in the air. A relief for everybody in close vicinity.

Several times Ernst makes an attempt to win Hilda back by leaving written notes on her night stand when she is in the garden. Like a schoolboy the man composes lyrical lines of devotion and admiration, begging for attention. She reacts to none of his efforts, ignores his pleas as if they never existed. To cave in cannot be love, not in her world. It would be pity, the worst kind of love imaginable, Hilda tells herself. And so she remains friendly but indifferent, caught up in her own world of building an even larger business within the walls of Ten Eicken. It helps to avoid thoughts. Ora et labora, as the Benedictine nuns practice. Hilda prefers the latter solution. No, she would not have made a good praying nun. But work, physical labor appeals. It is her salvation. There is no shortage of work to prove her point.

The business is flourishing, hundreds of guests frequent the restaurant now on a regular basis. Especially weekends crowd the beer garden, often young couples and students stay until three in the morning leaving hard-earned Deutsch Marks in Hilda's till. In addition, many customers order cakes and rye breads in advance for take-out. Even local grocery stores offer to carry her goods. The demand quickly surpasses the supply. Expansion is necessary. Again and again.

It's possible because of Lotte. Always by her side, she minds the business with just as much devotion as Hilda. Her share has risen to twenty per cent of all restaurant revenues. Two women working like one unit. They understand each other silently

"We have come a long way, haven't we?" Hilda says to Lotte who just put the children to bed.

"How many years has it been? Five? No six this month," Lotte responds. "And with so many changes, ups and down, six years seem like a lifetime. It truly feels as if we squeezed extra hours into each day in order to get all those tasks done, doesn't it?"

"We stole time from sleep," Hilda says. "That's where we made thousands of extra minutes count."

"And time generously rewarded this theft," Lotte says. They stay silent. No further chatting tonight. And never about the past, the shadows of the war are locked away. For the time being.

Only sometimes at night, when cuddled under warm blankets and westerly winds rattle the leaves of oak trees half visible within rays of moonlight, only then the shadows take a peek. Stretching their arms, reaching out to touch and wake what's seemingly at rest, ridiculing silence like a warning toward tomorrow.

Those shadows are not going anywhere, be aware and stay alert. Open the cupboard, let the moon sweep the shelves. Better tonight than the next day. Shadows won't fold their gowns without undressing.

Time is patient but most of all unforgiving.

Lotte turns on her night-stand lamp. Sweat is running down her forehead. Even Otto wakes up now. He looks at his wife knowingly. Wasn't he there too? Of course. A witness of unspeakable atrocities during their trek from Pomerania to the west. Not war any longer, but acts of revenge. Much harsher than battle. And always against women unarmed, vulnerable, easy prey. He remembers it well but keeps silent.

How many people are awake tonight, haunted by shadows they cannot tame? Lotte wonders. Perhaps millions. Friends and former enemies, victims and victors. All casualties of facts after the war.

Those memories take years to surface and decades to conquer, if at all. And by then they are larger than the issue itself. Growing with time, even within. While we tiptoe through the night, careful not to wake the sleeping past. Screaming inside without permission to exhale.

Such is the tragedy of silence in Germany. No provision for dialogue in a never-ending drama. In general for contemporary witnesses, in particular for a generation born after the fact. Silence dividing shadows from sunlight, inseparable for the effect but worlds apart in their cause.

28

"Don't you ever wonder about the past? How and why all of this happened? And what we could have done during those years? Don't you contemplate at times just for moments?" Lotte asks the next day when the women work in the large garden digging the black, heavy soil to aerate ground for new seeds. "Don't you?", she repeats while Hilda pushes the spade hard into the ground, forcing the blade even deeper by using her right foot as if searching beneath what cannot be found above.

"I won't go there," she finally says. "What's the use? Can't undo what's been done even if we contemplate for ages to come. Come here Lotte, let's rest for a moment." They sit down on a small stonewall, their colorful aprons stained with dirt. What can she tell her friend who wants to share and confide? Nothing uplifting, Hilda realizes.

Redemption cannot be earned. Not after this war. History will be unforgiving to a nation accused of fostering felonies, a people who kept silent during a dictatorship which few detected as such. But how much did common men and women truly know, what did they see? Most certainly not the camps with starving and dying people. Granted, there was propaganda full of hatred and threats throughout the war toward minority groups. But who anticipated such talk brought death to millions? Can the state of totalitarianism become a defense for helpless bystanders when put on trial? Perhaps not. No, history will be unforgiving to parents, their children and generations after that.

The analysis of the past, the pointing of fingers will go on and on. Contesting history will develop into a moral blame game. Back and forth.

Moments of turning a blind eye is considered a major sin. Sloth of the heart inexcusable. All this Hilda anticipates. Atrocities against displaced Germans by Russian soldiers, even the murder of millions of Prussians and Pomeranians during their trek to the west will not weigh in on the scales of international opinion. It won't even be mentioned for decades. Or acknowledged for that matter. History is written by victors. It always is, Hilda thinks.

Soon enough reality will drag hidden sins of a nation into courts. Searching for more German perpetrators. Nuremberg trials were only a prelude to crime and punishment. Her children will be taught self-loathing in schools. Parents will be found guilty without trial, because reeducation happens in the classroom. That's were they talk about the past instead of finding explanations at home. And there is nothing Hilda can do about it. Absolutely nothing.

Defending her life to her off-spring would be the confirmation of guilt. So she keeps quiet, carrying the curse and mark of Cain like the rest of a nation in silence. Hilda cannot share those thoughts with Lotte, that kind and often naive friend of hers. Such harsh anticipation of the future would only deepen her personal pain. Hasn't Lotte suffered enough? In what books will history record her reality.

"Let's make a pact," Hilda says now. "One day at a time, we'll take life as it comes. We'll do the best we can because that's all we can do. If it gets overbearing you can come to me. I'll always be there for you when the time comes. But let's not increase the size of shadows with early dawns. Are you with me?"

Lotte nods. It's good to have a friend with silent understanding. But she wonders how smart it is to avoid disturbing dialogue. Won't it catch up, later? Yes, later. But that's better than today. Why place more burden on weight right now? Contemplating and worrying seem like ingratitude in advance. No, neither of them wants to go there.

So they pick up their rakes to aerate the soil instead of souls.

"Here, let me use that spade, I am much stronger," Albert interrupts their silence. How Lotte's son has grown. A strong teenager, muscular and tall for his thirteen years. He loves farm work but most of all tending sick animals. Years of watching and assisting the veterinarian on Ten Eicken educated Albert beyond animal medicine in books. When Dr. Mertel is called, Albert most often presents him with a diagnosis before the doctor can examine those four-legged patients. Astonishing indeed. A natural talent that boy. His devotion cures in many cases. What a veterinarian he would have made.

"I am going to Metzkausen this afternoon to help father with the foundation of the house," he tells his mother now. "I've done all my chores. Is that okay?" Lotte smiles. With his enthusiasm their new home will be constructed in no time. Thanks to the 'distribution burden law' passed by the government, the Marlows like other displaced persons are receiving compensation for properties lost in Pomerania, East Prussia and other former German provinces.

Billion of marks will be paid to uprooted Germans who lost homes and farms during the war. And once again most Germans in the west curse their fate, because they have to pay that bill. In 120 installments over the next thirty years part of their earnings go into the pockets of newcomers they once took in. Property owners protest against this redistribution of wealth. But what can they do? It's the law, which awards most displaced persons initially with a lump sum of four thousand marks until further claims are settled.

Combined with low-cost land to build houses and generous loans from banks, *Reichsdeutsche* soon gain greater independence. In some cases their finances look better now than those who lost their house in the Rhineland. Although assessments of properties lost in the east are not easy to prove, the law stipulates that any land or house-value up to 5000 Marks will be fully compensated. For losses up to 10 000 Marks displaced persons get eighty per cent, up to 60 000 Marks thirty three per cent and if a million worth of property was lost, some nine per cent of the value will be paid by the taxpayers.

Even Otto's fears vanish, when he learns that farmers from Pomerania by no means lose the right to their property in the east. So he takes the money and buys three acres in Metzkausen, a small community outside Düsseldorf. He will build that house for his family, a small cottage with a large garden. Nothing huge, because to him this is only a temporary solution. Until he returns back east, he tells himself.

After the distribution of burden law is announced, within weeks displaced persons become the mockery of the nation once more. Ridiculed by envy and mistrust.

"Oh yes, you are one of those eastern farmers cashing in because you had a thousand acres of wind instead of land behind your house," people say. And they laugh, because they don't believe most claims are honest. At least not realistic within their knowledge of geography.

"Now we are paying for millions of acres which apparently were lost in properties, what a joke. Regarding those claims, the former *German Reich* would have extended beyond Moscow," west Germans mock. Although Hilda's husband also complains that the burden of the new law is just too costly to taxpayers, Ernst never ridicules the Marlows. He admires their work-ethic and loyalty. They did not leave Ten Eicken when better paying jobs were offered in factories two years ago.

"It's not your fault," Hilda says to Lotte, when she apologizes for the mockery displaced Germans experience again. "We are all in this together. Yes I know, people talk again. Uninformed as always. In essence the financial burden to compensate refugees for their lost properties only amounts to two percent of our revenue on Ten Eicken per year. The substance of the estate won't be touched. We'll make it back. And please, don't believe those horror stories of West German widows who have to mortgage their homes to pay this new tax for displaced people. It simply isn't true."

Hilda watches Albert who dug the vegetable-beds in no time while they were talking. She suddenly misses her son Wilhelm, hoping he shows as much keenness on her father's farm in Westphalia as Albert here in the Rhineland. And then she wonders. Was sending her son away the right move?

Who separates a son from the mother? The war? It was the war, circumstances left her without an alternative to choose, she tells herself again. But the excuse won't do when Wilhelm grows up and develops a mind of his own. Regarding that thought, Hilda trembles inside.

29

Ever since Wilhelm left, Albert and Trudi have become inseparable, a friendship founded on similar backgrounds. The boy from Pomerania and the displaced girl from East Prussia. In their spare time they idle afternoons on foreign pastures, exploring unfamiliar territory on the highest point of the valley beyond the forests of Ten Eicken. Those excursions into the woods almost always unearth remains of the war. Like today, when they find underneath dry oak-leaves a web of trenches leading to a tunnel.

Deeper and further they dig. With bare hands they clean the pathways, throwing leaves at one another playfully while on their quest of discovery. Last year they found a Walther Pistol 38 in a gravel pit, wrapped in a greasy cloth, still loaded and functioning. Remembering that scary moment when they tried to detonate a hand grenade with a hammer, they did not dare to touch that pistol but told a farmhand cutting grass in a pasture nearby to retrieve the weapon.

Today no help is needed. Albert detects a green burlap bag beneath the foliage. It weighs heavy, so Trudi gives him a hand to lift the bag out of the trench. However, the find disappoints the children.

Just letters, stamped envelopes, hundreds of them. Useless for their adventure. A waste of time. What to do with all that paper?

They could make a huge fire, Albert suggests. But Trudi is cautious. She knows the importance of letters, remembering how her mother once cried with joy when an envelope arrived from a cousin who she believed dead. Burning those letters is not a good idea.

"You don't even have matches," she teases. "And it's far too dangerous to make a fire in this forest." They decide to carry the heavy bag home to the farm. A find, which later brings two policemen to Ten

Eicken. Several farmhands assists the authorities when searching the trenches in the forest for hours. The sight of uniforms frightens the children. Perhaps a fire would have been a better solution.

"No, no. You did nothing wrong," Hilda tells Albert and Trudi. "You did the right thing." She opens the bag, glancing at some of the addresses of senders and receivers. Berlin, Munich, Hamburg, Moscow and even Stalingrad.

Field post. Mail from soldiers to their loved ones. Families deprived of thoughts and last farewells. How can they deliver those letters now, nearly eight years after the end of the war? The delay of time will raise false hope within families when reading lines of brothers and husbands who might be dead by now.

What is more cruel, a note from a soldier who already died or no news at all? That would always leave families wondering and secretly speculating what truly happened to a loved one.

It's better to read a last farewell from a distance, Hilda thinks. Quickly she scans through hundreds of addresses. But none of the envelopes is for Ten Eicken.

What did she expect? A letter from her dead husband Walter? A note from the other side? Dear God, she sighs, hope is a fruitless quest and most often in vain. She puts the letters neatly back into the bag before calling the police.

By nightfall the officers have found another two sacks of mail in the trenches of that oak forest. Further down the tunnel they come across empty brandy bottles, a pistol and finally a body.

They identify him later as postman Meier who has been missing since spring 1949. Once a soldier on the western front, he became one of two hundred letter carriers for Düsseldorf after the war. A carrier alright but not a deliverer of messages any longer.

For nearly six months before his demise, he buried the mail in the trenches. He simply could not do this job any longer. Not out of laziness, although after the war he drowned his memories with cheap schnapps. No, Meier was not lazy. Quite the opposite. He was a good soldier, obeying orders all his life.

But a messenger of death? That's what his job entailed, delivering letters which often confirmed the death of young men. He handed those envelopes to parents only to learn the very next day of another tragedy. His job killed hopes, anticipations. It created tears because he brought sorrow to those families.

Postman Meier embodied the grim reaper in the truest sense. He was only a mailman but Meier was not simply a messenger any longer. His mere presence at doorsteps became the message.

The authorities learn about his motives through a good-bye letter, which they find in his pocket. After a brief inquiry the delayed mail is none-the-less delivered with mixed emotions by new carriers. Families check dates on the stamps over and over especially when receiving mail from prisoner of war camps in the east.

When was that note sent? Three years ago or last month. Even a week in a Siberian camp can make a difference over life or death. More than a million German soldiers are still missing eight years after the war. No news is mostly good news these days when a total of two thousand letters from Meier's batch are delivered. The story makes headlines across the nation. Opinions are split regarding the mailman's motivation.

"I am glad we did not receive delayed field post," Hilda says. "Just imagine, you get that letter years later while your loved one is already dead. How cruel is that?"

Because there is still no word about the fate of her brother Hubert, the missing pilot who flew supplies to Stalingrad, Hilda continues to check on a weekly basis the publicly posted lists at town hall of deceased soldiers. No name is good news.

Often she wanders to the railway station where hundreds of people still wait daily in anticipation of spotting returning loved ones. But after all these years? Yes, why not? It's happening. Not many return this late, but some do. Thin and pale, sunken eyes, unrecognizable by waiting relatives. Mothers touch those faces of late returnees, search their eyes for familiarity while praying silently. Only to find out it is not their son but Ferdinand Schulte, the neighbor's son who stands there before them. Home at last but forlorn.

30

Nothing looks the same for late returnees. Not even their homes and families. Those houses only shelter memories of times gone by like pictures in a photo album. A reminder of the small boy that was but not the human wreck who found his way back home from Siberia. None of the German soldiers returning this late were in western prisoner of war camps run by Americans and Brits. No, most of those men came home one or two years after 1945. They returned like human beings from camps.

But look at those poor souls who return this late from the east. Look at Ferdinand Schulte. He is a shadow of his former self. An animals with trimmed claws in the wilderness of his nightmares. Even his parents hardly recognize their son. He was in Russia alright. It's written all over his face.

For two weeks Ferdinand stays in his bedroom. Interrupting sleep only by meager meals to recuperate. He cannot sit at the dinner table and look at those greasy sausages. Food, which turns his stomach after years of scarcity in labor camps. Nor can he listen to the laughter of children when his thoughts lead him astray to eastern Russia and faces of suffering comrades who are still in captivity. Those emaciated faces are imprinted in his memory.

When glancing out of the window, he now looks toward the east where the suffering of his comrades continues.

Such paradox, he thinks.

While in Russia, his view was constantly fixed to the west. Toward home.

Where am I now? he questions his existence. In no man's land. That's where souls hide to rest. And heal? Not likely. Perhaps forgetting is all he can pray for.

During the third week after his return, Ferdinand finally asks for his first visitor. He wants to see Ernst, the brother of his former high school friend Walter. But what can they talk about? Not the war. And definitely not labor camps.

"The estate is in great shape," Ferdinand says for the sake of uttering anything. Not that he is interested , but small talk is all he can bear at the moment.

"You did a fantastic job on Ten Eicken. I saw the fields when they picked me up at the railway station." He is leaning on a walking stick, taking one step at a time.

"How clever to open a restaurant. That's what I would have done on my farm if I'd been home. Yes, a restaurant. Intelligent indeed. People always need to eat. They are always hungry." He chokes on his last words and turns sideways to avoid the embarrassment. No, he will not cry in front of Ernst. He cannot, even if he wanted to.

Ferdinand has no tears left. His crying years are done.

"I want you to do me a favor," he says while pulling a note out of his pocket.

"Anything, just ask. I'll do anything for you," Ernst says while Ferdinand hands him the paper.

"You have to bring this to the headquarter of the Red Cross in Düsseldorf, you know the department that searches for missing soldiers. Bring it to them soon, people ought to know," he says.

"They have to know what?" Ernst asks.

"The living and the dead. Oh yes, it's better to know, isn't it? I certainly would rather want to know than live in suspense for the rest of my days," Ferdinand mumbles.

"Look at the note. Just look at it." Ernst unfolds the paper and glances at names, hundreds of words scribbled in small letters, lined up neatly like soldiers.

"From Siberia," he says. "I wrote down the names of German soldiers I met in the labor camps. "See here," he points to a name, "it's underlined. That man is dead, I saw it with my own eyes. He froze to death. Ah yes, and this one, he shot himself ..."

"How can you remember after all this time what happened to them?" Ernst wants to know. "It's been over eight years."

"Don't you see my system? Can't you spot it? Here, see the tiny circle. It stands for hanging. The period sign for shooting, the brackets for starvation and on and on. If there is no mark behind the name, that person is still alive." Ferdinand looks at his friend. Why can he not see what's so obvious?

"You better come with me to the Red Cross and explain. I'll bring you there," Ernst says. "But how do you know those soldiers without a mark in your notes are still alive?"

"They were alive and still might be, although some could have died later. You never know. Not in Siberia. Life and death, it's all the same. It happens so fast, within the blink of an eye."

"You want to talk about it?" Ernst says.

"No, I just want you to deliver this information to the authorities. And what do you mean, talk about it? What's there to chat about. The cruelty is beyond words, you have no idea." And with those words he walks away in haste. Enough for today. Let the living take care of the dead.

Ernst sits down on a bench in front of the farmhouse, looking at the scribbling beside names on Ferdinand's notes. Searching for places and names. For anything familiar. Suddenly he stops reading while screaming out loud.

"It can't be. Dear God." Like a wounded animal his outburst echoes in the yard. He runs toward the barn after the late returnee, grabs him by the shoulder, shakes him. Awake, talk to me. Is this real? "Who is the madman now?" Ferdinand says in a calm voice.

"Why didn't you tell me he is on your list? Why? And is he truly alive? There is no mark beside his name. What does it mean? The Red Cross declared him dead. They told us he died south of Stalingrad," Ernst says while handing the list back to Ferdinand.

"Wrong location. Not in my book, I met Walter north of Chita in Siberia. He was sent to a labor camp in the far north, I think close to Cap Deschnew or some other godforsaken place. That's were they mine lead, copper and cobalt. They call it the Gulag, slave labor camps where Josef Stalin imprisons millions to better themselves. That's where he even sends his own people, not just prisoners of war from Germany. I haven't heard of anybody who left there alive. But what do I know?" Ferdinand says.

"When, tell me, when did you see him in Chita?" Ernst asks.

"We went there by train, let me think. Yes, I remember the day because it was mother's birthday. Yes, I am certain, it was February 16th in 1944. Defiantly, that's the date." Ernst is pale like the freshly white painted window frame behind him.

"Impossible. My brother was declared dead a year earlier," Ernst finally says. "Walter's death date is the spring of 1943." Ferdinand looks horror-stricken. Is the impossible imaginable after all those years? For Ernst, the moment of joy is paired with agony. His brother is possibly alive, and if so, he is still married to Hilda.

That's all Ernst can think of. Himself, obsolete in person and on paper perhaps legally no longer a husband. What to think and hope for? It's been nearly nine years since Walter was seen alive. Siberia, dear God, a vast tundra of ice and snow for two thirds of the year with temperatures dipping to minus sixty degree. Pair that with hunger and hopelessness. Surviving such hardship would be a miracle.

Ferdinand puts his arm gently on the right shoulder of Ernst. What else is there to do? Poor man, just as damaged as those late returnees. They sit there in silence, for he cannot speak of those horrific acts of revenge he saw. Remembering the anger of young Soviet soldiers herding the enemy like cattle through a wasteland of ice and snow toward any of those five thousand labor camps.

"Nobody will be shot," Russian commanders say. "You'll die doing honest work in Russia."

With speedy trials most captured German soldiers are sentenced to twenty-five years labor camp. Guilty. Each and every one of them. No exceptions or leniency for enemies who are accused of destroying Russian landscapes.

Let them rebuild it, give them that shovel to dig. If needed, even their own graves. Although the war has been over for nine years, there is no chance anybody will be released soon. At least not as long as Josef Stalin is alive. He'll reign with an iron fist till his own demise. German prisoners of war cannot expect empathy, not from a dictator who even starves his own people. That reality is common knowledge not only among soldiers but also western politicians. Attempts of the new

German government to bring home their boys after all those years fail repeatedly.

And what about those displaced German civilians, caught during the hasty trek toward the west. Captured by Russian soldiers and also deported to Siberia. Nobody speaks of those women and children from Pomerania, Silesia and East Prussia who labor as living reparation payment in mines and bedrooms of the Russian Gulag. Wasn't the loss of their homeland as a collective punishment decided by Truman, Churchill and Stalin during their Potsdam Conference punishment enough? Ferdinand thinks.

Mustn't think or talk about it. Turn the page, lose the memory, Ferdinand tells himself. But how can he? So he just sits there with Ernst.

Two former soldiers.

Too young to be old.

Too old to feel useful.

Decimated to driftwood washed ashore.

Lifeless, useless, captured by individual agonizing memories. Hoping for a tide to take them somewhere. Anywhere but here.

Who do you talk to at home? Not to the women. Not to them about a man's world.

Alive or dead in Siberia, Ernst wonders. How often will I have to bury my brother? Wasn't once enough? Mustn't tell Hilda. It would only raise her hopes in vain. Giving her that straw would mean fire on both ends.

Damn hope. It's nothing but a seducer.

"I don't know where to go from here, what should I do? Should I tell my wife?" he now asks Ferdinand.

"No idea, I don't give advice. I am the wrong person to ask," he responds.

"But what would you do?" Ernst says.

"Nothing, absolutely nothing. That's what I would do. Let time take care of the future. It always does," he says. Ferdinand gets up, clinging to his beige walking stick.

"Made this myself, carved it from a weeping willow south of Moscow after I got shot in the leg. How ironic is that, a stick from a weeping willow in Russia. A present from the enemy. Stiff leg and a walking stick.

Nothing from the Germans, not even an Iron Cross. Ironical, no present from the *Führer*, don't you think?" Slowly, with small steps he walks away like an injured animal.

On his way back to Ten Eicken, Ernst stops at a familiar place to clear his thoughts.

The iron gate of the small private cemetery of Ten Eicken looks rusty except for the handle. Polished by many hands who reach out when visiting. For a moment Ernst pauses in front of his father's grave, Gunter. So many words left unsaid, questions unasked, chances missed. Too late now, the roads backward in time are closed. How Ernst misses his father. What would he do in his place? Inform the family about Walter's fate?

What do you want me to do? Ernst whispers now while looking at a pale wooden cross erected in memory of Walter, born 1920. Grandmother Agnes insisted to create this make-believe grave to remember the man when the Red Cross informed her of her son's death in 1943.

Ernst touches the cross gently. How often has his wife gone here? Too often, he knows.

"You miss him too," he suddenly hears a voice from behind. It sounds like a statement, not a question. "I come here as well when it get's unbearable. It's such a peaceful place." Hilda has spoken those last words with an unfamiliar softness in her voice. She places her arm around the shoulder of Ernst who is now quietly crying.

"There, there. I know, it's alright. Let's make a promise in his memory," she adds. "Let's bury our fights and try to get along for Walter. He would have wanted it that way."

Motionless Ernst listens while staring at the cross. Unable to respond to such sudden kindness his thoughts are frozen. He kneels down in front of the grave, pulling weeds and grass with awkward gestures.

"The cross, look at the cross. It only has his birth year," he now stutters while Hilda holds his right hand to stop his gardening.

"I know", she says. "We will engrave the year of his death too. In time, not now. Yes, in time, we'll close this chapter," Hilda says.

"Let's go home now. Let's find our own peace."

Without further talk they stroll toward Ten Eicken. He will not say a word about Walter's sighting in Russia, Ernst decides. Not now while he is on the mend with Hilda.

31

"What? He never told her that day about the possibility that uncle Walter was still alive," I ask Lotte after a long day of talking. "That is just terrible, really cruel."

"Dear girl, don't be so judgmental. You were not there during those years. Your father carried many scars from the war. And suddenly Hilda, who he always adored wanted to reach out to him. It was an opportunity for him to carry on, the truth would have killed that moment," Lotte explains.

"I don't believe he ever told her. Not that I know of. But maybe she found out another way? In any event, Hilda did not put the death date on Walter's cross as promised. Not for some time. Perhaps she knew more than we thought. I saw her a few times talking to Ferdinand, she even invited him over for supper. That late returnee was like an invisible link to the dead as well as missing soldiers. Although I must point out, Ferdinand never spoke about that list. At least, that's what I believe. But who knows?"

"Sometimes we say more with silence than with words. Anyhow, the relationship between Hilda and Ernst improved. We could hear the couple chatting and laughing at times. They were finally pulling on one rope into the same direction. They became a team. By necessity, with two small children. Birgit was now three years old, Manfred two. Adorable kids." Lotte looks at me. No need to explain. I know because I saw it later. She looked after my sister and brother, washing their diapers, making their meals, comforting them when they cried and reading stories at bedtime. It was Lotte, not Hilda.

"Don't judge, please," Lotte begs. "Your mother was a full-time professional entrepreneur. It's not that she did not care. She did but there was no time to balance family and business. Not during those years. It was a once in a lifetime chance to get ahead again, to make money. That was the priority for almost every family after the war. Pampering children like they do today just wasn't done. Time was a precious commodity not to be wasted any longer. Doesn't that make sense? After years of unrest and deprivations parents sought stability. And that, my dear, you can only gain with a solid financial base. Businesses and jobs came first. Naturally those baby boomers were not spoiled. At least not the ones I saw. Spartan upbringing seemed in order to teach values for a new beginning. It was different with my son Albert. He was born during the war, a child forced into adulthood before his time. Raising him with less authority made sense. Indeed, children born during the war saw enough cruelty. They deserved better."

"Tante Marlow," I now say softly, "don't we all?"

"I know, what you are getting at but you need to understand those times. Here we were with the trauma of a lost war and illusions, many with guilt and dark secrets in particular, but in general we were a nation of people eager to prove again worthiness as human beings by getting ahead," she says. "Building a nation once more, accumulating wealth became a priority in the fifties."

"And children?" I say. "So baby-boomers were just the by-product of the *Wirtschaftswunder* (economical miracle) families could afford once more? We were a commodity like the first Volkswagen?" Lotte seems angered when hearing those words.

"No and no once more. That's not how it was," she lectures me. "Having a family, giving birth to children also marked a return to normality. Your father adored the children." And Hilda?

"Her love was exhausted beyond capability, believe me. Caring yes, always caring for all and everybody. Loving? Well that's another story. We won't talk about that today," Lotte says.

She opens a photo album on the coffee table. It shows the Marlows in front of the main entrance of Ten Eicken. A smiling Lotte and grinning Albert. But husband Otto's face looks grim.

"My dear husband, bless his heart. So sad, he could not adjust or forget therefore he never felt at home in the Rhineland, not even on

Ten Eicken or later in our own house in Metzkausen. His body was here, his soul somewhere else. That constant inner split became unhealthy in time. In addition, politicians used the torment of displaced people for their own agendas and stepping stone in politics."

"Until the late sixties they kept our dreams of returning home to the east alive. Those promises were made by all political parties. Naturally, with over twelve million displaced persons, some three million alone from Pomerania, a lot of votes were at stake during elections in West Germany. We were valuable at the polls. Did we trust them? We wanted to but could not. At least not me. Remember this, displaced persons always arrive without a return ticket. Whoever promises the trip back home is lying."

"None of that propaganda ever touched me. I knew we were here to stay and master our own destiny in the west," Lotte says. "So I resigned my desires of returning one day. In addition I felt at home on Ten Eicken. I chose from day one to make it my new Pomerania."

"That's complacency, a form of treason, Otto complained. Never give in, never give up was his parole. And so he later went to every meeting for displaced persons, talked to organizers who mingled with politicians in hope of being among the first to return."

"What a waste of time, I told him. And what hours are you wasting serving Hilda, he'd snap right back at me. Yes, difficulties in marriages arise not only when money is scarce but also above a new found safety net. Because of new riches lifestyles were changing rapidly during the early fifties. Men demanded their former roles back as head of households and breadwinners. Even late returnees stopped whining. With their new found self-esteem they pushed women right back into *Noras Doll's House*."

"The surplus of seven million women in Germany was visible everywhere. We ran businesses, made deals by telling men what to do. No surprise, that's what we did for years when men battled on foreign soil forcing us to take the lead. But not any longer. Now men pushed to reclaim their former territory."

Lotte laughs. "Ha, ha, reclaiming ground. Not in Hilda's citadel, not one centimeter. She was not willing to share her reign after all those years. Not Hilda. She had plans, big intensions for Ten Eicken. Constant expansion of the restaurant business, remodeling of the interior to accommodate more guests and later adding a hotel kept all of us busy. On the estate we did our own thing, away from the visible scars the war left in cities."

"Sometimes I felt as if we lived on an island, cut off from the reality of political and social life of the times. We still didn't have television on Ten Eicken. We only had radio. But that's different. When you only listen, your mind has a chance to participate. Don't you agree?"

I nod because of what we know today about the uncritically view of everything American in the fifties and sixties, when the stability of the west was created on the foundation of fear for communism. Pictures helped to create that fear and cemented complacency.

"Germany made in the USA," new socialists complained. "Rather red than dead," was their parole when nuclear fear roamed the airwaves in Europe while in America people preferred to "rather be dead than red".

With money and propaganda the Americans intervened once again so that conservative German politicians prevailed. The financial support for the propaganda operations, as known today under the top secret operation *Pocket Book*, came from the CIA. They fashioned public opinion while modeling Germany in the image of America in culture, politics and economics. In countless cases they also placed former Germans with tainted histories in key political positions because of their expertise during the *Third Reich*.

"A joke and rather unjust, as we know today. But not then. We simply had no idea. And anyway, based on my personal experience of displacement, I did not mind the new American way. I would have rather wanted to be dead than red," Lotte explains.

"When after the fall of the Berlin Wall communism outlived itself with such a cruel track record by the likes of Stalin and Honecker, who would disagree today? Strange developments indeed. Who would have thought that east Germany would be reunited with the west after all those years? Maybe one day even East Prussia and Pomerania will be given back to Germany?" Lotte says.

"Did you know that the Russians, in particular Gorbachev, offered those lost territories back to German Chancellor Kohl and Foreign Secretary Genscher during their discussions about reunification? It was truly discussed behind closed doors. Imagine, Pomerania, my homeland. The village, our farm, the land. I still cannot believe it wasn't made public at the time," Lotte says.

"Of course, the Soviet Union asked for a high price, billions of dollars if they were to return those provinces. At least that's what Gorbachev wrote in his book. At the time, the German government apparently showed no interest in getting back Pomerania, Silesia or East Prussia. A pity. And yet, what would they have done with millions of displaced Polish people who were resettled there on former German territory after the war? Chase them back east? Impossible, those lands belong now to Russia," Lotte says.

"For politicians, borders are only lines on paper without individual faces. People and countries, ah yes, the pawns on the chessboard of kings and queens. We are a helpless bunch in essence, aren't we?"

"I have lived too long. I can't be surprised any longer," Lotte says with resignation in her voice. She straightens her apron while getting up slowly from the chesterfield.

"It's late. Go and see Albert to prepare for your trip to the east next month. I am certain, you'll have a lot to talk about."

"Why won't you come along? Aren't you interested in what it looks like now?" I ask her. "You must be wondering at times what happened to the house and land."

"Did you not listen?" she says. "Why go back and reignite desires? I understand that Albert wants to retrace his past. He was only six when we were expelled from Pomerania. And I realize you want to go along to write a story."

"You go, but let me be. After all these years some matters are best left alone," she adds. "And beware, sometimes we don't like what we'll find at the end of our search."

"I don't understand what she was trying to tell me," I say to Albert later.

"You may never find out but she definitely was not talking about our trip to Pomerania," he points out.

32

The nation is dizzy with excitement. Planning and building. Tomorrow has arrived. The early fifties take on speed.

Germans inhale the future by forgetting the past. Watch that train, it is racing far too quickly and getting ahead of the tracks. The conductor jumps off the engine, the passengers are on their own. Haven't we seen that before? Is that the station? Won't they crash again?

She screams and waits for the echo but the turmoil is only within. Hilda is bathed in sweat when she wakes up long before sunrise. So much to do with little time to think during her waking hours. But it's her choice, especially when it comes to the past.

Bury it deeper, put another shovel of soil on top.

Use your feet to trample the crumbs to even the landscape. No one will notice.

It's all good down there. Hidden for the time being.

How she longs to be there with Walter.

She brushes her shoulder-length hair while studying her face in the mirror. Sleep deprivation has left marks, her blue eyes bath in a ring of dark shadows. But they sparkle in anticipation of the day and tasks. So she wipes off her face last traces of sleepiness and braids her hair.

It is her hour in the silent hallways of Ten Eicken when husband Ernst and the staff are still asleep. She is usually the first to fire the stove with small pieces of quick burning poplar twigs to boil the water for coffee. Except today. The smell of freshly brewed beans lingers in the entrance of the kitchen. Lotte has beaten her to the task.

"I was too tired to sleep," Lotte says. "And I needed to see you before Ernst gets up." Her face looks worried as she hands a note to Hilda. "Your neighbor Ferdinand Schulte gave this to me just ten minutes ago."

"He was here at this early hour? Strange, he wants to talk to me privately," Hilda says after reading the note. "It's urgent. It doesn't say why in the note. I'll better go right away. Lotte, can you look after the children when they get up, please? And don't tell Ernst where I am.

Don't say a word. Or better, tell him, I went to town. He won't question my trip, we always need supplies." She grabs a red wool scarf from the hanger by the door.

"When will you be back?" Lotte asks but Hilda is already gone. She rushes out of the yard passes the cemetery and hurries up the hill toward Ferdinand's place. He is waiting for her, sitting on the bench in front of the cottage, watching her from afar.

He sees her red scarf like a lantern, marking the trail of a woman he also adores, the wife of his best friend Walter. When Hilda stretches out her hand to great him, Ferdinand points enthusiastic to his walking stick.

"Did you know, I made this from a weeping willow in Russia," he says.

"How fitting, weeping willow," she replies. "You haven't said much about those years in the east. Is that why you wanted to see me?" He shakes his head nervously.

"It's not about me but about you," he says.

But where to start? Not at the end. No, that would be a shock. So Ferdinand recalls the past, his transport as prisoner of war in Russia and the train station in Chita.

"And that's where I saw Walter in February 1944."

Hilda can barely breathe. What? Impossible. Did she hear 1944? What is he saying? Her husband died in 1943. She has the confirmation of his death in writing from the International Red Cross. Twice they told her.

What is Ferdinand talking about? Has he lost his mind. Many late returnees have, he would not be an exception.

"Have you gone crazy? It cannot be, it's not true. You've mixed up the years," Hilda whispers. "Don't do this to me, I cannot stand that pain again. When they informed me of Walter's death, I died too but was forced to keep on living. Which is worse, I cannot tell? Please, think again, try to remember that date. Look at me. Are you telling me he could still be alive?" Ferdinand nods without making eye contact.

"Who else knows about this encounter in Russia, tell me. Who knows?" she asks.

"I had to inform the Red Cross, you surely understand, don't you? I gave them a list with hundreds of names," Ferdinand says. "There is so much misinformation about the dead and missing. It's a tragedy in itself. Oh dear, if we could only rewind all those years. Hilda, Walter is my best friend and you are still his wife. I had to tell you in person before the authorities contact you." They sit side by side and stare toward the awakening of the day in the valley.

Soon it will be light. And life goes on because people carry it step by step toward the evening. Every day, often unwilling.

But they carry the burden of hours because the minutes rush their tasks.

"Hilda, listen to me. That's not why I called you over," Ferdinand says. "There is something else. And I don't know if it's all good news. I truly don't know. You see, when I went to the authorities with this list of German war prisoners in Russia to sort the missing from the dead for their archives, I may have made a mistake. Instead of being thankful that some records could now be revised to inform loved ones at home, I stumbled again over that precise German bureaucracy other nations hate us for."

"I don't understand, what are you saying?" Hilda asks.

"Well, the Allies have their own lists. Heaven knows from whom and under what circumstances they obtained those. In any event, Walter is listed as a person of interest who cannot be *denazified* if he should ever return from Russia. In essence, if he is alive they'll incarcerate him and put him on trial in Germany for crimes against humanity. For what exactly, I don't know? But it looks pretty serious, he will definitely be indicted." Ferdinand stops talking when he hears Hilda screaming and raising her fist.

"No, not Walter. I know him. No, not him," she says while pounding her hands on Ferdinand's chest. "He is a good man, I am sure he is innocent, he is a soldier like millions who simply following orders of wicked commanders. I won't have it, I will not believe it. Not Walter, not my husband."

"Calm down, please. I agree with you for I have known Walter since childhood," Ferdinand says, "But a good character reference from before the war doesn't matter to authorities now. We just lost a war, it only takes one person to denounce a fellow German these days and the hunt is on. The country needs individual perpetrators to white-wash a nation. Do you understand?"

"It won't come to that, he won't return," Hilda says with resignation in her voice. "You don't believe Walter is still alive, just because you saw him in 1944? He went to Siberia nine years ago. Do you know any survivors who reported back home from that frozen hell? And if so, are you telling me they can put them on trial in Germany after they have already suffered so much in Russian labor camps? Dear God, what world are we living in?"

"Hilda, listen. Please look at me," Ferdinand begs. "I want you to pay close attention. There is something else. Look at me, please. You have to be strong now. And you must promise to never tell anybody, not even Ernst or anybody else in the family. You can't even talk about this to your friend Lotte. Promise?" She is sobbing now. She is losing her composure. Can it get worse?

"Why, for heaven's sake why have you told me all this? You should have kept that information to yourself. It won't change anything except increase the agony of living with useless hope," Hilda says.

"I would have kept quiet, believe me," Ferdinand says. "Except for a promise I made to a friend yesterday. Walter begged me to talk to you, to prepare you with background information before you meet. Hilda, are you listening? Walter is here, your husband is back from the labor camps. Hilda, Hilda, can you hear me?"

She cannot. Not any longer.

Sinking within, her red scarf slides off her shoulders to follow the body.

Silence, quiet from sorrow and pain.

Drifting, perhaps floating with lightness further than far away. Neither up nor down.

Just there in space where stillness lives. Is this birth or death, day or night? No questions asked, no answers needed.

She once knew that place when she loved and was treasured.

33

Don't ask me about love. Talk to the lovers who endure years of agonizing separation without losing hope. Call it insanity to believe in the possibility of meeting again. It is beyond organized religion because it is pure faith.

Why do lovers believe? They don't, they simply know beyond reason. What has logic to do with love anyway? Nothing, not a thing. It's like energy in space beyond black holes. A knowing which cannot be calculated by mathematician because love is the sum of all uncertainties.

So don't ask me about those matters, speak to the lovers. Like Walter, who is sitting on a chair in the living room of that cottage and adoring his wife Hilda by simply looking at her. She fainted out there, the news was too much for her tired mind and body. Let her rest for a while. They can wait a while, if need be forever after all those years.

When Ferdinand brings a bowl of cold water and a cotton cloth, Walter shakes his head. Let her sleep, she will wake when she is ready.

"There is freshly brewed coffee in the kitchen, I'll be in the barn," Ferdinand whispers before he leaves.

Only the ticking of the floor clock interferes with total silence in the room while Walter just sits there. Waiting and watching her chest slowly moving up and down, breathing calmly. It takes another fifteen minutes, before Hilda finally wakes up. Her hand searches the edge of the couch sighing with relief when she touches his arm.

"I knew you were alive," she whispers. "I've felt it all those years."

Is she still dreaming or back in reality? Awake or asleep? She does not dare open her eyes to end this moment. How she longed to be reunited, to touch and caress. If only for one last time. She can feel him gently squeezing her hands. And then she hears his whispering voice.

"There were moments in that Siberian prison camp when I heard you calling out for me. Over and over I heard your voice," Walter says. He is hugging her now, his head is buried in her right shoulder. Like a little boy who has found his way back home in the dark. Their sobs melt. And then their bodies, hungrily they rise and dissolve. Touching and searching with her soft skin on his weather beaten and scarred chest.

If death is possible then let it be now. But the moment passes and later words follow. He brushes her hair from her forehead, following the lines of her smile with his index finger along her cheeks. Never, during all those years of desperation in the Siberian gulag did death cross his mind. Determination and hopes of returning home kept him going.

Now that he feels safe and alive, he is ready to die. This very moment. With or without her. That's what love can do to lovers. But looking at Hilda, he pushes his agonizing thoughts aside while watching his wife getting dressed.

She smiles but knows without saying. Walter is not the same man she remembers, the lover she longed for all those years. He is like a damaged package. Inside and out. When Hilda looks closely, now that broad daylight streams over his shoulders, she utters a faint cry. His once muscular body now disappears in his clothes. And his eyes, his beautiful sparkling eyes. They look gray, as gray as his skin, resembling an old man. Walter looks like his own father.

But there is something else, way beneath his boney body. Invested deeply beyond his soul. Removed, remote. A stranger within a familiar body. He is here with Hilda in that very same room. But is it him?

During his dreadful yeas in labor camp he fell out of love. Mainly with himself. Even Hilda's touch cannot reach him skin-deep. Frostbites linger beneath, no warmth to hold and melt what's petrified during lone hours of suffering in prisoner of war camps. Walter knows but he too keeps quiet. He smiles to help her remember the man she used to know. But war has fogged familiarity. He is still absent from the present.

Where is he now this very moment? She wonders while trying to recover pictures of afternoon strolls through the forests when they were younger, and pending war was only a conversation topic not to be taken seriously. What a handsome man her Walter was before the war.

But look at him now. In board daylight he appears like a stranger. The distance between them has no chance to shrink in this small cottage. She can hardly breathe to overcome the awkwardness of the moment. True, he is still her husband, the one she married on the eve of war. But looking at him now, Hilda suddenly feels as if she committed adultery with this man.

How is it possible to love someone and loathe yourself at the same time? What to say? How to overcome the gap time has widened? He needs me, she thinks. That's all. Like a child not the man she used to know. He is drowning, she tells herself. I owe him.

And it is pity, the worst kind of love, which motivates her now to speak.

"I will take care of you now, you'll get better soon," she says while caressing his forehead. She recalls Ferdinand's report prior to their meeting. "Don't worry about anything, just rest and recuperate. We will clear your name, all will be well. You'll see," she says. "And then I am going with you, I will leave Ten Eicken. Now that you've returned, the marriage to your brother Ernst must be declared void. We'll start anew. Just the two of us. We'll reset the clock to carry on where we left off. That's what we'll do."

She is talking herself into an optimistic mood, hoping it will be contagious. But Walter just sits there while watching her lips move.

Like a little boy he listens with intensity. The sound of her voice is like music to him. A woman talking, his wife. But her words of promise to clear his name quickly become meaningless, for he knows better. And while she talks about their son Wilhelm and how well he is doing on her father's farm in Westphalia, he smiles at her with encouragement. Walter begs her to keep on talking, to inform him of every event he missed while he was gone. She now speaks about his mother Agnes and the family, her own children with his brother Ernst and even about Lotte, her best friend from Pomerania.

Without interruption Hilda reports to the returned soldier the headlines of a life missed at home. For hours she chats while he watches her face, her full lips and strong gestures with both arms. He soaks in her presence like a man dying of thirst while drowning in the depth of her blue sparkling eyes.

"Now you talk, say something," she encourages him. For a brief moment he hesitates. But the late afternoon requires a sudden return back to reality.

"I cannot stay long, they'll come after me soon. The authorities know that I've returned to Germany. I am on the list of late returnees from Russia," he mumbles. "I have to leave the country, perhaps within a week," Walter says.

"Hilda, I know you mean well and want to help me but it's impossible. There is no way my name will be cleared within weeks. It may take months, perhaps even a year. And I cannot endure another hour in a prison cell. Never again. Not for a moment. I would suffocate. Do you understand that?" he asks. "My conscience is clear, I have not committed any crimes. For heaven's sake I was only a foot soldier, not a commander. The government can't hold that against me. What did I do? I don't even know the accusations against me. Who denounced me? I have no answers to all those questions," he says.

"What does it matter, they'll put me in prison and ask questions later," he speculates. "And that I cannot allow, not after what I've been through. I'd rather be dead."

Hilda shakes her head with bewilderment while hugging him. He then tells her that he even refused an order to shoot at civilians in Poland and was considered a war resistor by the Nazis. Shouldn't that make him a hero now in the aftermath of war?

"But forms of such heroism don't count because they don't get investigated. No Hilda, there is no chance for us. You must forget me. Stay with Ernst. My brother needs you," Walter says. She is crying now. What is he telling her? How can he utter such a request?

"It's you I love," she whispers. "I can't carry on if I lose you again. Please take me with you." He shakes his head while freeing himself from her embrace.

"You know I can't take you. You know that better than me," he says with a firm voice. "I'll be a fugitive. Wanted, a runaway. No Hilda, you have to stay. Think about your children and Ten Eicken. You are needed here." He takes a deep breath while pulling her once again close to him.

"Listen, it will be all good. There is an organization in Italia, I can't tell you the name. But Catholic priests help to obtain new identities and passages from Genoa to South America," he explains.

"Don't look at me that way, I know they call it the rat-route," Walter says. "But you know me better, don't you? I am not one of those scumbags who committed such unspeakable atrocities. I swear. You believe me, don't you? Like my brother Ernst and friend Ferdinand, I simply fought in battles where at the end of all wars illusions are send to the slaughterhouse. So gruesome …"

"You don't have to tell me about those years today. Perhaps one day you might want to. But not now," Hilda says. "We have to clear your name. Perhaps it's all a misunderstanding. A message mixed up during transmission like the declaration of your death? Bureaucrats make mistakes. We'll take them to court if we have to …"

"And drag the family name and Ten Eicken into the mud with a trial?" Walter says. "Never, I won't have it. Let me hide for a while at least until we find a way to sort out this mess. Promise you won't tell anyone that you saw me and don't tell anybody about my plans. You must pledge and swear," he begs. Hilda is crying again while he holds her tighter.

Their union is the desperation of love threatened by departures. A brief encounter of stolen moments during a lifetime of turmoil. Before the war, during the war and even now. Can it be that the depth of love can only be measured by anticipation and attempts to reunite? It that the base of its strength? The longing of naivety within chaos?

"I promise I won't tell," Hilda finally utters while hugging him. "But I must see you again before you leave. I just have to, please. There is so much I haven't told you yet. As soon as I get home, I'll probably remember what else I wanted to say to you. Always afterward, isn't it? That's when we remember. Mostly when it's too late." She hugs him once more.

"Ferdinand will know where I am, he will contact you," he says when they finally step outside the cottage. How can it be getting dark already? It wasn't even light when she arrived. On her way down the valley she turns around numerous times to wave back at Walter until the gloom swallows his silhouette.

She straightens her dress and tends to her hair before making her way into the yard of Ten Eicken an hour after supper time. Avoiding the main entrance, she uses the kitchen door to rush to her private room.

But her efforts are noticed. And a few minutes later she is startled by a firm knock on her bedroom door.

"Are you still awake?" she hears the voice of Ernst. "I was worried, we need to talk." When she opens the door, he is holding her red scarf.

"I think you lost this. It's yours, isn't it?" Of course, the scarf. How did she forget? She was wearing it when sitting outside the cottage with Ferdinand, when he spoke and she fainted. But then she woke up and lived. And loved again after all those years. Why worry about a silly scarf? Ernst stands there with her scarf as if holding a piece of evidence, demanding an explanation. But quickly she regains composure. He won't win. Not against her.

With anger, Hilda pulls the scarf out of his hand. Has he been spying on her? How much does he know? she wonders.

"Lotte tells me you went to town to buy supplies. So what did you get?" Ernst questions her. He is playing a game, she senses. And she is in no mood to go along.

"If you found the scarf you know that I did not go to town. So what do you want? Make it quick, I am rather tired," Hilda says. Ernst just stands there, he expected a lie and was ready to respond. But this? She is now in command, he is losing charge of the moment.

"I spent the day with Ferdinand, he called for me," Hilda says. "And you know damn well you should have told me, instead of keeping this a secret. How could you?"

"What should I have told you? What ...?" Ernst stutters now.

"I am talking about the list, the names of missing and fallen soldiers Ferdinand made in Russia. You kept that to yourself, didn't you? Had no guts to share that Walter might still be alive in a Russian labor camp."

There it is, out in the open. The half-truth, always convincing and defeating the opponent while making the king a pawn. Ernst looks speechless. So that's what this is all about. He looks at this wife, attempting to apologize.

"I am sorry, so sorry. I was jealous, I thought that Ferdinand and you, you know what I mean. I didn't know your visit was about the list," Ernst whispers.

"I should have told you, I realize now. Please forgive me but I was afraid of giving you false hope that Walter could still be alive in a Siberian labor camp? Nobody survives that gulag. Nobody."

Before she closes the door, Hilda pets Ernst on his right cheek.

"You are right, survival would be a miracle. That list is out-dated. Ferdinand made far too much fuss about it. Good night," Hilda says.

After she shuts the door she puts her hand over her mouth, afraid of screaming. She hears his slow footsteps on the wooden hallway, the echo of defeat. He doesn't know, she is convinced. His jealousy of Ferdinand placed blinders over his eyes. Walter's resurrection remains a secret for now.

34

Stay with the half-truth and avoid communication. Let the moment pass and hope for tomorrow. An attitude which saves the day for Hilda, because that next morning Ernst evades to continue that conversation from last night. Instead the couple chats and giggles around the breakfast table about menial tasks with far too much ease. An intoxicating euphoria is in the air. But it is too fake for Lotte's taste. She knows her friend and cannot be fooled. But is it her business? Not if Hilda is happy. Is she really?

Like a silly clown she entertains her husband and the children, louder and quicker as if the day after tomorrow can be caught before the fact. She races through the motions to avoid thoughts of clarification and self-reflection.

"Isn't it a marvelous day?" she says to Lotte.

"As good as yesterday and the day before," her friend points out. Hilda stops talking. Any more small talk and Lotte will become suspicious.

"Your son Wilhelm is coming on Friday to stay for the weekend," Lotte says now. "Yesterday your father phoned. He'll put the boy on the morning train from Soest so he should arrive around noon. Do you want Otto to pick him up from the train station?"

Not this time, Hilda thinks, she has her own plans. She will go herself.

The mother will meet her son, Walter's son at the platform. Friday, that's two days from now. Her father mentioned on the phone that the boy has been lonely. But not to see her, Hilda knows. He is coming for grandma Agnes who will be celebrating her seventieth birthday.

As always when Wilhelm visits, Hilda will pack presents and two pounds of coffee to bring to her cottage. They still don't talk but at least Hilda tries to communicate through kind gestures. Agnes has never rejected her offerings but neither has she thanked her. Not once.

"Before I forget it, the Red Cross phoned twice. Someone will be coming to Ten Eicken later this afternoon," Lotte says.

When the delegate of the organization arrives, the announced visitor is not alone. Two officers from the local police detachment have come along. In civilian clothes. It's a delicate matter. Bureaucrats screwed up twice, they now have to be careful while questioning the assumed widow. Or more precise, the wife of a suspected war criminal.

In silence, the officers sip their coffee at the kitchen table while Hilda is waiting for their questions. An awkward situation for both parties. But then it gets official. Without mercy it's government business. But Hilda is prepared.

Yes, of course she knows that Walter was last seen in Chita, her neighbor Ferdinand told her just yesterday. No surprise there. So what are they trying to say, he is still alive? And does that make her a bigamist sanctioned by the government who declared him dead in 1943 and therefore permitted her new marriage? What exactly do those bureaucrats want from her? Can't they leave her alone, hasn't she suffered enough?

"We have reason to believe that Walter Eicken recently crossed the border into Germany," the officer now says. "He was on the list of late returnees to that *Friedland* camp in the north. We assume, he will contact you first. When that happens we need to know it immediately."

"He has returned? What are you telling me?" Hilda yells suddenly. "You told me twice he is dead. And now you are saying he might be alive? Which one is it? What is true?" Hilda mumbles."

"Alive? How do you know? You've made mistakes before? Has anybody seen Walter? Dear God," she adds while jumping up and leaning against the wall. She will faint if she has to. One officer now gently holds on to her while grabbing a chair. Silently they wait while Lotte puts a glass of water into her hand.

"You better leave now," Lotte says to the men. "Can't you see, what this is doing to her? Don't you people have any empathy?" Hesitantly the officers retreat into the hallway. But they are not done yet. After opening a black leather briefcase one man hands a letter to Lotte.

"You give this to Frau Eicken, make certain she reads it immediately," he says while glancing into the kitchen where Hilda has now buried her face into her hands. She is sobbing.

"As soon as she feels better you give her this note. You may as well let her know this is not over. We'll be back."

But Lotte is no hurry to comply after the officers leave. She watches their car pull out of the yard. Slowly she returns to the kitchen where Hilda is setting the table for supper, attending to chores as if nothing happened. A surreal situation. For both women who just stand there without searching for words. One knowing, the other suspecting. Both understanding the dilemma in one form or another.

When Lotte hands her the note, Hilda just folds it before putting it into her apron pocket. She cannot be bothered to read the details. They are looking for him, that she knows. And now it is documented. Her assumptions are confirmed later when she is alone in her room. She has to inform her neighbor Ferdinand to warn Walter. The accusations against her husband now have a place and apparently even eyewitnesses.

"We cannot discuss this over the phone, why don't we meet at the Eicken private cemetery around noon tomorrow. It's only a short distance from your cottage," she urges Ferdinand the next morning.

Sneaking out again. Lotte watches, as Hilda hurries through the back entrance to avoid Ernst and farm workers who crowd into the kitchen for lunch. But their hectic schedule leaves little time to pay attention. Lotte keeps them busy, she feels like a collaborator in a story where plot and characters are missing while protecting Hilda. From what, she does not know. But secrecy needs allies. Lotte is more than a willing friend.

Why is it always so quiet in graveyards? Hilda thinks. We whisper and tiptoe carefully as if we are afraid to disturb the dead. Is it because we are dismayed of waking them? They surely cannot hear us and neither do they care.

Hilda slows down her steps before she opens the rusty gate. The squeaking sound interrupts the stillness but cannot surprise the man standing in front of a wooden cross in awe. But it's not her neighbor Ferdinand.

"That is more than unusual. It's not often you get to stand in front of your own grave," Walter says while turning around. He reaches for her hand. They sit in the shadow of an oak trees. When Hilda shows him the note the officers left the other day, Walter is not surprised. What else was there to expect but a warrant for his arrest. The accusations are ridiculous, he tells Hilda. He has never been in that Polish town of Nowy Sacz where he apparently committed those atrocities against unarmed civilians.

"How do you pronounce that Nowy Sacz? Where is that anyway, wasn't that in Silesia, German territory before the war," Walter asks.

"I looked it up on a map," Hilda explains. "It's a community southeast of Krakow. It has always been Polish. "Where you there with your unit?" Walter shakes now his head angrily. Why is she asking? Doesn't she trust him either?

"This is a lie, a set-up. But by whom and for what reasons? Who will gain by defaming me?" he says.

"We need the names of those two men who apparently witnessed the shooting of civilians in that village during the war," Hilda says. "That's the only way to prove that the story has been fabricated." She looks at her husband. His thinness makes him look even taller than she remembers.

"You say, you don't know the town of Nowy Sacz?" she says. "Why don't you tell the authorities to clarify the situation? I'll go with you, we'll do this together."

"So you think they'll believe me? No chance," he says. "Those Nazi tribunals. Do you have any idea how arbitrary they are meanwhile, replacing old injustice with new injustice? No, I cannot risk to expose myself to that kind of revenge." He turns sideways to look at her.

"If you only knew how it is. How often did I want to give up during those past nine years? It would have been so much easier. Many of my friends did, they just vanished by choice. Walked right out there into the Siberian landscape at night during fifty below. Couldn't take it any more," he says without looking at Hilda.

"No, we can't go to the authorities. Ferdinand is helping me, I am going to Italy to sail to South America." Walter is angry now. Outraged and aggravated. This is not his fatherland any longer.

Why wasn't he born thirty years earlier or twenty years later. Too old or too young then to participate in prescribed aggressions. But no, time decided his fate as well as the destiny of millions of other men.

"Nonsense. Born earlier, how would we have met? And later? We wouldn't have had our son Wilhelm," Hilda says. And then she tells him with excitement that his son, the boy who was born after he left, is arriving at the railway station on Friday.

Is he listening? Wilhelm, his son is visiting Ten Eicken. He is coming tomorrow by train. She tells him to make certain Walter will be there to take a glimpse. A brief hello and a long farewell. The child won't realize who that man is, she won't tell the boy.

35

How she misses the tranquility of the ride by buggy and horses to town when anticipation rises by slowing down time. Not any longer, now that gasoline is available again. They too use a motor vehicle now.

Hilda is prepared. She packed a rather large bag last night which neighbor Ferdinand now quickly shoves into the backseat of his car, a beige 1938 *Opel Kapitän*. Within twenty minutes they reach the railway station. Ten minutes ahead of the train's scheduled arrival.

"What's with the bag?" Ferdinand asks.

"I am leaving, I am going with Walter to South America," she says without hesitation. "I am certain he'll be at the railway station to see his son. And then I'll hop on that train to go with him. He needs me. I have thought it out well. You'll take Wilhelm to the farm, won't you?" The firm tone of her voice disallows any further discussion. They wait in silence in the car, starring at the railroad tracks as if determination could speed up the arrival of the train.

But the train is late and the minutes grow longer. Ferdinand steps out of the car to smoke a cigarette. He glances at the brick station where few people wait. Who wants to travel anyway after just returning home from a long war? he thinks.

Going somewhere is the agonizing absence of being at home with yourself. No, he will not leave for some time to come. He has arrived. His hand reaches for his right pocket to feel the envelope. Money for Walter. He will need it to buy a new identity when he gets to Genoa. But what about Hilda? He cannot afford to take her. A second fugitive slows down any trip. And doesn't she realize the consequences of her decision, leaving behind three children, a second husband and Ten Eicken? Blinded by love or her own entrapment of a predictable future? Which is it? You can't have it both ways. Make up your mind.

"I know what you are thinking," Hilda says when Ferdinand sits down in the car again. "But I have to go, I am drowning in this valley with Ernst by my side. I need to leave. Don't you get that?" She stops speaking abruptly when she hears the whistle of a train entering the station.

She rushes out of the car followed by Ferdinand without grabbing her bag from the backseat. Hilda's eyes are glued on the train. Which door will her son exit?

When she spots Wilhelm, she runs toward him while the boy slowly climbs down those stairs from the train. Her arms, not his are holding and caressing for minutes. How tall he looks. Wilhelm has grown another six centimeters since his last visit. She takes his suitcase to leave the station. Only when walking toward the car, she suddenly spots Ferdinand with Walter who is wearing a long green coat and black hat, pulled down over his forehead. He looks somewhat disguised wearing a fake grey mustache.

While the boy admires Ferdinand's car, asking numerous questions about make and speed, Hilda is now whispering to Walter. Although few words are exchanged their gestures tell the story. Her waving arms extend the urgency of phrases until Walter finally shakes his head.

Several times.

"I want to meet him," he tells her now.

"But you can't tell him, promise," she says. He nods while they walk toward the car.

"This is Ferdinand's friend," Hilda says to Wilhelm. The boy just glances with little interest at the stranger. He wants to know more about that automobile in front of him.

"Here, you want to sit in the driver's to get a closer look?" Walter offers, while lifting the child into the car. Wilhelm gets exited.

"Can I drive it?" he asks.

"Not just yet. But maybe next year when your feet can reach the clutch and brakes, perhaps then we can give it a spin," Walter says.

"Promise?"

"Yes, we will do that."

And then they just stand there in the parking lot waiting for the next train to Munich which connects to Genoa. The train is due to arrive in twelve minutes. It is the child, who finally brakes the awkward silence of the adults.

"Ferdinand is a soldier, are you a war hero too?" the boy asks Walter.

"A hero? I don't know. No, I don't think so," he answers.

"Well, my father was a hero but he died in the war," Wilhelm explains.

Hilda has stepped behind the boy and hugs him now, while looking at Walter.

"You climb into the car now, we'll be off soon," she says with an urgency in her voice. "Go now." She quickly embraces Walter one last time before opening the side door.

While hesitating for a moment, the child seizes with keenness the appearance of the stranger in front of him. He climbs into the backseat of the car while pushing a heavy bag on the backseat aside.

Only later when the car pulls back into the farmyard of Ten Eicken, Wilhelm starts wondering why his mother hugged this stranger at the train station. Perhaps because he is a friend of neighbor Ferdinand?

No way, the boy tells himself. Outside the family, Germans don't hug, they only shake hands. That's how they are raised, to keep distance.

However, Americans hug all the time, he has seen that in movies. Maybe that man was an American. A plausible solution, Wilhelm decides. But then again the stranger had no accent. He spoke German like Ferdinand.

"Stop nagging me. What is this? Are you a detective now?" Hilda says while showing her son to his room. "The man's name is Roland Schmidt and he is a good friend of Ferdinand. They were in the war together. They are buddies. And talking about buddies, Albert has been waiting all afternoon to see you."

Stupid and foolish. Hilda curses her own actions while putting on her work-clothes. Of course, Walter rejected to make her a co-conspirator on his trip out of the country. He refused to discuss the matter of her leaving the farm and three children. It would be foolish, selfish and even childish to think about something like that.

But how his eyes shone, how proud he was when he saw his son Wilhelm. It was worth the risk. And when he said good-bye, Hilda hugged Walter. A careless act in front of the boy. An activity which, of course, created suspicion.

How could she jeopardize a secret so lightly? That's not like Hilda. She usually takes control. Like now, when she pushes the suitcase she took to the station back under her bed and pretends nothing occurred that day.

Further precautions need to be taken. What, if she is pregnant with Walter's child after that day in the cottage? She decides right then that she will visit her husband's bedroom tonight. Just for one night.

When she later returns to the kitchen, Lotte's son Albert is still waiting. No, he has not talked to Wilhelm, that boy went right away to the cottage of grandmother Agnes. He left an hour ago. No use for Albert to wait here any longer, he needs to finish his chores in the barn.

That's were Wilhelm's absence puts him. In a place with the farmhands, not in the pastures which once they roamed as children in search of adventures. They were small then.

But the tall teenager Albert feels even smaller today.

36

Only two more days and her son will return to the farm in Westphalia. Will Hilda notice? Wilhelm spends nearly all his time with Agnes without showing any interest in his half-siblings Birgit and Manfred. The work on the farm and in the restaurant leaves little time to pay attention to such details.

Even Albert resigns his desire to rekindle the past with his former friend.

Ten Eicken functions like a well-oiled machine.

All parts are in place.

No spares needed.

Wilhelm realizes he is only a visitor on the estate he was born.

His family membership expired.

"What is she doing here?" Ernst says to Hilda while pointing out of the window toward the garden. For over six years he has not talked to his mother Agnes and now that woman is walking toward the mansion.

If she comes through that door, Ernst thinks, I'll throw her out. But his mother keeps her distance by some twenty meters to the entrance. Between the rows of potatoes and peas in the garden. She stands there, uncertain how to proceed.

She is leaning on a walking stick to the right while grandson Wilhelm is holding her left hand. They stop in front of a pale wooden bench. Slowly she takes a seat. Tenderly the boy wraps her silk-scarf around her shoulders.

"What boldness to show her face here. It doesn't matter what she wants, I certainly won't talk to her," Ernst says. But Hilda is not listening, she has left the house and hurries toward the garden. What if the old woman is sick and needs her help? Never in all those years has Agnes found her way back to the mansion. Considering her pride, this path takes more than physical efforts.

When Hilda pauses in front of the bench, Agnes tells Wilhelm in a kind voice to leave. The adults need privacy.

"This is not a courtesy call, you know that, don't you?" Agnes says after the boy disappears into the house.

"I am here because of Wilhelm, I wouldn't have come for any other reason, believe me. But he is just a child. My grandchild." She looks at Hilda with a keen sense. Her daughter-in-law looks prettier than she remembers.

"So why don't I get right to the point?" Agnes continues. "I realize how much you must despise me but I am what I am and I won't make excuses. I am too old for such nonsense ..."

"Your behavior wasn't always fair to say the least, but I don't hate you," Hilda says. "I dislike what you did but not enough to condemn you." Hilda points to the window where Wilhelm and Ernst watch the encounter of the women from a distance. They cannot hear what is being said but watch with fascination.

"Yes, he is just a child but he is my son," Hilda points out. "And you are not responsible for his education. Why do you think I sent him away to stay with my father? You surely don't believe I am that disinterested and cold hearted to part with my son for my own convenience. Or is that what you think?" But Agnes is not listening, her mind is lining up her own thoughts to formulate words which will launch her surprise attack on the present. Not the past. She needs to know as all mothers need to know.

"He was at the train station, wasn't he? You hugged him," Agnes now says. "I know it was my son Walter, don't even try to lie. The Red Cross informed me as well about the wrong death certificate. Little Wilhelm has no clue, but when he described the man you hugged at the train station I knew instantly."

"I am aware the authorities are looking for him but you must tell me. No one else needs to know, nobody, except you and me. Please, I am his mother. Is he well, is he healthy?" She is sobbing now, the old woman has lost her composure.

What predicament, Hilda thinks. If she tells the truth she will break her promise of secrecy. Staying silent will surely break a mother's heart. The dilemma of love. There it is again. No one must know that he is on his way to South America, Hilda decides for herself. As long as his secret is safe, the former German soldier will only be one of thousands who are leaving Europe. Unrecognizable to authorities, a man on a trail without a path. Hilda cannot risk his safety by talking now.

Old age has made Agnes lonely. Once she knows, she will tell. Her urge will grow to share. And in time her daughter Gisela and husband Fritz will lure the secret away from her. They'll suck it right out of her sparkling eyes, her new-found happiness and purpose. Gisela will serve freshly brewed coffee and chocolate cake on a windy afternoon just before dusk. The creation of coziness will offset suspicion of falsehood. It will overwhelm and weaken the old woman's resistance. Agnes will finally succumb and share whatever Hilda says today. And Walter will be failed by the two women who love him most.

Carefully Agnes watches Hilda's face as if searching for unknown expressions to read what stays unspoken. Finally her daughter-in-law reaches for both of her hands and caresses them tenderly. Hilda's unexpected empathy overwhelms the old woman. Within seconds Agnes recognizes the honesty and sincerity of love by the kind of daughter she always wished for but never had.

While they look at each other without saying another word, Agnes now smiles with relief. She came for Walter but his absence gave her Hilda. It will do for now, she thinks. It's more than she hoped for this morning. She quickly hugs Hilda before getting up from the bench.

"For whatever it's worth now after all those years," Agnes whispers, "but Walter chose well when he married you. You are more than his keeper, thank you."

With steady steps she walks past the property line toward her cottage. Not once she turns back to look at Hilda. Their moment has past. No need to share it with spying eyes behind curtains. Here and across the yard.

37

"Perhaps it is easier to let go, when the distance to your final destination gets shorter," Lotte tells me the next day during lunch. "Age not only tires the body but also the mind. Letting go of grievances is a relief. Too bad we don't realize that when we are younger. It could spare us a lot of pain. All this secrecy, the ballast and garbage we carry with us for ages. It's tiring, it drains you. And for what?" She looks at me as if expecting an answer. "Don't say to protect others, that would be too easy," she adds.

"I can still see the two women in the garden that day. Such a tender, forgiving moment. We felt like thieves behind those curtains, stealing with our eyes what we could not hear," Lotte continues. "No, we never learned that day what was said. Only many years later we found out. At that time we still did not know the fate of uncle Walter. There were accusations of war crimes but that was common during those years. Returning soldiers were picked up ever so often, questioned and released soon after."

"Oh yes, the search and justification. You know, the hunt for perpetrators is still on today, nearly fifty years after the war. Not only in Germany. As you know, they are also looking for collaborators in France, Poland and Italy," Lotte says.

"That search intensified especially in the sixties and seventies. Your mother would get a fit when she saw on television ninety year old men being dragged into courtrooms to stand trial. Of course, the likes of Eichmann and Mengele needed to be hunted down and sentenced. Such atrocities during the war. Terrible. But your common soldier? How guilty was he?" Lotte shakes her head.

"Show me a soldier anywhere who always behaves like a caring human being during times of conflict? We don't know the half of it but we judge. We assess matters from a distance without taking a look up close. But let me get back to the story. To those glorious early fifties."

"Somewhat absurd, when I think about it today. Naturally, it was all about money and prosperity. Everywhere. We now chased shadows casting the path ahead without looking back to see what was trailing us. Economical miracle years catapulted us into a lightness of existence we never dreamed of. Everything was possible. Otto and Albert finished building our private house in Metzkausen while the restaurant on Ten Eicken flourished. Even farming made money for a change. Your father specialized in dairy products and potatoes. Two tractors were purchased while horses retired to the pasture. How Otto missed plowing the fields by hand. Automation was not for him. He rejected driving a tractor. In Pomerania we got the work done without such fancy machines, he argued."

"Of course, with more technology fewer farmhands were needed. Even on Ten Eicken. And among those leaving to work in the factories was also my husband Otto. It was not just the money, although he got paid twice as much in the city. No, he was still restless, he needed to move toward something new. Or away from familiarity. Meanwhile I continued working on Ten Eicken. I could not let Hilda down. Our common project, the restaurant, made us inseparable."

"But it was more than the business. Our struggle after the war had brought us closer. It was this kinship women develop, an affinity out of necessity without the help of men. In addition, we both loved the farm. Even Albert spent most evenings and weekends to help on the estate. He felt more at home on Ten Eicken than in our new house in Metzkausen."

"Those were wonderful backbreaking years Hard on the body but easy on the mind. Always forward without looking back. No wonder, that only nine years after the war, history was collecting dust in archives. Silence. No talk. Until the next generation went to school."

"They were taught in classrooms what no one dared to even whisper at home. Soon children began questioning their parents. Dear Lord, the accusations that came out of their little mouths. The teacher told them, so it must be true. Why are their own parents lying about Nazi Germany? What are they denying, it's right here in those books. Teachers don't make up stories. Or do they? We are all bad. That's what we learned today."

"Time was catching up," Lotte says. "The silence at home and the teachings at schools clashed and exploded everywhere. Imposed history lessons in schools resulted in self-loathing for a whole generation. It created self-hatred while in addition the rest of the world began pointing fingers at us. I don't have to tell you or?"

Still haunted by the sins of our fathers. No, there is no need for Lotte to expand on that chapter. I leaned early enough when visiting neighboring Holland how vendors in Venlo refused even fifteen years after the end of the war to sell candy to a German child because their country was invaded by those Krauts. And twenty years later, when a professor wanted to fail my grades in an American college because of all the atrocities my people had done to his family in Belgium. Or thirty years on, when a reporter in Canada accused me of running the office like a Gestapo camp because I asked him to work a little bit harder.

Often I tried to explain my heritage; but to people who uttered offenses it made no difference when I pointed out, that I was born long after the war and my parents were good people, country folk, farmers.

"We will never be forgiven, will we?" I ask Lotte. "Even the generation after me will carry the torch burning on both ends. Politicians will make sure of that, won't they?"

Tenderly she strokes my cheeks. "You had nothing to do with that. But ignorant people don't differentiate, they view the world in black and white while missing the beauty of colorful rainbows. That's what they were taught," she says. "So there, don't you ever sulk in self-pity, show them who you are and be proud while doing so. You have nothing to hide or loathe yourself for. Not you, not your generation."

"Let me go back to the story in the mid-fifties when you were born," Lotte points out. "What a beautiful day it was. The cherry trees were in blossom and scents of spring filled the air. What a time to awake. Your father was beside himself with joy that day. It rejuvenated his sense of family he believed lost. We'll name her Christina in honor of my favorite aunt, Ernst said. Even Hilda, who was never a baby-person suddenly showed extreme tender maternal care when you were born. She was holding and cuddling you, unwilling to let go. It was strange, rather unusual."

38

She is snuggling Christina tightly while thinking of Walter. Where is he now? Will she ever see him again? Her husband Ernst reaches for the baby with pride. His third child with Hilda, a gift during these months of upheaval within the family. First his mother Agnes shows up on the property and then those court officers who claim his brother did not die during the war but was released from a Russian labor camp a year ago.

Hello, he said to them, it's 1954 and nearly a decade since the fighting stopped. Nobody returns this late except as ink on a printed piece of paper that lists the names of fallen soldiers.

Why can't his family be left in peace to simply live life with revived lust? Hasn't this country stolen enough time from his generation? What else? But the officers persist when revisiting Ten Eicken. Walter is wanted in connection with war crimes in Poland. So they say. Not as an eyewitness. No, it's a much more serious matter.

"Just phone us if he shows up," they order Ernst.

Yes, phone them? As if his brother moseys from the Siberian Gulag straight into the mansion of Ten Eicken. Really, perhaps during a surprise visit? Who phantoms such wild imagination?

"For sure, you'll be informed right away," Ernst says mockingly.

"I tell you what, if he shows up, I'll drive him right over to your office. How about that?" As if that will ever happen, Ernst thinks, but when the officers warn him that harboring a fugitive is a punishable offense, he utters no further words. His brother Walter on the run? Never, not his proud brother.

But there it is again, the threat of punishment by German bureaucrats. Before and during the war, the Eicken brothers as all young men were conditioned to absolute obedience within the *Wehrmacht* (German Army). To follow orders or be shot as resisters. And now a new German consciousness seeks punishment in the aftermath because soldiers obeyed? Annoyed Ernst shuts the door after the bureaucrats leave. He suddenly feels old, way beyond his years. Contemplating about the past, his generation has no permission to forget.

He cuddles little Christina. Perhaps there is hope for her.

For another hour he sits alone in the library, rocking the baby back and forth. Humming children songs while holding her close to savor this moment. From the kitchen he hears the faint sound of dishes rattling. Lotte and Hilda are cleaning up the remains of a busy day in the restaurant. It is way beyond midnight.

Another cup of coffee, perhaps two. The late hour on the clock is no indicator of bedtime. They are wide awake. Both of them.

How similar these women are. Both want something that is out of reach.

"I've been wondering lately," Hilda says, "what happened to our husbands during the war, and what did they do. They don't talk about it. Maybe they speak about the past among themselves but not to us."

"I've never asked Otto, I don't want to know. I think I would fear the truth," Lotte says. Hilda is starring out of the kitchen window into the darkness.

"But what if there is nothing to fear, wouldn't you want to know?" she suggests. "I mean, after all these years now politicians are telling us this and that. We are bad, we are good. Depending on what shade of color their parties subscribe to. Don't you think it's insulting to get secondhand information? Why don't we ask our husbands? They were there, they know."

Talking to eyewitnesses could be one way of getting to know the truth. Or not at all? Lotte thinks. Take ten people and let them watch the same occurrence and you'll get the equal amount of different stories. Varied recaps which seldom match reality.

She will never ask Otto, he can barely handle the present, let alone the past. And what is truth anyway? Isn't it simply a story we tell ourselves to feel better.

"They were there alright on the battlefields but what did they know about the politics of the day?" Lotte asks.

"Well, only their own stories, certainly not the big picture," Hilda points out. "Coherency is seldom apparent in the moment. But now, nearly ten years later distance could help. Don't you think?"

"How far can anybody run from his past?" Lotte says. "It's stories, all of them. Just stories. We were not there, we don't know anything." She has touched a nerve with her last statement. Hilda wonders, what if Walter simply told her a story too.

What if the truth is hidden? Quickly she pushes that thought aside. No, he is a good man. But people change, don't they? Time makes the soft hard, the gentle brutal. That's what war can do to people. Better men have faltered during unpredictable and cruel situations. Or?

There has to be another way to find out and clear his name. Hilda needs to locate those witnesses who defamed Walter. However the authorities won't disclose that information. That she knows. But perhaps somebody within the bureaucratic apparatus can help. Pull some strings to access government files. Hilda knows just the right man for this task. That sneaky cousin Bernhard. He has contacts. That man is a good source of information, for digging up details. She will invite him to Ten Eicken and load his car with home-made farm products as an incentive. He'll come. She is certain. Why didn't she think of him earlier? He is also Walter's cousin. The family name is at stake. He'll care.

When Hilda phones Bernhard early that next morning, she avoids telling him that she has seen Walter and that he is on the run. That is her secret. But she mentions the details of the warrant and the officers who won't leave her family alone. The key are those eyewitnesses who signed affidavits. Can Bernhard help? she pleads.

No problem, that's easy for the scholar. Doesn't Hilda know those files are public? The government must provide insight. Yes, she knows, but what she need is deep insight, details which are not in ink on paperwork. Perhaps addresses, dates and places as well. Ah yes, Bernhard agrees. That is a bigger challenge. Just right for him because he has contacts, people who where in charge then and are once again running the show within the new government.

Recycled German bureaucrats. Why aren't they prosecuted by the Allies? Because they are useful. They know how the system works best. Recycled in every system, he knows. But Bernhard won't tell Hilda such details. Country folk. What do they know about political games people play? Not a thing. But they are extraordinary when making those wonderful smoked sausages. Perhaps Hilda can set a dozen aside when he visits Ten Eicken, he will share them later with his informers at city hall.

Nothing is for free, Bernhard points out. Especially those official document addendums, information which will be concealed for the next fifty years. That's how governments work. Sit it out. Wait a while. Let the mob complain that the truth was withheld at the time. But it does not matter then, half a century later, because guilty and innocent people are equally dead. No harm done. Yes, Bernhard knows the repetition of history. The trickery and deceit are not news to him.

39

That Teutonic work ethic, often a curse but a blessing today. It comes in handy when the task seems impossible. Bernhard's persistence is rewarded within days. He is not simply surprised, he is stunned about the results. Details in Walter's file leave him speechless. He did not anticipate this outcome. And by the way, how ignorant can people be? Bernhard needs a copy, right away. Details in printing. It cannot wait, people are aging here. Lives are wasting as we speak, he says to his informer.

"People are extremely stupid, we know. But this?" he says to Hilda when visiting her on Ten Eicken three days later. He rushed to the farm as soon as he received those copies. He could not phone her. Not with news like this. He places his find, eight pages of papers on the table. Walter's fate in ink. There it is. Look for yourself. With hesitation Hilda reaches for the documents, uncertain what to expect.

The truth? And if so, will it set her free or confirm her worst nightmare that Walter is not innocent after all? She cannot guess. Bernhard talked about stupidity.

"You have to explain this to me," she finally says. She is shivering with anticipation. And while Bernhard reads sentence after sentence, stopping here and there to expand with explanations, the tension becomes unbearable. Confirming the accusations of polish civilians shot by German officers in Nowy Sacz during a raid in May of 1940 is no news to her, Hilda knows from the warrant she discussed with Walter. But who are the perpetrators? And more important who are the witnesses?

"Here, see on page two. They mention four names Meier, Geiger, Schmidt and Eicken. Walter Eicken, to be precise. Four German soldiers are accused," Bernhard points out.

"What about witnesses to the massacre? Only two names. Micha

Piecek and Pawl Jalowy, both polish citizens. At the time they were in their mid-twenties and worked for the resistance in Poland. That's what it says on this page. Are you listening at all?" he asks Hilda.

"Of course, but you are only confirming the government's accusations against Walter. You sound like the prosecutor. How can this information help us?" Now Bernhard's face opens up to a bright grin. He is not finished. Just wait he is saving the best for the last page.

"Here comes the defense. It has to be about money and greed in particular. Isn't it always?" he points out. "Did I mention that we found a second file on those witnesses. Yes, their names popped up in another case. Pawl Jalowy and Micha Piecek are presently partitioning the German government for financial compensation for their years as forced laborers during the war. They worked on a farm near Munich in Bavaria." Bernhard pauses for a moment while looking at Hilda.

"So?" she asks. "Shouldn't they be compensated?"

"Of course," Bernhard says, "especially because these Poles were forced laborers in Germany for over two years, from January 1940 to August 1942." Hilda now looks at Bernhard bewildered. Forced workers in Germany uninterrupted from January of 1940 to 1942 and at the same time witnesses to atrocities in Poland in May of 1940? Impossible to be in two places at the same time.

"That's really dumb. Those men are lying, but why are they defaming Walter? Fake witnesses mean false accusations which voids the hunt for Walter, right?" Hilda says. "We have to inform the government right away, they'll have to drop their case against my husband. Surely Walter can now clear his name without incarceration." She has to tell him, he can return to Germany. Tomorrow she will go to her neighbor Ferdinand, he can bring Walter back to Düsseldorf.

Hilda closes her eyes while taking a deep breath. Perhaps there is justice.

While she is talking, Bernhard looks over the documents a third time. He avoids sharing Hilda's euphoria.

"Slow down girl, one step at a time. Authorities won't back off immediately just because we found this new evidence," he says. "That's not how it works. They'll take their time to investigate, if those two witnesses were in fact forced laborers in Germany during said time instead of resistance fighters in Poland. Our evidence has to be confirmed and acknowledged in writing by bureaucrats. And that takes lots of time. Just imagine, there are tens of thousands of cases pending in front of the courts. Defamations, accusations mixed with truth and lies by perpetrators and witnesses. It all needs sorting out. That is a tremendous task. It takes a vast number of government employees and time. We are not talking about a few months but perhaps years. The mills of the system grind rather slowly. And who knows if our former enemies Poland and Russia will even cooperate to exchange information? I strongly doubt that," he says.

"Why should a Polish official help to rehabilitate a former German soldier?" Bernhard points out. "I can't see it. Not yet. The cold war in the east against the west and visa versa is escalating. I doubt those eastern governments will open their files for simple German foot soldiers. No, we have to do this differently. We need to find those Polish witnesses, talk to them and convince them to retract their accusations. That's our only hope." Bernhard points again at the documents in front of him.

"I think I found something. Here, check the last line, down there, where they signed their names. Pawl Jalowy and Micha Piecek filed their petition for compensation just two months ago in Cologne."

Bernhard is grinning now.

"Our Polish witnesses still live in Germany," he points out. "Look at the address, they live on Glockenstrasse, Apartment number 27. That's only forty minutes by train from Düsseldorf. Want to go for a ride?"

40

They did not announce themselves, they simply barged in. And now Hilda feels terrible, like an intruder. Look at that poverty. Those Polish families live like beggars in a shabby two-room apartment on Glockenstrasse in Cologne. Not counting children, she spots six adults sharing less than sixteen square meters. The smell of garlic and onions is mixed with mildew.

Why don't they open a window? She can barely breathe.

Miracle years in Germany? Not here, not among those Poles. What did she expect? Is she forgetting those thousands of displaced Germans from East Prussia and Pomerania who still live in camps nine years after the end of the war? What about her own kind? But then she thinks, what about people in general. You cannot sort displaced people by nationality and compare sinister fates. Aren't civilians in every country victims of war?

Hilda pulls Bernhard's sleeve. She is now ripping his jacket while mumbling some excuse and urging him to turn around. She cannot go through with this. But yet, there is also enough anger to step forward. Torn between empathy and fury she needs to see this through. It's them or Walter. Isn't it? Someone has to lose.

She had a plan before she stepped into the apartment. Now her mind seems blank. What does she wish for? She wants to turn the clock back to happier times before the war. Hilda sees herself running through pastures with Walter. Live and love. Raise children. And love some more.

What was the question?

"So what do you want?" she now hears one of the men asking with annoyance in his voice. "You force your way in unannounced and interrupt our supper. I warn you, those times are over. You cannot do that any longer, do you hear me?" She can hear him alright but also needs to clarify, make them realize they are wrong by defaming other people. It's not about being German or Polish, it's about the truth. And their defamation of a German soldier in particular. Isn't that what happened?

But the words stay stuck in her throat. They won't come out. It is Bernhard who finally takes charge. He places the documents on the table and points to the signatures beneath the affidavit against Walter.

Suddenly two men step forward. They must be Pawl Jalowy and Micha Piecek. They seem surprised. But don't deny that they signed those papers.

"It was us alright. So what? That's what happened back home during the war. Why shouldn't we have confirmed those allegations?" Pawl and Micha act overconfident. It's a bit too much for Bernhard. He quickly pulls another document from the pile and points to the compensation claim for two years of labor in Bavaria. The overlapping of the time period becomes obvious. The evidence is right there. In ink.

"Perhaps you have twin brothers if it wasn't you who signed those compensation claims. Yes? Oh, no, you were in Poland working for the resistance at the time, were you witnessed atrocities. Or what? Which is it? It can't be both ways. You better talk now," Bernhard demands.

Micha looks at the claim form and then his signature. He picks it up and even looks at the blank backside. What to say, how to react? What game is this man playing with them? How much does he know?

Of course he signed that paper as well, Micha finally admits. He should be compensated for all those years of forced labor on a Bavarian farm. Mind you, he says, they were nice people, treated us fairly and always fed us well. But those German farmers didn't pay him once. Two long years Pawl and Micha labored on that farm. Nothing to show for. No money.

"You definitely deserve compensation," Bernhard says. "I can help you. But dammit, stop lying about Nowy Sacz. You were not there, where you? No, it's a lie. You stayed on that Bavarian farm for two years. You could not have left there during the war, you did not witness any war crimes in Poland, did you?"

Micha and Pawl look stunned. What is he suggesting, they are liars? The men check the documents again, handing pages back and forth. How did these strangers get those papers? In disbelief they reconfirm dates and places. It's right there on paper. In writing. Attempts of denial are useless. It is time to come clean.

"I warned you, they'd find out," Micha now yells at Pawl. "You got too greedy, needed to cash in twice. Why did you pull me into this mess? Why didn't I refuse? But that woman, she was so convincing. A signature for five hundred Marks. Easy money without a risk. She said, nobody would ever find out. She lied, she is the liar, not us."

Micha looks pale. Will he and Pawl now go to jail? Not if they withdraw their accusations, Bernhard suggests. They nod, of course, injustice has to be set right. There are lives at stake. But that woman?

A woman? Hilda asks. What did she look like? What's her name? Micha and Pawl don't know a name. She looked like a German lady. And there was another man, rather arrogant. That woman came later with an advocate to deliver the money. They met in the *Kleister Pub*, close to the Cologne Cathedral. That's all. The two men have nothing in writing from that deal.

"You have to retract those accusations right away, go to the local authorities in the morning. Is that understood?" Bernhard says on his way out of the apartment. "I will know if you don't. And then I'll be back. Not alone but with the police. Do you get that? The men nod in agreement.

When leaving, Hilda quickly turns to the women, apologizing for barging in like this. But they understand, don't they? It's for her husband. They would do the same. While looking at one another, Micha's wife Brigitta suddenly reaches for Hilda's hand.

"It's me, who has to apologize. Such foolish men. They are ignorant. But we needed money, we hardly can afford to buy groceries. I am only telling you how it is. Of course, that no excuse for what they did." She looks into Hilda's face, the face of a former enemy, steady with much more empathy than expected.

"We'll fix this, I'll see to that," Brigitta says. "At the end men always listen to us. But you have to believe me, I did not know anything about those false accusations." Later on the train, Hilda suddenly starts sobbing. Not for Walter but for those Polish women. For the way they live and struggle even now that the war is over.

41

Bureaucrats don't apologize when their reproaches deflate. They simply keep quiet when proven wrong. Not a letter or phone call acknowledges several weeks later the clearance of Walter's name. The record has been set straight? Hasn't it? Bernhard is certain but he will check again like he did yesterday and the day before. When he finally catches up with Hilda, he is the bearer of more bad news. Walter's name is still tainted although those Polish witnesses withdrew their accusations. But now a new government file on Walter Eicken has surfaced. Apparently he was also a member of the notorious *Waffen SS*, Hitler's private army. Didn't she know?

Feared even by most German *Wehrmacht* foot soldiers, uncounted atrocities originated from their ranks. Paperwork the Allied Forces and German bureaucrats exchange apparently cement those accusations. That's why the government digs deeper in search for individual guilt. A task, which keeps bureaucrats and courts busy for decades to come.

That's why they go after Walter, his name was tainted before. His identity is on file in archives. And bureaucrats need faces to match the number of former *Waffen SS* members.

The small detail of guilt or innocence can be resolved later. Let's find them first.

Somebody needs to go to jail. The world is waiting for resolve.

"Yes, that is the problem. They'll also catch innocent guys. But that's the beauty of peace, it allows time to investigate what happened in the past on battlefields, excavating what's gone while preparing the future for the next campaign. Lucky for those bureaucrats, it keeps them busy because there is always another war right around the corner. Need I mention Korea?" Bernhard says.

"Bad conscience only lasts within nations until another world-moving bloodbath is committed. Look at history, it never takes long before guns talk again. That's not an excuse but simply reality. Regarding Walter and those new accusations, I don't know what to make of this. The whole case stinks. Looks like someone's personal agenda, a crusade of revenge."

Revenge? Who wants to harm a late war returnee? Who started this when paying for the help of two Polish men? For Hilda the thought of payback seems far fetched but she will talk to her neighbor Ferdinand. He knows the mind of soldiers, he dwells on it day after day since his return from Russia. Yes, she will ask Ferdinand, he'll have a clearer perspective of reality.

"Walter with those people? I cannot imagine that he belonged to that organization. In later years he so despised their rites, this talk about obedience unto death," Ferdinand says after listening to Hilda's account. "But don't forget, many German soldiers were in the *Waffen SS*, some joined by involuntary servitude after 1942. Although now we tar all with the same brush. Membership doesn't prove they were all thugs and committed crimes."

Words of relief, perhaps hope. Hilda ran over to Ferdinand's cottage as soon as she heard the bad news. Who else can she confide in? No one, not a soul on Ten Eicken because she still keeps her inquiries and Walter's whereabouts a secret. But Ferdinand, Walter's best friend, is different. He understands her agony.

"Nobody wants to be connected personally to the *SS*, especially now that new political attitudes hold iron brooms to sweep the house," Ferdinand says.

Beware of those self righteous cleaners although their boots are still stained with red Polish soil from the invasion. Who are they to preach? They think they are better. Especially at the end of a war when they crush the scales of justice over the heads of foot soldiers.

Give me a soldier and I'll find you a crime, they utter with their personal promotion in mind. And then they go to work. Whichever way they choose. They have permission from way up on the top. Since the Nuremberg trial, the thirty eight divisions of the SS are condemned by the Allies as a criminal organization due to war crimes. The *Totenkopf - Verbände* (Skull organizations) were the worst. As if that is news.

SS members are easily recognized. They are branded with a Gothic-style letter identifying their blood-type. A mark which is one centimeter in size and located eight centimeters above the elbow; it is well hidden under the left armpit. But not for authorities who know where to look.

So raise your arms, the cleaners say. Let's see, if you have that tattoo. Don't show me that self-inflicted scar you got when trying to burn out the SS signature and claim it's a war wound. We know better, because we are better.

Or so they think. Did they forget to mention, that the worst of the worst, the likes of Mengele and Eichmann did not have that tattoo? Must have missed to brand them. But those beast are out of sight anyway. Probably somewhere in Argentina where President Peron shelters them with other refugees. Some even innocent. Ah well, can't do anything about that situation from a distance. Need to find some foot soldiers right here in Germany to fill those empty jails and meet the quota of perpetrators.

Such is the face and farce of justice during and after postwar Germany. "So why an additional investigation?" Ferdinand mumbles. "Why him? I get it, combined with the accusations of those greedy witnesses, the SS membership is an ideal canvass on which premature conclusions can be drawn. It might stick, dammit, I hope not. But I am certain, Walter won't be coming home soon if he hears about this."

"But you told him the other good news, didn't you. You wrote to him?" Hilda asks.

"What news?" Ferdinand says. "Ah yes, of course. I told him all about it few months ago, right after your husband Ernst came over. Euphoric, bursting with pride. I think he was a little bit drunk that night. No wonder, his third child. He was beside himself with joy over the birth of Christina. Called her his little princess. Finally a father again. Who would have thought?"

"Your told Walter about the child?" Hilda asks.

"Yes, why not? Walter is Christina's uncle. Shouldn't he know?" Ferdinand says. "Here see for yourself. Those are his words, he is somewhere in southern Argentina, on a hacienda near Bariloche. It looks like Austria down there. Anyway, in his last letter Walter responded how happy he is for you and his brother Ernst about the birth of another child. Shortly afterward, I sent him another letter about the closure of the proceedings, the clearance of his name regarding Poland, thanks to you. I expected, he'd be overjoyed. When I didn't get a response, I mailed another letter reminding him that all charges against him were dropped. Why don't you come home now? I even asked. But he did not answer that letter either. Of course, I did not know about those new accusations regarding membership in the *Waffen SS*. But weird, that he did not answer. I'll try again. Tomorrow I'll write another letter. I won't give up. Eventually he'll answer. Unless he moved on. But wouldn't they forward his mail? We'll see."

Hilda touches the letter. She reread Walter's words of joy for her and Ernst. Their apparent rekindled marriage. Overwhelmed by his handwriting but more by the words, she suddenly gets up and rushes to the bathroom. She feels dizzy, sick to her stomach. Cramps find relief while vomiting. Over and over until her eyes water.

"Is everything alright in there? Are you pregnant again?" Ferdinand asks after knocking on the bathroom door. But Hilda stays quiet. She is staring in the mirror without seeing her own face. She can only see Walter. But he is lost again. Especially to her. Perhaps this time permanently.

His absence from her life is a familiar repeat. During the war and later. And now once more she'll wait in anticipation while the clock winds down her remaining years.

Waiting and wasting. No, there is no place for this extraordinary love story in her life any longer. Not with those dark memories of the war, the agony of postwar years with uncounted tragedies. And Walter still out of reach. It's all an illusion to hope for the impossible. She has to let go of her dreams or she'll go mad. On Ten Eicken bread needs to be baked. That is her reality.

"Don't bother to write, he won't answer any more letters," Hilda says knowingly after she steps out of the bathroom. "But I am glad, you told him about the partial clearance of his name. Thank heaven. I am happy he knows. Without his awareness of the latest accusations, Walter can come home now if he wants. We cannot force a decision, the choice is his."

Her last words, her tone of voice confuse Ferdinand. Why is Hilda acting so cold and distant all of a sudden? She seems different from the woman he knows so well. What about that day in the cottage, when she spent those long romantic hours with Walter? Has she forgotten? Is this a game?

Don't ask Ferdinand for answers. What's love to him? He is a loner, he just wants peace and quiet for the rest of his life. The end of the war was his divorce from his partner, his mate the battlefield. That's the only relationship he knows. Since coming home his life has been bearable in this cottage. And undisturbed. Content, not necessarily happy. For him this will do.

But Hilda and Walter? Now that's a different affair. A true love-affair.

"I'll write anyway, perhaps one day he'll answer," Ferdinand says. With compassion he looks at that tall, slender woman in front of him, wishing he could be of more help.

"Hilda, you have never been homesick, I mean, really homesick? Have you?" he asks. "It's more painful than thirst. A reality I learned during the war. I am certain, Walter remembers that urge of homesickness as well." She looks at him somewhat bewildered, wondering if men truly believe emotional despair is their sole domain. As if only battlefields away from home give people the ultimate insight view? Hilda gets ready to leave.

When shaking hands to say good-bye, she smiles at Ferdinand. Perhaps he doesn't realize that homesickness isn't only a yearning for the homeland, a house or place. No, it also means the painful craving for a person who shelters your life. Hilda is homesick without ever leaving Ten Eicken. Her unhappiness is not about location.

42

The endeavor of forgetting is a laborious task. As time goes by Hilda digs deeper and quicker. Day after day. Hiding her feelings, entrenching in work. A salvation which even creates contentment at times. Those are rare moments but they exist. Especially when working with Lotte. Companions by fate, not blood. But closer, much closer than in-laws.

Sisters. Chosen by circumstances from two different worlds, detoured from their individual path, merged to walk together for a while. Side by side. Mellowed and melted under Rhineland skies during times when the worst brought out the best in them.

She must confide in her friend, Hilda convinces herself. The air weighs heavy. Sharing meals becomes a chore with all that secrecy lingering like gray shadows, clouding anew, creating space while confining free spirit. Yes, Hilda needs to talk. Like most women. And the moment has arrived. Now, this minute.

For hours Lotte listens. The story is not entirely news to her. She suspected more than she realized at the time. Those meetings with Ferdinand, that trip to the train station. Rosy cheeks and bright eyes. In hindsight it was obvious. Hilda now only given rhyme to rhythm. And the good news. Walter is far away from Germany and secure from self-proclaimed prosecutors. What joy. Or is it?

"Bitter and sweet like that wine we make. Isn't it," Hilda says. "Walter has changed so much I miss him the way he was. Yes, I want to have him back home but not if it means prison. I'd rather imagine him carefree in the pampas of South America. Who knows what they'll do to him once he comes home to Germany. The search for warlocks will continue for years. What am I to do?"

Lotte has no answer. Not for Hilda or her own story. She suddenly misses those fuss-free postwar years, when thinking was an unaffordable luxury. But the economic miracle changed all that. Their lives, also easier economically, now appear much more complicated.

It's harder to make it through the day with a full stomach and a new found lightness. Shouldn't it be the other way around?

"Now we should be so lucky to finally be happy. If only we could," Lotte says more to herself than to Hilda. "I miss that uncertainty. At least excuses were justified."

"You never talked about your personal ordeal," Hilda says.

"Were you, I mean, did they also ...?"

"No, not me but my aunt Berta. I saw it," Lotte says. "Over and over. For days, until she could not take it any more. When a Russian soldier came for me, my aunt snatched his gun and shot herself. Right in front of him. Here take this, she screamed at him. This is what you want? Isn't it? And then she killed herself." Lotte looks at Hilda in bewilderment while talking. Her wonderful aunt dying while committing a last deed for her niece Lotte. Out of devotion, for the sake of the younger.

The soldiers were so shocked by this tragedy that no further rapes were reported that afternoon.

They lost their appetite at the sight of the sacrificial lamb on the muddy road.

During the night, the rest of the Marlow family escaped unharmed, hiding in the forest until the Red Army moved on. But fear was their constant travel companion for several weeks. The fright of getting raped by beasts who wear uniforms crept like shadows along the ditches of solitary country lanes. The Marlows shunned crowded roads with refugees who would have shared a loaf of bread. They rather went hungry to avoid soldiers.

"Give a man permission and he'll be at his worst," Lotte says. In every war. On both sides of the trenches. She remembers it well. Thousands of Germans could have escaped earlier, when they heard the gunfire coming closer from the east. But no, the *Gauleiters* (German district officials) prohibited any evacuation in the East when the enemy was literally at their gates. By order from Berlin, they said. The land and farms, these towns have to be inhabited by our kind. We'll show those Russians who lives here. Germans. And they stay. Nobody will abandon the fatherland in the east. Not under their watch.

And so by decree they all stayed like animals, waiting for the butcher. Those few Germans who tried to run toward the west, were shot in the back by their own soldiers. Fleeing, even with the enemy at arm's length, was considered treason. Punishable by death.

"The choice was death, either way by German fanatics or revenging Russian soldiers," Lotte recalls. Just imagine how many refugees could have been saved if *Gauleiters* had not delayed people's escape from eastern villages and farms? Of over fourteen million displaced Germans more than two million died before and during their trek to the West.

The run from the Red Army began after a barbaric incident in the small village of *Nemmersdorf*, East Prussia in October 1944. That's were Russian soldiers first broke lines and marched into Germany. The Red Army held that position for only a few days. But when German soldiers came to the rescue it was too late.

Streets, houses and fields were littered with dead civilians, most of them children and women. All of them raped and later shot. The victims were as young as eight years and as old as eighty. Many women were nailed to barn doors, visible from a distance.

The *Nemmerdorf* massacre was reported world wide. It created fear and the urgency to leave even before the war was lost seven months later. But people like the Marlows were not allowed to leave before they saw Russian uniforms. And the Allied Forces made no attempts to stop the massacre of civilians.

"Such inhumanity, such tragedies. *Nein, nein* (no, no), I don't want to think about that ever again," Lotte says. "Talking about it doesn't help, it just stirs up emotions and pictures I am trying to forget." She is crying now, cannot help herself or those she left behind. Hilda takes hold of Lotte's shoulders rocking her gently back and forth. Soothing the pain for a moment, sharing the incomprehensibility of undocumented atrocities. Against Germans. For a change. Write that down and try to share it. Not possible at this time in history. You'll get accused of crunching numbers. The who and why and how many. Need to stay silent and swallow the dust which you swirled up. Those thoughts leave Hilda agitated and angry.

"Mustn't dwell any longer," Lotte finally says. "We have work to do, and you have four children now. That's a huge responsibility. Reality is bigger than our own grievances." She looks at Hilda with expectation, but there is no response. She is thinking about him again. It's always Walter, never Ernst. Lotte sees what isn't uttered. She shakes her head, straightens her apron and walks toward the stove. More coffee is needed. It always helps.

Whoever said life is just? Where? Show me a place or a man. But Ernst, the father of Hilda's children. He deserves better, doesn't he? Lotte thinks. Like a ghost that poor man moves around the house. Always second, never up front or in the center. A shadow of a man. A man who did not commit any crimes. But simply forgot to die in the war to make room for his brother Walter, should he ever return.

"We must try for the sake of our children," Lotte says while placing the coffeepot in front of Hilda. "I think Ernst deserves better. He is a good man. And he is right here on this farm with you. Do you hear me? Ernst is right here."

"But not in here," Hilda points to her chest while banging her fists angrily against her bosom. "He is not in here," she repeats. But what can she say to Lotte, her dear Lotte who married a man she knew from childhood. The son of a farmer in Pomerania. They married because of commonalities. That's the kind of marriage Albert will choose. He'll wed Trudi one day. How could he not? Who else is there to share his memories of eastern lands, heritage and familiarity? That will be the solid base of their union just like it was with Lotte and Otto. Honest, strong and lasting. A bondage which rides smoothly through the years without feeling the torment of violent storms. The ups and downs of love and consumption. Those fierce longings for a loved-one. That immortality of love which is felt only by mortals who believe.

No, that depth of agony her Lotte will never know. But Hilda does. Her love is like the legends in Greek mythology. But don't they always end tragically?

What is it about love? And in particular Walter? His absence has deepened Hilda's love. Or is it meanwhile the idea of love she has fallen in love with instead of the man? Like in Richard Wagner's Tristan and Isolde. Perhaps Hilda is Isolde? But Walter not Tristan. At least not the way he sees himself in a far away land with no dragons to slay, but alone with his miserable memories of Russian labor camps.

They only spent a year together before he went into the war. Hilda saw the best of him before the worst could surface as it does sooner or later in all of us.

Would their love be as pure and longing if reunited with daily quarrels about chores and money? Routine, the disenchantment of all illusions. But Hilda does not want to think about that. His absence is the time capsule, the preserver of her immortal devotion. And there is not one person who can convince her differently.

43

That constant pain, this ache. Always within never without. His Argentinean doctor considers Walter Eicken physically healthy but he feels sick.

Homesick. Tired of foreign pastures as all soldiers when the guns fall silent. Nothing else to do but wait. Biding the hours, counting the minutes. Hoping of discharge. But from what? The war has been over for nearly ten years. And he is still fighting.

Walter tackles once again a familiar feeling he remembers well from Siberia. Hopelessness. Only the geography has changed. In the east it was Russia, in the south it's now Argentina. And his homeland is somewhere in between. Thousand of miles away from this rotten society of uprooted people who long for national identity while hiding in the pampas.

How he despises some of those fellow Germans who fled to Patagonia. Former so-called elite soldiers bragging about the war, embarrassing immigrants from Bavaria who came to Argentina two generations ago to make a living. But now they have to listen to those German newcomers who raise their voices in restaurants and bars. Those jabbers, noisier than pigs in a barn.

Who are those people anyway? They are former pencil-pushers from Berlin and guards of civilian camps now hiding while wanted on international warrants for war crimes. Can't they shut up? Must they exaggerate to make matters worse? No wonder, locals turn away, rush back to their stores and houses to avoid eye contact and conversation.

"They are sick those bastards, still believing they did the right thing." Walter informs his friend Ferdinand by letter. "I feel ashamed of being a German when I hear them bragging with those stories. Is that what we fought for in this war? I feel like a foreigner among all those *Landsman*, questioning myself constantly."

"Am I better? Surely not. I came here under false pretense as well. Therefore I am one of them as long as I stay. Ferdinand, I want to come home. I need to. This is not my country. The worst of the worst has found refuge in Argentina, blemishing what little is left of our German integrity. I have not felt this bad since Siberia. At least in the Gulag we conserved some of our human pride. But this? It's so disgusting. I need to leave soon. Can you help?"

Yes, of course he received all those letters from Germany. He was just too preoccupied and depressed to respond, Walter reports. What a relief to hear that his name was cleared regarding that incident in Poland. But now they want to charge him for being a member of the *Waffen SS*? On what grounds? He did not commit any crimes.

"I will come home now for certain to set the record straight," Walter writes. "You remember, how we gossiped about those fanatics who swore obedience until death? Those dangerous minds who in most cases lacked formal education to amount to anything but gun-slinging? Well, some of them are here as I write. And worst of all, did you know that Adolf Hitler is presumed to be living right here in Patagonia? Imagine that, alive and well. That's what they say. Eva Braun and the Führer apparently live north of Bariloche on a huge hacienda surrounded by brick walls and guards. Near Lake Nahuel Huapi, or so many believe."

"Ha, they say that coward did not commit suicide in his Berlin bunker after all but escaped by submarine to Buenos Aires. Wouldn't that be a joke? I am certain government officials will never make this story public. No, nations help one another, don't they? Leaders are never canon fodder. They get away without a bruise. It's us they are after, the little people."

Walter stops writing. What else is there to say? He cannot ask about Hilda and Ernst in his letter. Not any longer. Didn't his wife give birth to another child after he left? Ferdinand will surely let Hilda read his letters. Mustn't get specific but rather talk about general events. The big picture always makes the small one look more attractive and less agonizing. In addition, it helps to forget.

But how can you, when mild summer winds find their way into your bedroom after midnight to caress your cheeks? When leafs flutter out there in the dark, humming *Schlaf Kindlein schlaf* (sleep child sleep), that familiar melody from childhood. How is sanity possible so far away from home?

On a farm in southern Argentina he labors among locals like the Marlows on his estate in the Rhineland? He, who should be master, is also a servant now. Displaced as well. How he understands the feelings of those East Prussians and Pomeranians.

One could laugh at the irony of the situation if ignoring the tragedy, Walter thinks. While the Marlows were displaced by force, he removed himself from the cradle of his forefathers by choice. The Marlows did not have the luxury of choosing.

While writing personal notes, Walter turns another page in his diary. The account of his life. Moments in no order. Only some sorted by days and years. He began recording events in Poland and during his imprisonment in Russia. In small letters to save space and ink. His stories fill meanwhile five volumes. They are his most precious possessions. Three notebooks he left with Ferdinand in Germany while two more diaries about his time in Patagonia are on his night stand.

There was a time when he wrote down those thoughts for Hilda. To share. But not any longer. Now Walter writes to himself and out of necessity. Everyone needs to talk once in a while. And Walter talks to blank pages. He places words to fill his own emptiness.

"Walter, *puedo pasar?*" After a firm knock on his door he hears the soft voice of Isabelle, a woman who lives three doors down the hallway. He knows why she is coming but he won't open the door. Not tonight. Too many memories. Not enough distance to himself to be with her.

"*No, no esta noche. Talvez manana,*" he says, while listening to her footsteps disappearing. She is ten years his junior but she wants to marry him. Or so she says. When Walter told her about his wife and child in Germany she only shrugged her shoulders. Who isn't married? Isabelle responded. And what does it matter? It doesn't. Not in Argentina. And anyway, nobody uses their real names. No harm done.

Walter won't tell her that he'll be leaving soon. As if it means anything? Not to her. She has several lovers but Walter is a hard working German, he would make a good husband. A secure relationship could help the rest of her kin. And Isabelle has a large family.

What about Walter? He loves her soft dark skin, the warmth she generates under the blanket when he shivers at night thinking about Siberia. That frozen hell is his first and last thought every day. He can't help himself. Not even the visualization of familiar faces can soothe those horrors implanted in his memory.

Tomorrow, he thinks, on Friday I will go home. But there is always something else. Another day passes and then weeks. Walter is working the fields to bring in the harvest. He needs money to return to Germany. His false passport has only value in Argentina, the precision of German bureaucrats will surely detect such amateur forgery upon his return. He needs his original papers, his true identity for his return. Ferdinand can send him those papers from Germany.

Yes, he will come home as Walter Eicken, under his real name. With haste he sends another letter, urging his friend to prepare his departure from Argentina.

44

Walter wants to return for the right reasons. Ferdinand feels relieved. It's not entirely the woman but foremost his personal honor as a man. Only a former soldier understands.

Within three weeks Ferdinand organizes the return-trip to Germany for his friend. He intends to send Walter's original papers as well as the money for the ship passage by registered mail to Argentina. This time around Ferdinand even keeps his preparations a secret from Hilda. They are rather self-involved on Ten Eicken as it is, settled into mundane daily routines with constant talk about expansion. One day it's a bigger restaurant and next the construction of a large hotel.

Avoidance of thinking indeed. It's now about money. Everywhere. That's how Germans feel about their new-found wealth. They make it but they refuse to share it; especially with the taxman. Split all profits? Not just yet. Not after all they've been through and endured.

"Government, you owe us," they say. "Don't you get it? You owe us big time. Didn't we sacrifice our fathers and sons in bloody battles? Not enough? Here you are again, increasing taxes. What for? To buy new cannons for future invasions? Not from the sweat or our labor. Never again, or at least not now when the future looks bright for a change?"

It's always about money. But what does it really matter? Ask Ferdinand if he cares? Talk to the former soldier. But not about taxes or politics. Let's stay trivial, let's do that.

Although he spends most of the time by himself, he needs to talk to someone once in a while as well, when his cottage becomes too small for his shadows. So Ferdinand goes over there on occasion. To Ten Eicken where the future is outracing itself with constant visible changes.

He visits late at night when most guests have left and only a few lovers sip fruit wine on wooden tables in unlit corners of the patio.

Lotte is clearing the tables after a busy weekend. Still full of zest for action at this late hour. She even hums a merry tune.

"Yes Lotte, that Hilda is lucky to have you," Ferdinand says while drinking his cool beer out of a stone mug. "What would she do without you?"

"Why do you think it's her who is lucky?" Lotte responds. Words, which make Ferdinand smile. It's good to see such harmony and honest devotion. Characters like Lotte restore his faith in people. Not that he seeks their company. But it's refreshing to be an observer. A change from the monotony of his secluded life. They chat for a while until Hilda and Ernst join them.

"Still only a farmer, won't have anything to do with the restaurant?" Ferdinand inquires.

"I grow food. I don't serve it," Ernst says. "The farm and restaurant are a good combination. It works out for both of us," he says while turning for approval to Hilda. She nods without looking at Ferdinand. He knows better, she cannot hide from him. Can he from her?

He has told her more than once that there is no news today. Those letters from Argentina don't arrive overnight. It takes time. But Ferdinand said that last Friday and the week before. Does Walter not write any longer? Perhaps the mail got lost or worse, the government confiscated those letters? That's foolish, Ferdinand told her when they were alone. The mail never has a return address. That's the arrangement they made. Just in case. Walter's letters are delivered to his aunt's house. Another measure of precaution from spying government agents.

He'll write when he is ready, Ferdinand reassured her during her last visit. And now? Sitting there at the table in her restaurant, he doesn't blink. And she cannot read his thoughts. Or can she? So they talk about everyday life. As if that truly matters to anybody around this table.

"The children, oh yes. Growing like weeds, soon they'll be big enough to help around Ten Eicken," Hilda says now. "And Lotte's Albert is a teenager now. A fine young man who has set his eyes on Trudi. He'll marry her one day, I am certain."

Chit-chat. And more small talk for another hour. Enough for today. Time for Ferdinand to go home. This is not his world. He just likes to peek into it once in a while. His aloneness always becomes bearable after those visits. Perhaps that's why he goes there in the first place. To Ten Eicken for a reality check.

What would Walter make of all this familiarity and revived Bourgeois way of life? After fighting in the war, his additional ten years in Russian labor camps and two years of hiding in Argentina. How can anyone adjust to that middle-class life-style in the aftermath?

How? Just imagine yourself, a witness of so much agony and atrocity. Deprived of basics. And now this? Abundance overnight, like thunder and lightening. You'd lose your senses, wouldn't you? But the others would request that? Wouldn't they? They cannot phantom your inner torture and nightmares. How could they? They expect the original Walter to step forward and carry on as if nothing ever happened.

That's the anticipation.

So you return. And then what? Dive right in, sit down. You are now back home. All is well. The past was yesterday. Today we'll eat and sing. And if possible be merry. See how we live in the late fifties, notice the *Speck* (fat) around our bellies and necks. A sign of the economic miracle, to be worn like a pearl necklace with pride.

Yes we eat again. Pounds of pork and schnitzel, because we can. And we drink lots of beer and wine as well. It dulls the senses. Hurrah.

But what about the past and those shadows lingering about? Shouldn't we try to undress the past and chase those shadows away? Shadows, which secretly torture us day and night? Nonsense. Leave that to the women. They wear the gowns.

For an instant Ferdinand feels sad. Not for himself but his friend Walter. He will have to return to such a life and play duck down till the day he dies. Can he cope with that new prescribed lightness? How so? Uplifting that darkness deep down which sticks like molasses to the bottom of your soul? Impossible. Not Walter. Ferdinand has reached the gate of his property when Hilda steps out of the dark. Fumbling in her pocket she pulls out a letter and hands it to him.

"Here, he has to read this, please. Make sure Walter gets this letter right away. It's rather important." And without further explanations, Hilda disappears again. Like a shadow which dissolves with the gray of the night. But not unnoticed. Not this time around.

Ernst is watching. He is not a fool despite those cheerful hours in broad daylight month after month when Hilda jokes with him and the children. When make-believe almost convinces to trust again.

He is aware his brother Walter is alive. Somewhere. So rightfully he is still Hilda's first husband. The marriage to Ernst has been minimized to an interlude of a drama still unfolding.

There can't be two suitors when the curtain falls. He knows. They all do. But the audience is out for snacks, they won't be back for a while to fill the theater. Meanwhile the actors bide their time. Waiting to perform the grand finale. Listening to the ticking of that clock in the hall, watching as time steals itself out of the side entrance into the dark back-alley. A shadow in the pale of the night. Impossible to locate and pin down.

If talking was possible, Ernst thinks. But isn't this a dilemma beyond words? Who is he to spy on Hilda, the rightful and first wife of his brother Walter? I am second choice, he thinks. That's the way it has been since childhood. Standing back and waiting for his brother to outgrow his pants, so the younger can wear the hand-downs. But can Ernst also fill his shoes? They don't fit, never will, he realizes.

Absence is a mighty warrior which grows stronger in time. He cannot fight Walter's shadow which lingers over his own existence and love for Hilda like a dark cloud. No, he cannot battle thin air without his brother's presence.

45

"So what about the letter Hilda gave to Ferdinand to send to Walter in Argentina," I inquire the next afternoon when I sit with Lotte on the porch of her house in Metzkausen. "You have not said anything about it, what did she write to him?"

"Patience, girl," Lotte says. "But yes, that note. Not a good idea. I told Hilda, when she showed me the draft of that letter. Don't send it, I warned her. It will make things worse. But Hilda had it all figured out. She was convinced Walter needed encouragement to return home. Good news. The better, the quicker his return. I think, she felt guilty."

"Can you imagine her inner turmoil from the past? Walter still in a prison camp in Siberia and Hilda in the Rhineland with the notification of his death, her new marriage and then the news that her first husband is still alive. She coped with it. She managed. But sending that note years later to Walter in Argentina was stupid. I know, she meant well. But I told her several times, such information does not belong on paper. It should be communicated in person. She didn't listen. The very next day she gave that letter to Ferdinand."

Lotte shakes her head. "My father taught me, think twice and then once more before you put anything in writing. You can say what you think, but if you write it down prepare to face the consequences. Because what's written in ink can't be denied later. Trust me, there is always a moment when those written words will come back like a boomerang. And so they did. But I won't say anything more about that incident today."

I feel puzzled, she is only giving hints instead of concrete content regarding that fateful letter. I want to know what Hilda wrote. But I cannot pressure Lotte to go into detail. She'll shut down. So I simply ask her: "So did he come home that summer?"

But Lotte stays quiet, her daughter-in-law Trudi brings sandwiches with homemade liver sausage, the way they made it on Ten Eicken. Trudi learned the art of cooking, baking and butchering by watching Hilda and Lotte. But later she only had eyes for Albert. Although Wilhelm, heir of the land Trudi's father plowed, made several attempts to date her, she rejected him. Her choice was Albert. From the beginning. No contest.

How is your memory, Trudi asked Wilhelm one afternoon, when he tried to ask her out to a dance? Didn't you call me a Pollack without a backpack when I first came to Ten Eicken? Wilhelm looked bewildered when she talked. That was then, we were children, he quickly argued.

Kids don't know any better, such ignorance can be forgiven, can't it? If they change after growing up, Trudi responded, but not if the adult is the carbon-copy of that mean child.

That's the last time they talked, she left the future master of Ten Eicken standing there on his own land, abandoned him with his secret longings for a girl he would never possess.

Lotte scopes with her knife some liver sausage to sample it without the bread. She closes her eyes to combine pictures of the past with the taste on her tongue.

"Spot-on, outstanding Trudi, you haven't forgotten," she praises. "Just the way we used to make it," Lotte says. "You don't get that kind of food in America, do you?" Lotte says while looking at me. Not on a regular basis, I tell her, but there are lots of bakers and butchers who have German ancestors.

"Yes, I have tasted liver sausage in California but not as good as Trudi's creation," I add quickly. Trudi gives me a light pat on the shoulder before she leaves.

Gently I guide Lotte back to her story, I want to know about Walter. Did those words, whatever Hilda wrote, convince him to rush back to Ten Eicken?

"No, he didn't come home that year," Lotte finally answers my question. "But something else, rather earth-shattering happened meanwhile on the estate. It was the disguise of the perpetrators who defamed Walter in the first place. Incredible, who would have thought?"

The truth surfaced by coincidence when least expected. It happened on a rainy Sunday afternoon when Bernhard stopped by to visit his aunt Agnes. And although the rest of the family cut all ties after those court battles, Bernhard still felt some sort of responsibility for the sister of his mother. You have to forgive and respect her age, he used to say when visiting.

"So he went over to the cottage for a visit, chit-chatting about politics. Agnes did not even get a chance to participate, her daughter Gisela and husband Fritz took over the conversation. Complaining again about the financial burden, displaced people placed on German taxpayers. That's ridiculous, Bernhard argued. Those people from the east suffered a great deal and they pay taxes as well.

"Maybe some do. But I can name quite a few of those suckers who try to squeeze the state dry," Gisela argued. "And what about those Poles we had in Germany. Take Pollacks like Micha Piecek and Pawl Jalowy. Here we have two foreigners, who want compensation for forced labor on Bavarian farms during the war. Dear God, what about our German soldiers who were required to work in Russian labor camps and on farms in France. Shouldn't someone pay them as well for all those lost years? Perhaps Germany should give our people compensation before paying those aliens. "

She was furious now but not as agitated as Bernhard. As soon as Gisela mentioned those Polish names, he connected the dots. Where in the world would she have known about those two men? Micha and Pawl were only two persons among thousands of forced laborers in Germany? She heard those names from a neighbor, Gisela tried to elude when pressed for an explanation. And that was the end of the conversation for her, but not for Bernhard.

A week later he came again to Ten Eicken. This time in the company of two men. Micha Piecek and Pawl Jalowy. Spontaneously they pointed at Gisela and then Fritz Becher.

"Yes, we are certain. We saw them. And it's that woman who organized the payment. No doubt about it, they were both there when we swore those affidavits against Walter Eicken."

Lotte is clapping her hands together. Bernhard's description of all those faces in the room resurface. There was pure consternation and at first disbelief. Such utter betrayal within a family? Was that possible?

"That Bernhard was quite the detective. He exposed them right then and there in front of Grandma Agnes. He showed the old lady the true face of her princess Gisela," Lotte says.

"Why did she denounce her brother? Simple, after learning that Walter was still alive in a Russian labor camp and soon to return to Germany, Gisela and that lazy husband of hers were afraid they would have to leave Ten Eicken. The father of the rightful heir Wilhelm on that part of the estate was on his way home to end the cozy life of his sister in a nest which was not her birthright."

"After the truth was revealed, Bernhard also asked the authorities to further investigate Walter's apparent membership in the *Waffen SS*. Perhaps that initial inquiry was also instigated by Fritz Becher. Or was it not? Who knows, many paper trails were lost during the war. But the police picked up Fritz for further questioning. And although he returned the next day because the authorities considered this case only a matter of defamation, punishable by a small fine, Grandma Agnes spoke a much harsher sentence," Lotte says.

"Banished for life from Ten Eicken, was her verdict for Gisela and Fritz. Agnes simply kicked them out. Off the estate and down that private drive-way to get a taste of their own nastiness. Acting like that was not easy at her age and against her own daughter," Lotte says. "But how Gisela conspired against her own brother was unforgivable."

After that episode Hilda visited Agnes and invited her to move back into the main mansion. Let's forget the past, we should live together again. We are one family.

Are we really? Agnes simply asked. Her son Ernst still didn't speak to her after all those years. His pride, her pride. The same old story was relived year after year. Hilda knew. And there was nothing she could do to reunite mother and son.

"I manage just fine in my cottage", Agnes said, "there is nothing I lack. Not even friendly company." To the surprise of everybody on Ten Eicken, Agnes was seen that summer nearly every day in the company of Trudi on her short walks around the farm. How caring the teenager tended to that woman, like a granddaughter.

"Trudi later told me although some children do not change, like Wilhelm, adults like Agnes still can. Agnes, once full of prejudice against displaced Germans suddenly saw the world with different eyes. I think the debacle with her own daughter Gisela took her blindness away. Trudi accomplished that with her kindness," Lotte says.

"Perhaps the war screwed us all up in one way or another but this utter confusion was also a chance for Agnes and Trudi to became a perfect match. The first one was too old to seek redemption and the teenager still too young to feel guilty about the sins of a nation."

"They became inseparable. Quite a sight, the girl from East Prussia and the old woman who once despised those strangers. Her relationship with the young girl was definitely not born out of neediness. No, Agnes was far too proud to seek assistance Their friendship seemed genuine when you saw them strolling through the gardens and down that road to the lake. We often watched them from the kitchen window. Hilda was delighted at the sight of those two.

Lotte looks at me, as if waiting for a comment. But I am only interested in one topic. And it's not about Trudi and Agnes. It's Walter, the uncle I never met. The man who seems to be present everywhere on Ten Eicken. Except in flesh and blood.

46

Walter is bathing in sweat, but shivering under the gray blanket. Resting on a bunk in a shed of a farm in Argentina, his mind is wandering again to the camps of Siberia. As every night when high and humid temperatures keep him awake. Or is it his conscience? He has lost track of himself. Not only in time.

How much longer can he postpone his departure? Walter is running out of excuses. He received the papers for his return to Germany and Ferdinand sent him enough money to sail back home. But then came that letter. That darn note from Hilda. How can he now face her or even talk to his brother Ernst when he returns to Ten Eicken.

What was Hilda thinking? Walter contemplates. And why did she put it in writing? It's a lie, he knows. But does she realize it too? Perhaps not. How could she? She wasn't there in those Russian camps, has no idea what people will do to other human beings.

Again he glances at the note on the table, remembering every word. And suddenly he brakes out in loud laughter. Like a madman he cannot stop, until he finally hits his fist on the table to return to his senses.

I have to end this misunderstanding, he thinks. Clear words need to be spoken to end this confusion. He owes it to his family. And within a week he packs, books his passage to Germany and boards a steamer to

Bremerhaven. Walter needs to be home to explain. Foremost he has to speak to his brother.

On Ten Eicken they don't know he is returning. Nobody is informed, even Ferdinand is not aware of the exact date. The late returnee is overdue for years. Unexpected and on nobody's mind these days. Walter has overstayed his absence.

The farmhands in the fields have never seen Walter, they only know the brother. So as he walks down the private road toward the estate with just a knapsack on his back, the workers take him for a wanderer. They greet him out of courtesy by baring their head to the stranger.

Walter slows down his steps as he gets closer to the mansion. What will he say? Estranged from himself, alienated from others, he cannot think of any explanations to vindicate his sudden reappearance. Words are needed. Phrases? Excuses?

Surprise? Look here, it's me. I am back. Guess what, the war has been over for more than ten years. Sorry for the delay but those Russians just couldn't do without me. And what about those German war prosecutors who forced me to flee to Argentina? Well, how time flies. Another two years passed. It's been twelve years. Yet it seems like a hundred long agonizing winters. Trust me, you don't want to know.

That's what he could say. Or something like it.

If there were only trenches beside this road, he thinks. How he would like to jump right in there and hide. This very moment. But someone has spotted him while stepping out of the front door. He hears a scream, a loud cry like that of a wounded animal.

From afar he sees a body hit the gravel in the yard. As if gunned down by the enemy. A body sinks toward the ground, not in slow motion but speedy and hard. As Walter rushes forward several people come running from several directions. They are not coming for him but the person on the ground. For Hilda. His wife. She recognized his movements from afar. Knowing instantly and then she fainted.

"Who are you to scare a lady like that," foreman Gustav scolds Walter. "Here, give us a hand, we have to carry her inside. Careful now with the mistress. Watch those steps." But before they enter the hallway, Hilda regains consciousness. She fights those strong hands which lift her.

"Stop it, I am alright. Put me down, I can walk," she says in a shaky tone of voice which echoes in the hallway. The commotion brings out more spectators, they are coming from the kitchen and the dining room. Ready to assist. But Hilda simply waves them away. "Go back to your lunch. Yes Lotte, you too."

They are standing there now, face to face. Close, but yet further away than two years ago when they met in secret. At a loss of words, they just look at each other in anticipation.

"Walter, dear God, Walter," they hear the voice of Ernst. Slowly he walks toward his older brother, arms stretched forward, ready to hug and hold. For minutes he won't let go of Walter. They are sobbing now, both men. Quietly Hilda retreats to the kitchen.

"What was that all about?" Lotte asks while getting a roast out of the oven.

"It's my husband," Hilda says.

"Yes, I know it's your husband," Lotte responds. "But who is the other man?"

"My husband," Hilda repeats. And now it dawns on Lotte. She lets go of the frying pan and grabs a chair.

"Dear God," she says, "we finally have a miracle." Overwhelmed by exuberant joy she spontaneously hugs Hilda. Both women silently start weeping until they hear more commotion in the hallway.

"Out of my way, let me through. I want to see him, he is my son," they hear Agnes harsh command in the hallway. The firm tapping of her walking stick on the wood panel precedes her approach. And then the old woman stops a few steps short of the embracing brothers. The mother simply stands there while looking at Walter. She only has eyes for him.

"It's about time you came home," Agnes says. But her voice is without the harshness Walter remembers. It sounds soft and caring. He turns toward his mother to sink into her arms. They don't talk. She strokes the back of his head while he buries his face on the left side of her shoulder.

It is quiet now. Only the faint footsteps of Ernst retreating toward the backdoor are audible. He withdraws because he is not wanted here any longer. Nobody needs to tell him that.

The firstborn has returned to the estate.

47

The aches of joy. On one hand brimming with mirth, while subliminal a reality-check is waiting to reveal itself. But not just yet. Maybe later, when the initial excitement subsides. When all is said and nothing left but the inevitability of actualities.

While Lotte comforts Hilda in the kitchen, Agnes is holding her oldest son in the hallway. She cannot let go. Her boy, the pride of her family is back. After all those years she is finally hugging him again. What felicity to listen to his words, the account of events which now come thick and fast.

His mother does not interrupt him. She simply holds on to his hands while trying to read the lines in his face. They take her through ice desserts, along barbed wire and into total isolation. And the eyes, his beautiful blue eyes. They remain the gatekeepers of unspeakable sufferings. Once in a while she utters a sigh but it stays beyond her imagination.

Only later when the rest of the family gathers around the supper table the absence of Ernst is noticed. By Lotte, of all people.

"I think, he went to the barn. I saw him crossing the yard earlier," she says to Hilda. "Shouldn't someone fetch him for supper?" But the family is preoccupied with Walter and his many stories. First about Russia and then Argentina. Even Hilda is fascinated by his new enthusiasm with which he colors his trials and encounters. Like a globetrotter, not late returnee, he recollects anecdotes in an adventurous way for his listeners.

Yes, Walter it a fine actor like Agnes. He has the charm and discipline to play his part tonight. And his listeners are buying the fable of happy endings.

After another twenty minutes, during which nobody from the family makes an attempt to search for Ernst, Lotte leaves the table.

She finds Ernst in the barn, preoccupied with fixing a leather belt for a saddle.

"We are having supper," Lotte says. "You are coming?"

"I'll eat later, when mother has left," Ernst says matter of fact. Lotte looks at him, unwilling to retreat.

"Later, I said. Can't you see I am busy ...?" he adds. Taking a small screwdriver from his toolbox, he tries to punch a hole into the leather belt. He doesn't even look up when suddenly Hilda appears beside Lotte.

"They are gone, both of them. You can come back to the house now," Hilda says with anger in her voice. "Your mother went home and Walter is staying with his friend Ferdinand tonight."

"Good," Ernst mumbles while continuing his task. He doesn't get up to follow his wife and Lotte back to the mansion. Putting his tools aside, he just sits there. Alone, abandoned by choice, like a small boy wondering. Mostly about himself.

"We can clear the table," Hilda says to Lotte. "He won't come in, he won't eat. You know it's his pride. He'll probably rather sleep in that barn than give up whatever he is hanging on to." Lotte just nods. She hesitates to comment. The situation is complicated enough for Hilda. The joyful reunion is stained by the harsh reality of circumstance. Lingering like a dark cloud over the valley, waiting to exhale thunder and lightening.

What am I going to do? Hilda thinks. She is not the only person on Ten Eicken who dreads the end of that long night. Better to lie awake in the dark than wake up to face the new day. Someone will have to say something. Who will step forward?

"You will have to talk to her," Ferdinand says to Walter, who is still sipping coffee in the kitchen of his cottage at three o'clock in the morning. "You have to explain, it isn't right to just let it go." He glances at the letter his friend shared with him earlier. That damn letter Hilda sent to Walter when he was in Argentina.

"We'll see. Maybe later," Walter says. He points to those two diaries, he wrote during his time in Argentina. "You'll store them for me with the other books I gave you. Keep them safe. Maybe one day someone in my family wants to read those accounts. Perhaps years from now, when silence about those terror years isn't an option any longer for our nation. People need to talk. Who knows when? But in the end time always creates that urge." He is leaning back on his chair, glancing at his old friend.

"I like the way you live here. Alone, undisturbed. A life fit for a war veteran," he says. And before Ferdinand can respond, he continues with a gesture of mutual understanding. Their generation lived through youth, maturity and death within a few short years.

"We don't fit in anywhere, not any longer. We lost the war. What's left is shame. And more disgrace for generations to come," Walter adds.

"I can't forget the horror I saw, and now at home I must play nice, settle in and pretend it was all a dream. Can't do it, can't lie to myself. Lucky you," he says to his friend. "You can hide here by yourself. Impossible for me, look at my clan. They won't allow that seclusion."

"I understand." That's all Ferdinand can say. He will not contradict those statements because he feels the same way as Walter. Contemplating about the war has brought nothing but self-loathing, a tiresome activity. Consider it penance for having been born in Germany and worn that Nazi uniform. At least self-hatred shows some form of character after the fact, he tells himself.

In silence they sit there at the table for another hour. Two weary soldiers, tired of excuses and defenses handed out like coupons by civilians who don't know any better.

48

After Ferdinand finally retreats to his bedroom, Walter steps outside, aimlessly wandering the countryside around Ten Eicken in the dark. He needs to think while retracing steps on pathways familiar from his childhood in an attempt to reconnect to the person he used to be. Idealistic, honest, trusting. A good man once.

He is trying to concord. But it's useless. In the dim light of a half moon he loses that young proud man. All he can see is shades of Siberia and soldiers. Starving soldiers. Germans and Russians.

Overwhelmed by despondency Walter begins to shiver. While he looks for a place to rest, he finds himself back on his property, in front of the barn. How did he get here?

With childish joy he remembers his favorite hiding place. Under the wooden stairway which leads to the upper level where hay is stored for the winter.

He played here with his brother Ernst when they were kids, when possibilities had landscapes full of adventure. The wooden stairway was their secret place of happiness and innocence.

But it's occupied.

"What are you doing here?" Walter utters with surprise.

"I live here, remember," his brother Ernst responds while getting up and brushing some hay off his trousers.

"But not under the stairway," Walter mocks. "Why are you here? Why aren't you in the house?"

"I could ask the same questions, you are also her husband," his brother responds.

Walter nods while patting a black mare, who has stuck her head over the gate to his right side. He grabs a bunch of hay and holds it close to the horse.

"A fine animal," he remarks. "You always had a special affinity with livestock."

"Not as good as you. No, never as superb as you. And that goes for everything you did. Mother's darling. Ha, you think, I didn't know? But I got used to that over the years," Ernst says.

"So it's my fault you are the youngest in the family? Is that it?" his brother says. "You are your own man. Can't you see what you've become? Look, what you've made out of Ten Eicken. You should be proud. I admire what you did here on the farm."

"All will be good. Are you paying attention?" Walter says. "Listen closely because I won't repeat myself. I will not stay on Ten Eicken to play family. I won't be in your way. I only needed to come home once more. Do you understand what I am saying? Home, that's all. It's too late for me to play family, this isn't my life any longer. It's your turn now, your responsibility. And don't forget, you have three children with Hilda to take care of ..."

"Three?" Ernst interrupts him. "Did you say three children. Ha, don't try to convince me. I know you were with Hilda a couple of years ago before escaping to Argentina. Do you think I am stupid? I know of that romantic afternoon in Ferdinand's cottage. It was right after your release from that Russian labor camp," he says while looking with hatred at his brother. "And I know why you came back. It's the youngest, it's Christina, isn't it? You fathered her, didn't you? You lying bastard."

His words feel like bullets from a machine gun. This has to stop, Walter thinks, while stepping forward. Taking a wide swing with his right fist, he hits his younger brother below his left cheek. He goes down while wiping with his thumb blood out of the corner of his mouth.

Ernst is falling so hard that the barrel of a pistol, a Luger P08 underneath the hay becomes visible to his brother. Beside it on the ground he spots an extra eight-round magazine. The Luger, their father's most valuable pistol wasn't turned over to the Allied Forces when Germany was disarmed, but hidden on Ten Eicken until Ernst inherited the pistol from the old man.

Looking at the weapon Walter gets confused. Is his brother afraid, he will steal his life with Hilda? Is he that desperate?

Pointing at the weapon, Walter asks, "is that for me?"

"No, for me," Ernst responds. And then the picture becomes clear. So that's why he is in the barn, hiding under the stairway. He wants to end it right here, Walter thinks. Wants to be first in this family for once in his life. No longer second but number one before anybody else gets the same idea to steal his moment.

"You moron, can't you see," he yells at Ernst. "Christina is your child. She is not mine despite what Hilda thinks or hopes. She sent me that bloody note to Argentina, trying to lure me back home. I know. But it's all lies. Christina isn't mine, she is yours. I cannot be her father. It's out of the question." With those words he sinks to the floor right beside his brother. He takes out a handkerchief to wipe his brother's cheek. Both men are breathing heavily until Ernst finally speaks.

"Nobody said a word or gave a hint, not even Hilda. My suspicion was mainly based on observations, the way she acted," he mumbles. "Why do you deny? You could be Christina's father. How can you count out that possibility?" He looks at his older brother, but Walter shakes his head.

"Me, the father? Impossible, biologically infeasible. That I know for certain. Let me tell you a story. An anecdote about the life of German war prisoners in Russian labor camps. Something that is so dreadful that you cannot devise it. I will tell you the truth, an account of hatred and revenge that happened in Russia, in those labor camps against German soldiers they captured," Walter says.

His descriptions are brutally precise and factual without emotions. Like an onlooker, Walter reports as if recalling scenes of a motion-picture although he was part of the script. He talks until daybreak.

Sentences have no punctuation, no endings. Like bullets they fly into space without resistance, disappearing into nothingness, lingering undetectable.

First with fascination, but later with disgust as well as anger and empathy, Ernst listens to agonizing details, unspeakable pain hidden underneath plain descriptions.

He wants to ask questions here and there but remains silent to not interrupt the flow of words. There is brutal testimony which until today, Walter only shared with his diary.

"You understand now, don't you?" he finally says to his younger brother.

"Any further clarification needed? I didn't think so. So why don't you get rid of that gun now? Promise? And for heaven's sake Ernst, go home, join your family. They'll be rising soon." He hugs his brother before getting up to leave the barn.

"And you always thought my shoes where too big for you," Walter says while turning around one last time at the door. "Guess what, they don't fit me either any longer."

49

It only takes a few hours that next morning before they find Walter. Foreman Gustav spots his body at the lake behind the Ten Eicken mill. Walter is dead. Drowned. No medical examiner needed. The case is clear, he took off his trousers, shirt, jacket and shoes to go for a refreshing swim that night. That's what happened, his mother Agnes alleges. Her boy drowned by accident. Oh dear, he was never a good swimmer, always afraid of the water from childhood on.

Yes, an accident, of course. Why else would he have folded his clothes so neatly at the shore of that lake? It's obvious. Her boy just returned home, eager to get back to his former life, she laments while three farmhands carry Walter's body into the house.

Bewildered Ernst watches the procession move toward the living room where his brother will lie in state until burial on Ten Eicken's private cemetery.

Didn't the younger feel the pain of the firstborn the night before in the barn? Did he not see this coming? And if so, why did he not prevent this tragedy? Maybe there was something there, but this? No, he did not expect such a tragedy, Ernst tells himself. He was too overwhelmed with his own problems that night. And later, when he returned to the house, he put the Luger pistol back into the safe before he went to bed. For the first time in days, he slept well. The conversation with his brother was liberating. His death is not. Ernst knows, his brother did not drown. He is certain, that's not what happened. But he won't say a word for the sake of his mother.

The women close the living room door to wash and dress Walter for the last time. With tear-stained eyes Hilda dips a washcloth into a bowl with lukewarm water. But she cannot move, she just stands there, frozen. When Lotte pulls the cloth out of her hand, she willing lets go.

"Sit down, I'll do it," Lotte says while pointing to a chair in the far corner of the room. With tender movements she washes his face. Gently. And then his chest, before she lifts his arms to finish the ceremonial cleaning.

The tattoo is small, but clearly visible. Under Walter's left armpit, Lotte spots the *Waffen SS* branding. She stares at the blood-type *B* in Goethic letter. Mesmerized, she holds up the arm of the dead man longer than necessary. A movement, which has not escaped Hilda who has been observing Lotte from afar. She is now beside the body and sees what Lotte has discovered. The women stare at one another. Both are shocked.

A Ten Eicken man in the *Waffen SS*? Impossible. Not in this family.

But it's right there in front of their eyes. Don't these women realize what they see? It's the tattoo of Hitler's elite soldiers, the marking of his private warriors. It's there on the arm of a man who now seems like a stranger.

"We did not see this," Hilda quickly whispers. "Do you hear me? Nobody needs to know." Lotte nods. She is stunt but acknowledges Hilda's request.

With haste the women dress Walter with a white shirt and his best black suit.

"He looks peaceful and somewhat relieved now. Don't you agree?" Hilda says while finishing the task. They leave the room and open the door for friends and neighbors who have arrived to pay their last respect.

"At least he is home," someone mumbles. "He is here, no more guesswork." And then they talk, most of them at the same time. They tell their stories of brothers, husbands and fathers who are still missing in Russia. Not one family is unaffected. But a decade after the war, missing means dead. Hope wears itself out. No, their loved ones won't come back to be buried at home. They know, time has run out for miracles. They are dead. All of them. This they sense without proof. The reality of time needs no eyewitnesses.

They tell Agnes how lucky she is. Her son is right here, he'll be close to her for eternity on Ten Eicken's cemetery. The old woman nods. Yes, better here than in Russia.

"But he was so young. His whole life was still ahead of him," she says. "Why him and not me? I am old, I am not going anywhere. It should have been me, not him. Not my son." Ferdinand is now standing behind her. He touches her shoulder slightly not necessarily to comfort but to make a point.

"You have two sons," he whispers into Agnes ear. "Do you hear me? Two." But she brushes his words away. Even uses her left hand as if getting rid of a fly that's bugging her. That neighbor of hers, what does he know? Nothing, absolutely nothing. Her favorite son is dead, that's all she cares about. So don't talk about the living. Don't even try. And with firm steps she walks toward the door. Her eyes are fixed forward without attempting to glance right or left. She cannot bear another word from anyone in this room. Only for an instant she hesitates, when Hilda steps into the hallway to bring a pot of fresh coffee. But why stop now? What's there to say?

"I will visit her tomorrow," Hilda says to Ferdinand while placing the coffee pot beside the empty cups on the table. "Yes, I'll go to her cottage. For heaven's sake. She is an old woman." And yes, she has another son. But Ernst is unforgiving. When he sees his mother, he recalls the court case, the battle over Ten Eicken. He sees an old woman who tried to disinherit her own son. That he cannot forget. Never. And he has told Hilda more than once.

"Yes, somebody should see her tomorrow. It's not easy for a mother to bury a son," Ferdinand says to Hilda. "But what about you? Are you okay? You look rather pale."

"We'll talk, after the funeral. Later, not today," she says.

"Yes, we should," Ferdinand agrees. "You may want to take a closer look at something Walter left at my cottage."

Two days later more than a hundred people gather at the small cemetery on Ten Eicken. Walter's son Wilhelm came by train the night before. He is attending the funeral of a father he believed dead. Hilda has not told him yet that the stranger he met at the railway station two years ago was his father. Wilhelm met him once without realizing his identity.

Mustn't think about it now, Hilda tells herself. There is always time for the truth later. Much later.

The boy is clinching his grandmother's hand. He is staring at a white wooden cross. He played here as a child to be close to his dead hero, the father he never knew. Yes, the boy knows this place rather well. It bears the cross which was there before he was born, the memorial Agnes created twelve years ago when the Red Cross by mistake informed her of her son's death.

That cross now has two dates, Walter's birthday and finally the exact date of his death.

With obvious rejection Wilhelm glances at his mother Hilda. Why was he not informed that his father had returned. He could have met him, hugged him for once in his life. Bewildered the boy squeezes his grandmother's hand even tighter.

It is quiet on the cemetery. Every person is rapt in their own thoughts. Only the words of the minister break the silence. But is anybody listening to the cleric?

Walter must be smiling at this sight, Hilda thinks. He was standing right here, just two years ago with her while joking about his final resting place. And later, what happened to him? Could I have helped him? No, I didn't have that might, she thinks.

How many late returnees are tormented in similar ways, she wonders, while opening her hand to let the dark soil trickle through her fingers onto the pale beige basswood coffin below.

From a distance, Ernst watches the ceremony. "It should have been me. My brother deserved better after all those agonizing years," he thinks. He looks toward the crown of an oak tree above the grave. Wondering, contemplating. And suddenly a strong absence of faith overwhelms his feelings. Slowly Ernst walks away, swearing this day marks his last attendance of a church service. Ever. He is done believing. He is through with hope.

50

Like a shadow which grows larger during late evening hours, the events of the past two days cast further darkness upon Ten Eicken. Leaving questions unanswered, causing more confusion. Except for Ferdinand. He understands. But when Hilda visits him in his cottage, he is in no mood to explain. He simply points toward the living room table covered with five notebooks, different in volume and size.

"His life, his diaries, three from Russia and those on the left are from Argentina," he says. "It's best you start with his last entries, because they relate to the letter you sent him to South America." Without further explanations, Ferdinand opens the front door to leave Hilda alone. It's has to be, he thinks. Let the words of a dead man speak for themselves, because nobody wants to listen to the living anyway.

For hours Hilda turns pages, reads and rereads passages. Some events and observations are recorded in ink, others in pencil. In small letters, Walter dated all occurrences during the war, prison camp and his time in Argentina.

With meticulous precision he recorded a life lived in pain and at the end in vain. She is staring at the entries, trying to see through the eyes of a soldier. But it's impossible. Shocked, she puts the last diary back on the table. Pushing it as far away from her as possible, as if distance can refute reality and cruelty for that matter. When Ferdinand steps back into the cottage, it's already dark outside.

"Why didn't you tell me?" Hilda asks him.

"Would you have wanted to know what happened in Siberia. That awful truth against our own comrades," he responds. She shakes her head. He is right. Women bear their own cross, they have no strength left to carry the emotional weight of former soldiers.

"Death would have been a blessing for deported men and women to eastern Russia," that's all she can utter.

They sit in silence at the kitchen table for another ten minutes. Absorbed in thoughts, paralyzed by their own helplessness after the fact they keep each other company. When Hilda gets up she puts her right hand on Ferdinand's shoulder. For a momentshe stands there, uncertain what else to do.

"Dear friend," she finally says, "please store those diaries in your cottage. Keep them safe. I will cherish Walter's words forever. But I am done reading and thinking about the past. If we only look back we see nothing but our shadows. What are we going to accomplish with that?" She takes her hand off his shoulder, hugging him briefly before disappearing into the night.

Walter's notebooks remain on the table but some of the words have disappeared with Hilda. They are chasing her down the hill through the night toward Ten Eicken. She finally halts her steps, and while clinging onto a wooden fence post she starts weeping. Uncontrollably she sobs. No she will not look back, not any longer. She has to stop this or she'll go mad.

What is her generation anyway if not wreckage of a fanatic system run by madmen? Finished, dead inside. A generation damned to live without the luxury of forgetting.

Except Walter. Fortunate are the deceased who no longer cast shadows to obscure the past. Because talk is often nothing more than laundering the remains of their souls.

She will not be part of that any longer. She'll turn the page and try to forget. Hilda will never tell her children about those diaries, about the war and all those atrocities. Let future generation figure it out for themselves. She lived through those times, no further history lessons necessary. She will stay silent. That she promises herself while she wipes off her tears before opening the front door of the mansion.

"They've all gone to bed," Lotte says while looking at Hilda's messy face. But she pretends not to notice.

"I'll make us a fresh pot of coffee," she points out. "It will help."

"Yes Lotte, it's that simple. Coffee will do that," Hilda says. "Thank heaven for your friendship. What would I do without you?"

51

"I still miss her every day," Lotte tells me after talking about that particular day in 1955. "Believe me, life isn't the same without her." She looks at me with empathy. "I know," she adds, "it was too early, for both of them." She is referring to my parents who both died before they reached the age of seventy. First Hilda, then Ernst. He followed her only eight months later. Couldn't be without her, even in death.

"We can continue another time, if it is getting too much today," I suggest to Lotte, realizing what a strain these conversations must have been for her.

"No, I am fine, I am certain Hilda is listening and she wants you to know," Lotte says. "That's why you came back, isn't it?" I have moved over to the couch, hugging Lotte, placing my head on her apron collar. It smells of fresh potato peels and onions. Scents of my childhood when I watched her in the kitchen getting supper ready for the farmhands.

"That's not the only reason why I am here, you know that. It's you I wanted to see," I point out.

"Me and my information, be honest," she giggles while holding me close. We sit like this, leaning on one another for several minutes before I straighten up.

"So, tell me, was my uncle a Nazi? Was he? I ask "You saw the tattoo on his arm. What happened to him? What did he do? Is Walter perhaps my real father?" When she hears my last question, Lotte gets up with anger on he face.

"Stop it with those assumptions," she jells, "you don't know anything. I thought you are a journalist. Think and check your information before you ask questions which seem to expect predetermined answers. That's all you kids do these days, anticipate answers that fit your uncomplicated picture of things. But this isn't how it works; sometimes the truth isn't that simple. Understand?" I nod, ashamed of my impatience.

"You are right, forgive me. But that's how we were schooled, that's what authorities told us in the sixties. And our parents didn't say anything at all. Never talked, even when asked. So please tell me what you know," I now beg.

"I have nothing more to say. I told you everything. That day, after we buried Walter, your mother never said another word about the past. Neither of us ever mentioned the *Waffen SS* tattoo we saw under his armpit. No, we kept quiet. It was our secret. And to be honest, we didn't really know, what it meant. At least, I didn't. Perhaps Hilda had more information. But she didn't share them. Once in a while she still visited our neighbor Ferdinand. Because he was Walter's best friend it seemed to me that she wanted to be close to him."

"Perhaps Ferdinand knows what truly happened. I certainly don't ..."

"He is still alive?" I ask with surprise.

"Why shouldn't he, Ferdinand is only two years older than me. He still lives in that cottage beyond Ten Eicken," Lotte says. "A hermit, doesn't visit anybody, not even me although I have known him for over forty years."

"Would he talk to me, do you think?" I ask Lotte.

"Why not? He might talk to you. The question is, will he tell you anything?" Lotte says. "Even decades after the war he kept quiet about his experiences. But he said something, I never forgot. If you always look back, you see nothing but your shadow. Yes, that's what he said. Hilda told him to spend the rest of his days to look in front of him, toward the sun to avoid those shadows. I suppose, he took her advice."

"Maybe you should visit him. He is a good man," Lotte adds.

52

This is the path she went, the trees she saw and flowers in blossom so many years ago when she reunited with Walter, I think while climbing the steep hill to Ferdinand's cottage that afternoon.

I left my car at the Ten Eicken cemetery further down the valley. For at least an hour I must have stared at the graves of my forefathers. Grandma Agnes beside grandpa Gunter, Hilda between Walter and Ernst. And Otto, good old Otto. Lotte's husband was buried on Ten Eicken's private cemetery as well. He died of a heart attack during work in a factory. He should have never left the farm. He was happy on the land. It was Hilda, who promised Lotte, that Otto would not be forgotten on some public graveyard. He was part of the family, that's why he is here.

When Otto died, Lotte brought her small brown worn-out suitcase to the cemetery. "This belongs to him", she said to Hilda. "It's all that's left from his homeland. He needs it more than me," Lotte said. Later she told Hilda what they buried that afternoon with that suitcase. Inside was a box of soil from Pomerania, the good earth from their eastern farm; a last farewell from home. Regarding all those other missing soldiers, like Hilda's brother Hubert. Their fate is still unknown to this day.

I am getting closer to my destination. From afar I notice the bench in front of Ferdinand's house, that very same spot where Hilda fainted after Walter's return from Siberia.

Several times I knock on the front door in vain. Perhaps he is not home, but I could not announce myself earlier because Ferdinand does not possess a phone. When I lift my fist again to tap once more, I hear movements on the other side of the door.

"Coming, easy now, no need to hurry," I hear. And then he opens the door and stares at me for the longest time. His eyes widen as if seeing a ghost.

"Hilda?" he whispers. "Hilda, it can't be. No. But you look just like her." He stretches out his hand to shake mine. I quickly step forward to embrace him.

"That's how we do it in America. No handshake, just a hug," I say cheerfully.

"What a wonderful custom," Ferdinand acknowledges. "You must be Christina, Hilda's youngest. I should have known right away. But girl, you certainly look like your mother. You shocked me there for a moment." While pointing to the living room he goes into the kitchen.

"This is a pleasant surprise, we'll have coffee," he says. "I don't get that many visitors, in fact I haven't seen any for several weeks ..."

"Lotte would sure love to visit," I point out. "I've talked to her nearly every day these past few weeks. Why don't you contact her? She still lives in Metzkausen with her son Albert."

"I may just do that one day," he mumbles while bringing a tray with cups, cream and sugar. He watches me while I wander around the room, looking at his bookshelves and desk. No pictures, no photographs at all I notice. A man separated from his past personal life?

"You are looking for personal pictures? Won't find them on the shelves," he says. And then he points to the side of his head. "All in there. And in here," he adds while placing his hand over his left chest.

"I detest frames for memories," he says while walking back to the kitchen to get the coffee.

He is eighty two years old, but looks ten years younger. Still lean and physically in good shape like many of his generation. I once asked a former soldier why after all those years he still nurtured that fitness needed for combat without a war in sight. He simply replied, it's habituated. Out of fear and also a precaution. Obese people can't run, he said.

"I know, what's on your mind," Ferdinand says while pouring coffee into both cups. "Your face is an open book like Hilda's, I usually detected what she wanted before she spoke. She was easy to read."

"Are you going to tell me?" I ask.

"What? If Walter was a national socialist, a Nazi as you call them? Who wasn't excited at the beginning in the early thirties? Tell me who, and I'll respond they are lying. We were all enthusiastic during those years before the war. There was promise of new jobs and better lives. But by 1938 many detected the lies. Especially Walter. He was a good man, an honest man. But that's the problem with politics, war and bigotry. It begins slowly before crawling under your skin and into your mind. And then with speed it develops into an avalanche. Once detached you can't get out of the way. It overwhelms you, buries you in its path. You cannot fight or outrun that force. That's how it was during those years in Germany. And before we knew it we were wearing uniforms and marching east." He shakes his head before looking straight into my eyes.

"Nazi? Ha, what does your generation know about that time? Nothing, and yet everything better than us who went through that mess. But let me assure you under similar circumstances that kind of dictatorship could have happened in every country. It's the beast in man paired with opportunity which brings such agony. It will happen over and over. Just give it some time ..."

"Well, was he?" I interrupt him.

"Not by heart, although I did not know he joined those elite soldiers, the *Waffen SS*. He was an idealist, perhaps somewhat naive. When he saw where all this was going he became defiant. Walter had too much character for the party's constant brainwashing. But you don't last in a club if you speak your own mind. Maybe that's why they sent him to Poland right away. As a sort of punishment. Lotte perhaps told you, that Walter refused to shoot civilians after they had killed one *Wehrmacht* soldier.

We don't kill women and children, Walter complained to the German commander. We do now, he was told. It's ten of them for one of our men. Get on with it.

"When Walter disobeyed he was placed immediately into custody, branded a war deserter and later sent back to Berlin to face trial," Ferdinand says.

"That's how it was in those days. My friend ended up in a punishment unit on the eastern front. Without a weapon, easy cannon fodder for the Red Army. And then Siberia for ten years. Damn it, damn it all ..." He stops talking while banging his fists on his knees.

"Hilda once said, if you only look back, you see nothing but your shadow. I took her advice to forget about the past. Until today," he says while getting up to walk toward the window. "I want to live in the light, let it be. Why all these questions after so many years? I can't go there again. That pain, those horrible pictures of the war. Why do you think I live like this? Alone, a hermit ..."

Is he crying? I hear faint sobs when I move closer. And when I embrace him, he puts his head on my shoulder. I keep silent while listening to his now wistful weeping.

53

Ferdinand has stopped sobbing, he appears calm now, somewhat relieved. He needed those tears. While freeing himself from my embrace his face lights up. He even smiles.

"Go on then," he says to me as if nothing happened before. "I assume you have one question in particular. Am I right?" I nod, surprised at his speedy recovery.

"Well then tell me, was Walter my father?" I ask.

"That's what everybody thought at the time, including myself,"

Ferdinand says. "Considering that romantic afternoon with Hilda in this cottage, the time-line would fit. You were born nine months after his visit. Darn, Hilda even wrote to Walter in Argentina. I sent that letter to him although I didn't know what it said. But I can imagine. And it must have worked, he returned soon afterward to Germany. You really want to know, don't you? I can't tell you but there is a way to find out. Wait here, I'll be right back." It takes ten minutes before Ferdinand appears again. He is carrying a small wood-box.

"Couldn't find it right away, had it stored in the cellar," he says. He opens the case and takes out several notebooks. They look withered, worn out.

"Here are your answers. Find out from the man himself," Ferdinand says. "These are Walter's private diaries. He always scribbled something, even as a young boy. See for yourself. Hilda did, she knew the truth."

"And you?" I ask.

"I am only the keeper of his diaries. No, I never had the urge to read them. I was there myself, I don' t need written words to remember," Ferdinand says.

"Who else took a look at those diaries?" I ask. "Perhaps Wilhelm? Shouldn't these accounts be in the possession of Walter's son?"

"Don't make me vomit. That boy? Ha, no way. He was only interested in himself, never asked any questions, didn't want to know anything unless it had to do with money. I doubt he even knows these diaries exist. What do you think? Have you talked to that brother of yours lately?"

"Not since he sold his part of Ten Eicken right after his twenty first birthday," I say. "Can't say I even remember his face. I was only eight years old at the time. As he did not live with us I never really got to know him."

Looking back I can see Wilhelm sitting with Grandma Agnes in the garden of the foreman's cottage. He didn't visit us in the main mansion when he came to Ten Eicken. I only saw him once more five years later at the cemetery. Wilhelm didn't speak to any of us during grandmother's funeral, not even to Hilda. And Ernst wasn't there. He kept his oath to never speak to his mother again after those court battles over the inheritance. So naturally he refused to attend her funeral. He went to the fields, plowing his land as if so nothing special was happening that day.

"Oh yes, tragic, I remember. That's the only mistake Hilda ever made, fighting for that kid's inheritance. Wilhelm didn't love the land. When he sold his part of Ten Eicken to those developers for the expansion of the autobahn, it marked the end of the whole estate as we knew it," Ferdinand reminds me.

"Those politicians had their claws in the valley, Wilhelm opened that door when he sold. And after that it was easy for the city to expropriate the rest of Ten Eicken for the so-called greater common good. Now it's all gone, the forests, the fields and buildings. If you ask me, that boy killed Hilda and Ernst. Not immediately, but slowly over time. Without Ten Eicken they lost their purpose. Both of them."

"I wonder if he realizes that?" I say. "Forget it, stupid question. Of course not, it's all his mother's fault, that's what he thinks. I am certain." I point out of the window where once the mansion of Ten Eicken stood. The humming of cars on the busy freeway has replaced the twittering of birds in the valley.

"Only the private cemetery is left. It was not in the way. I suppose, the dead are seldom a nuisance to progress," I mumble.

"Were there ever any good old times? I mean really carefree years when looking back?" I ask.

"That happens only when you are young. But I can't confirm that for my generation. We grew old before our years during the war," Ferdinand says without bitterness in his voice.

"You did the right thing, when you left all this behind to immigrate to America."

"Did I?" I ask. "I mean, did I truly leave everything behind? Can anyone discard their own heritage?" He doesn't respond while carrying the box with Walter's notebooks down the hill to my car. But he grins, a bright grin covers his face. He looks somewhat happy now.

"I tell you a secret," he says. "All those years I was clandestinely in love with Hilda. Of course only from afar. I didn't dare tell her. Now that

I am old, I wonder, if she ever knew? Can't see, what difference it makes now." He doesn't wait for my reaction. Slowly he walk back up that hill to be alone with his thoughts.

54

Possibly I have a sense of smell for foreign places. It could be imagination, a trickery of the mind. But when I pick up one of Walter's diaries I hold it close to my nose. Sniffing, exploring the cover for scents of the past. The odor is hart to place, the aura elusively. It's been too long. Slowly I turn the pages to read at random passages while attempting to sink into the mindset of the man who wrote those words.

Wizna, Poland, September 1939

"We are camped at the river Narew, near Wizna. Tomorrow we will cross. I am here with a battalion of the Leibstandarte. The Waffen SS wants us east to see some action. If I am wounded, at least I'll be the first to get a blood transfusion. That's the privilege of tattooed elite soldiers. This war will be over soon, we haven't seen much resistance in Poland so far. It's so still in this countryside. It feels homey like Ten Eicken in the fall. But I miss my wife. I think of Hilda all the time."

Lublin, Poland, March 1940

"Those animals, not only some Polish partisans, but also a handful of our German commanders. They've become beasts these past few months. Behaving like killing machines, they don't differentiate between soldiers and civilians. I can't do it any longer, can't lift my gun at young mothers and old men. Had a dispute about that with my squadron leader today. They have taken me into custody as a war deserter. I won't tell my family, they'll despise me as coward. That's it then, I'll never see home again, my valley, my Hilda, my love ..."

For a brief moment I stop reading. I have to go forward in time. Quickly I turn pages while glancing at dates until I find the entry about that fateful day Walter received Hilda's letter from Germany.

Bariloche, Argentina, July 1954

"What is she saying? I am a father again? It cannot be. Why would Hilda write such a letter? She wants me home, I understand. But it's not my child. Christina is the daughter of Ernst, I know for certain. But does Hilda know? I need to explain. I will contact Ferdinand that I am coming home. Tomorrow, right away. This cannot wait."

Again I pause reading. Wondering how Walter could have been that certain? The answer lies in the past, somewhere in Russia. For hours I read page after page until I come across his fateful years in a Siberian labor camp.

Cap Deschnew, Northern Siberia, November 1946

"They say the war is over, we lost. But no one knows for certain. We don't need to know, we are dead in this frozen hell, damned to wither away. What did Stalin promise? We don't shoot German war prisoners, they'll die of hard and honest work rebuilding mother Russia. You are reaping what you sowed. That's what they hammer daily into our heads with rifle butts. Minus forty this morning, even the trucks won't start to bring us to the copper mine. Still dark, although it must be nearly noon. They have a surprise for us as we are not working today. Lined us up at the fence, a few hundred of us. I hope they shoot us today. It would be an act of mercy ...

We are still alive, barely. They picked out twenty of us. Only the strongest and tallest, the Russian commander said. And make certain you get those with the *Waffen SS* tattoo, they are preferred customers in my camp. In a barrack the Russians went to work. I saw rusty tools on a filthy cloth by a sink. A grinning doctor. No surgical alcohol left, he said while shrugging his shoulders. You must understand, it's the lack of vodka, my men drank all the ethanol. And he laughed while going about his business.

We are not allowed to ask, but I can tell by the screams. It's beyond inhumane. They are cutting us with dull blades. A specialty in this camp, forced sterilization. So you cannot produce any more little Nazis, the doctor grins.

Blood poisoning, no antibiotics. And if so, certainly not for prisoners of war. Not for Germans. Three comrades die a few days later. Bless them, their pain is done. If I make it through the night, I don't expect to ever leave here, so it doesn't really matter that I cannot father children any longer. Nothing matters any longer ..."

The pain is bouncing off the pages. Hurting like horsewhips after all those years. Exhausted I put down the diary, I cannot absorb another word, descriptions which create horrific pictures in my mind. I feel like crying for all that has happened. But I just sit there, paralyzed by history in motion.

"I thought we could get rid of those shadows by just talking about the past," I tell Lotte on my last day before leaving with Albert on our trip to Pomerania. "But instead, it seems worse. I am a shadow collector, that's what I have become."

"Nonsense. What are you talking about?" Lotte says. "You have to look at the past to understand the present. We are all eager to learn about our ancestors. Just don't nest in the past. Once you know it, let it be. You cannot change the run of events in hindsight." She looks at me in a loving way.

"Nobody's life is without shadiness," Lotte says. "If you undress all those shadows by taking away their gowns, you'll need to abandon the light in the process. Would you want to live in the dark for the rest of your life? Don't forget, variations of light and shade are part of our existence. It's how you wear that gown, that's the solution to the secret."

Epilogue

We are finally travelling east. Albert believes this trip can cure homesickness. But after more than eight hours on that tour bus, he gets increasingly tormented by doubts. What's he doing here, going back to Pomerania and checking out his former homeland? The border sign said Polska, can't he read? We are not in Germany any longer. Since 1945 Pomerania is part of Poland.

Along those tree-lined linden roads which bring us further east are the unmarked graves of thousands of expelled Germans. The road we now travel in haste was one of several exodus routes fifty years ago. While Poland lost 180 000 square kilometer of territory in the east to Russia, it gained 103 000 square kilometer in the west. Germany lost one fourth of it's territory.

"Stalin played musical chair with millions of lives," Albert says. "Wasn't it Churchill who said at the end of the war that the allies slaughtered the wrong pig? Makes no difference at all any longer. Not to the dead." He glances out of the window with melancholia as most travelers on this bus. The majority are seniors on a quest to rekindle their past. Few talk, all eyes are on the countryside.

Our destination is the town of Köslin, now called Koszalin, where we are met by Stanilaw Gozek. I found his service on the internet. He speaks Polish and German. When he doesn't guide western visitors around the countryside, he works on a collective farm.

"German tourists are good business since the Berlin Wall came down," he tells us. "Last week I had two busloads. They all want to see, what it looks like now. I have to warn you, it won't be the way it was when the Germans left. The upkeep, you understand? There was no money during communist times."

"You want to go to Strezepowa, Strippow, as it used to be called?" he asks. "That's not that far but it might be difficult to find your former farmhouse. So much has been torn down or withered away." He has stopped the car. "Look at your right, that used to be the German cemetery for the district some fifty years ago."

I follow Albert through the pasture toward a small hill. He brushes away thistles and stinging nettle along gravestones overgrown with weeds while trying to recognize names.

"And?" I ask.

"I was so young then, only six," he says. "But look here, I know that family. The name Treulow rings a bell. I played with their kids. Didn't they escape to the west as well. I thought, everybody did. Look here, it says Magda Treulow died here in 1976. That's strange." We leave the cemetery, Stanislaw is getting restless. Only two hours daylight left to search for the former Marlow property.

"Could be that some of those Treulows stayed behind," our tour guide points out. "I mean, they probably had to hide, pretend to be Polish, change their name at the time. Don't ask me how they survived. Our government estimates that today some 150 000 Germans still live in the east. Not immigrants but families with their offspring who went into hiding during expulsion."

Albert is not listening any longer, he walks off toward the north-side of the pasture. The playground of his brief childhood years.

"I can smell it now," Albert says. "Yes, it's familiar. Pomerania has the scent of that far-way sea breeze from the Baltic. There, look. Can you see them? Cranes." Like a little boy he reaches up his arms, pointing toward a flock of birds crossing above while spinning his own body in circles, carefree and happy. And then he stops in mid turn.

"It's here, over there," he points to a farmhouse nearly five hundred meters away.

"There, that building on the left. I recognize the grove nearby. That's where I was born."

"That's now the home of the Wozek family," Stanislaw acknowledges. "Good people, have lived here for two generations. I know them well. So, let's go." But Albert is not in a hurry any longer. He doesn't move. I pull him gently toward the car.

"Come on Albert, we'll just drive by. You don't have to go into the house," I say.

Stanislaw has shifted into first gear. Slowly he drives down the mud road to avoid all those potholes. We inch our way along the property which belonged to the Marlow family until 1945. I have no comparison to the past but the place looks pitifully. All around the lack of money for repairs is visible. A grim sight. I dare not to look at Albert.

"Just keep going, don't stop," he whispers to Stanislaw. But it's too late. A man has stepped out of the farmhouse. He is waiving at our driver. We cannot ignore the gesture so we stop at the gate. The stranger is now right beside us talking in Polish while pointing at the house.

"That's Krystian Wozek. He wants us to come in. It's not often, that visitors from the West stop by at his place," Stanislaw says. "It's your fine clothes, that's how we detect westerners in Poland."

"*Niemka*?" the man asks.

"He wants to know if you are German," Stanislaw says. Albert nods somewhat hesitant. Still uncertain what to do or say. The man laughs.

"*Lepiej Niemiec niz Rosjanin.*"

Our guide joins the laughter. What did he say, what does it mean?

"Better German than Russian. That's what he said. You must know, in these parts of the country we dislike the Russians more than the Germans," he says. "Understandable, considering the past. It has to do with forced displacement. You see, the family of Krystian Wozek lost their farm in eastern Poland when the Russians took over. They were chased out as well and relocated to this place."

Similarity of fates. Both expelled to foreign pastures. Albert can see it now in the eyes of the man in front of him. He takes his hand to shake it. Over and over while tearing up. And then he talks about his past. Tells him all about Pomerania, exhaling years of hidden anxiety under the roof he once called home.

"Translate, translate," he urges Stanislaw, while the flow of words take speed from both men now. A woman places a coffeepot on the living room table.

"Sugar and cream?" she asks in perfect German with a Pomeranian accent.

"My wife Anita," Krystian says. "And you?"

"Albert, my name is Albert Marlow," he stutters while getting up to shake hands with the woman. But she refuses to take his hand. Instead,

Anita pulls Albert closer to embrace him.

"You don't remember me, do you? Try, think. Start with Saturday afternoons at the lake," she says. "Mind you, I was three years older than you and a much better swimmer."

"Anita Treulow," he utters while hugging her over and over. He tells her that he saw a grave on the cemetery. Was that her mother? And she died here in the late seventies? Why didn't her family join the trek to the west when the Russians moved in?

"Grandma was sick that winter. Pneumonia. She would have died on the march to the west. We could not risk that. My father was missing in the war, so mother decided to stay behind until grandma got better. Those Russian soldiers are only humans like us. They won't harm us, we'll be alright. That's what my mother believed." Anita whispers those last sentences visibly afflicted while looking at Albert.

"But she had the foresight to cut my hair short and dressed me like a boy before sending me into the forest to hide. Later a pastor took me in. I did not dare to return to our home," she says.

"We should have left with you. Trekking westward was the only salvation during those months. Because when the Russians moved in they immediately apprehended mother and sent her off to Siberia. Grandma was battered to death in her sickbed." Anita is wiping away tears while Albert is holding her hands.

"Mother was released ten years later from a labor camp in Russia. She looked like a mad dog, didn't even recognize me for several weeks. No, we should have left too. We didn't accomplish anything by staying." For many years Germans lived like outsiders on their own soil in a new Polish society. The government made sure of that. And if it wouldn't have been for her loving husband Krystian, Anita's years even as an adult would have been unbearable. But she settled into her new life, learned the language while keeping a low profile with her heritage. It was a coincidence that she ended up in the house which once belonged to the Marlows.

"Promise to tell Lotte this," Anita finally says, "inform your mother that Pomerania doesn't exist any longer. It was wiped off the map the day she left. We have nothing left but memories and the illusion that history could have taken a different turn if only all of us ..."

It is silent now in the living room. No one dares to utter a word. There is so much heartache. But also bittersweet hope. Two generations after the war, Polish-Pomeranian children are being raised under this roof. They have fun in Lotte's former yard.

Carefree and untroubled they play as if nothing ever happened on the soil of Marlow's forefathers in a former German countryside once called Pomerania.

ABOUT THE AUTHOR: Born and raised in Germany, Ursula Tillmann immigrated as a teenager to Canada and studied journalism in Calgary, Alberta. She worked for Canadian and German newspapers for over twenty years, focusing on politics, history, investigative journalism and human interest stories. After the fall of the Berlin Wall, she reported extensively about changes in eastern Europe. She received several awards for writing, photography and poetry in both English and German. Ursula has published a selection of her poetry as well as two photography books. Now a Canadian citizen, Ursula Tillmann lives in the Rocky Mountains, in Canmore, Alberta.

UNDRESSING SHADOWS is also available as an e-book on KINDLE and as a paperback on AMAZON.COM worldwide.

Made in the USA
Charleston, SC
24 July 2013